...ignorant

'Y...
ba...t as...
fe...hting him sooner, her...
fig...ed **with scorn, every in**...
la...**ughty lady.**
hau...

'The barbarians were not as ignorant as you might imagine. In some ways their culture outstrips our own.' Justin smiled, more amused than angry. 'Had I been the ruthless devil you would have me, you would be warming my bed this night before I gave you to my men for their sport.'

Maribel drew back in shock, her eyes wide with horror.

A smile touched his mouth. 'Nay, I shall not treat you so ill. You may be a shrew, but you are a lady and I shall treat you as such. You will not be harmed while we hold you for ransom.'

'How can I trust your word?' She would be a fool to believe him for an instant, but something inside her responded despite herself.

Anne Herries lives in Cambridgeshire, where she is fo
of watching wildlife and spoils the birds and squirr
that are frequent visitors to her garden. Anne loves
write about the beauty of nature, and sometimes put
little into her books, although they are mostly about l
and romance. She writes for her own enjoyment,
to give pleasure to her readers. She is a winner of
Romantic Novelists' Association Romance Prize.

Previous novels by the same author:

MARRYING CAPTAIN JACK
THE UNKNOWN HEIR
THE HOMELESS HEIRESS
THE RAKE'S REBELLIOUS LADY
A COUNTRY MISS IN HANOVER SQUARE*
AN INNOCENT DEBUTANTE IN HANOVER SQUARE*
THE MISTRESS OF HANOVER SQUARE*

*_A Season in Town_ trilogy

and in the Regency series
The Steepwood Scandal:

LORD RAVENSDEN'S MARRIAGE
COUNTERFEIT EARL

and in _The Hellfire Mysteries_:

AN IMPROPER COMPANION
A WEALTHY WIDOW
A WORTHY GENTLEMAN

THE PIRATE'S WILLING CAPTIVE

Anne Herries

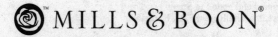

All the characters in this book have no existence outside the imagination of the author, and have no relation whatsoever to anyone bearing the same name or names. They are not even distantly inspired by any individual known or unknown to the author, and all the incidents are pure invention.

First published in Great Britain 2010
Harlequin Mills & Boon Limited,
Eton House, 18-24 Paradise Road, Richmond, Surrey TW9 1SR

© Anne Herries 2010

ISBN: 978 0 263 87580 5

Harlequin Mills & Boon policy is to use papers that are natural, renewable and recyclable products and made from wood grown in sustainable forests. The logging and manufacturing process conform to the legal environmental regulations of the country of origin.

Printed and bound in Spain
by Litografia Rosés, S.A., Barcelona

THE PIRATE'S WILLING CAPTIVE

I thank all my readers
for their continued support.

Prologue

The man walked away from the hostelry on the water-front deep in thought. He had booked passage on a ship bound for France and it might be many years before he returned home. He was filled with regret and anger for he had parted from his father with bitter words.

'You take the word of others above mine, Father—you would believe a stranger above your own son.'

Justin Devere's blue eyes had flashed with pride, making Sir John snort impatiently. 'You were a damned fool, Justin. By God, sir! There is no excuse for what you have done. You are the great-grandson of Robert Melford and a more devoted supporter of the Crown could not be found. Your grandfather was much favoured by King Henry VIII—and my own family has always been loyal. By becoming involved in this con-spiracy to murder Queen Mary and replace her with the

Princess Elizabeth you have let your whole family down. I am ashamed of you!'

'No, sir. You wrong me…'

Justin raised his head defiantly. He was a handsome devil, with pale blond hair and deep blue eyes; reckless, arrogant and dismissive of rules, he stood head and shoulders above most men, including his father. His grandfather said he was a throwback to Robert Melford in temperament and build, though not in colouring. He was also fiercely proud and it pricked his pride to hear his father call him a fool.

'You have spoken treason against the Queen and that cannot be tolerated.'

'It was no such thing, sir!' Justin declared passionately. 'I will grant that some hotheads have talked of such a plot in my hearing, but I am innocent of any conspiracy—as is the princess herself. She was gracious enough to grant me an audience; many of us wished her to know that we support her and if any attempt were made to disbar her from inheriting the throne when the Queen dies we should rise to her—'

'Be quiet!' John Devere thundered. 'Do you not realise that that in itself is sufficient to have you arrested for treason?'

'I shall not be silent, sir. I am as loyal an Englishman as any, but I cannot love a Catholic queen who puts good Englishmen to the fire in the name of religion.'

'It is not so many years since we were all Catholic and proud of it,' Justin's father reminded him. 'King Hal saw fit to break with Rome and we were all forced to follow or lose our favour at court, but that does not mean—' He broke off, for the anger was writ plain on Justin's face. 'While the Queen lives 'tis treason to speak of her death and well you know it.'

'We did not plot to murder her, merely to protect our own Elizabeth.'

'Surely it is enough that talk of your conspiracy has reached her Majesty? The Princess has herself faced questions from the Queen regarding treason and was lucky that her Majesty was in good humour because her husband has promised to visit her soon. Had it not been for that fortunate circumstance, she might have found herself in the Tower once more.' John placed a hand on his son's shoulder. 'Go to France or Spain, Justin. I know that though you have done wrong your heart was good. You have my blessing. Send me word of your situation and as soon as I think the coast clear you may return.'

'You would have me flee like a coward?' Justin's face reflected his disgust.

'I would have you live, sirrah! Stay and I may have no son to inherit my estate—and that will break your mother's heart.'

Lost in the memory of the bitter quarrel with his father, Justin did not notice the shadows behind him. Not until it was too late did he realise that he had been followed from the hostelry. Even as he turned, about to draw his sword, a crashing blow to the back of his head sent him to the ground and he lost consciousness as he was carried aboard a ship, not as the passenger he had paid to be, but to serve before the mast.

Chapter One

Spain—autumn 1558

'No, Father, please do not ask it of me.' The girl faced the tall man with iron-grey hair defiantly. He was a man of wiry stature, elegantly dressed in black with only one jewel of note, which was a ring made from gold and black agate to denote his mourning for his late wife. 'I am not ready to marry again. I know you are grieving and you wish a better life for me, but I would rather stay at home with you.'

'It is nearly a year since Don Pablo died.'

Don Miguel Sabatini's face was cold as he looked at his beautiful daughter. With her dark hair dressed in ringlets in the Spanish way, she reminded him of his first wife, whom he had come to hate after learning she had played him false with a lover. Her eyes were those of a temptress, a wanton wretch who had betrayed him, leaving a scar that would never heal. When he looked at Maribel's face he saw the pride of her English mother, a pride he had never been able to break despite his treatment of her, and the hatred burned cold and deep within him. His first wife had been a wanton, deceiving him with a man he had believed his friend. He had never forgiven her and his unkindness had driven her to the decline that led to an early grave. She swore that Maribel was his child, but he had never been certain and because of it could not love his daughter.

However, his second wife Juanita, a gentle kind-hearted woman, already past thirty when he wed her, had loved the motherless babe, and, unable to bear a living child herself, had taken the girl as her own, forcing him to show acceptance of a child he despised. It was she who had arranged Maribel's marriage to her young cousin. Unfortunately the bridegroom had died at the hands of bandits while riding in the hills a few months after the wedding, and Juanita had insisted her much loved stepdaughter return to live with them. Maribel had been grieving for her young husband ever since.

'You must marry, daughter. It is a woman's duty and her destiny.'

'But I cannot put aside my feelings for Pablo so easily, sir. I loved him truly and I do not wish to marry again.'

'I have written to a gentleman in England with whom I have business. He imports wine from our vineyards and a marriage between you would seal the alliance, make it stronger.'

'But I do not know this man…' Maribel protested, dark eyes flashing a protest. 'You have not even told me his name.'

'His name is not important, but since you will have it—he is Lord William Roberts of Helbourne.' He waved his hand as if to dismiss her.

Maribel refused to be dismissed so brusquely.

'An English lord?' Her gaze narrowed as she looked at him, saw the cold proud stance and felt again the hurt he had inflicted so often. Why was he so often unkind to her? What had she done to make him hate her, for she felt that his feeling went deeper than mere dislike? 'How old is he? What manner of man is he? Please tell me, Father.'

'What can his age signify?' Don Miguel demanded with an icy stare. 'He is of good character and rich—what more could you wish for?'

'A man such as Don Pablo. He was young and handsome and I cared for him,' Maribel said proudly. 'He left me a fortune—so why should I marry for wealth when I do not need money?'

'A woman alone cannot properly care for her estates. I have done what I can for you, daughter, but you should think of marriage. It is the right and proper course for you to follow. Surely you wish for a husband and children?' His voice softened, took on a persuasive note. 'You cannot wish to spend all your life in mourning for a man you hardly knew? He would have wished you to be happy.'

'Yes…perhaps,' Maribel faltered. When her father spoke softly to her she almost believed that he truly cared for her, and yet in her heart she knew that it was Juanita who had always stood between them, sheltering her from his anger. She thought sometimes that he had hated her from the moment she was born. However, Juanita had told her that he was a good man despite his stern ways and she believed her stepmother. If he felt she should marry this English lord, it might be for the best. To openly disobey him at a time when they were both grieving for the woman they had loved would be to show disrespect to Juanita's memory. 'I beg you will allow me time to consider this marriage, sir. I should like to meet the gentleman before making a commitment.'

'I will write and invite him to visit. He is a busy man. He may send someone in his stead—perhaps a portrait would ease your mind?'

'I should like to see his likeness.' Maribel moved forwards, her hand outstretched. 'Please, give me a little time, sir. I have not yet recovered from my stepmother's death. I loved her dearly.'

'As did I, God rest her soul,' Don Miguel said piously. 'For Juanita's sake I shall grant you a further few months, but I want you to make yourself ready, Maribel. It is my wish that you should marry soon.'

Maribel inclined her head. From the tone of her father's voice she knew herself dismissed. He had no more to say to her and considered the matter settled. No doubt he would invite Lord Roberts to visit them and arrange the wedding without further reference to her wishes.

Going outside to the shaded courtyard, Maribel blinked to stop her tears. She had no wish to leave Spain for England, which was a country of which she knew little. Her mother had been an Englishwoman, but Maribel could not remember her, though she had lived until past her child's second birthday when she had died of a fever after giving birth to a stillborn son. It must be because she was half-English that her father had decided she should marry this English lord.

Maribel's throat caught as she thought of her handsome young husband. He was but sixteen when they married, her own age at the time, and beautiful to look upon. Pablo Sanchez had a gentle nature. He was loving and kind, and he had treated Maribel as a sister. They had had fun riding together and playing foolish games. Something that no one else knew was that their marriage had never been consummated. Maribel was as much a virgin now as she had been on the day of her wedding.

Perhaps if her father understood that she was still virgin he would have some sympathy for her, but she could never tell him for it would shame her.

The future loomed dark and forbidding before her. She had been granted a few more months, but she knew the time would come when her father would force her to marry the man of his choosing.

'Cut him down and carry him below,' Justin commanded of the sailors. He had just been compelled to order the flogging of one of the crew for disobedience and it had taken all his self-control not to snatch the cruel whip from the bosun's hand. 'We must tend his wounds.'

'Aye, that we must,' Higgins growled. ''Tis a wonder the poor lad bore it as well as he did.'

'I know it well enough.'

Justin did not remind the man that he had been lashed the first time he disobeyed the monster that was their captain. On waking with a crashing headache that first morning to discover that he was aboard a strange ship and bound for the east, Justin had at first refused to take orders from Captain Smythe and his bosun. However, a lashing at the mast had made him realise that he had little choice but to obey. It was entirely due to the first mate Higgins's care of him that he had recovered.

Gradually, over the months, Justin had found his sea legs and gained the respect of the rest of the crew. He knew that they looked to him for a lead, and that most of them were at the point of mutiny. The time was coming when he must act, but for the moment the injured lad was his main concern.

Once they were safely below decks, they laid the young sailor on a mattress of blankets and sacking and Higgins began to wash away the blood as carefully as he could. The sailor had fainted after forty lashes and was unaware as the man tended his wounds with a salve. When he had finished, Higgins looked up at Justin.

'The men can't take much more of this, sir. They are looking to you for a lead.'

'You are talking of mutiny?'

'Aye, sir—common justice, I call it. The captain and his bosun must be put overboard in the night. Some of the officers are ready to join us, but any that refuse will go with the captain. The men think you should be their captain. They will follow you, sir—wherever you lead us.'

'I have heard the whispers. I am honoured by your trust in me, Higgins. Do the men understand that if we do this we shall be outlaws—forced to earn our living by piracy? If we were taken, we should all hang. This ship sails under the Queen's flag. Some of you may have signed of your own free will. I was press-ganged against my will, but it would not save me. I should hang with the rest of you.'

'Aye, we'll all hang if they take us, sir—but some of us think it worth the risk. A year or two as privateers and we can live like kings for the rest of our lives.'

'We'll be pirates, make no mistake, Higgins. A privateer sails with the Queen's blessing and I think we shall not be granted such a dispensation.'

'Aye, sir. The men know it.'

Justin's gaze narrowed. 'If I agree to this, there must be as little bloodshed as possible. I shall not stand by and see old scores settled. If I am to be master then the men will obey my rules. I shall not flog a man for a petty offence, but if a man murders a comrade he will hang. I am no soft touch and it is best the crew understand it before we begin.'

'We'll sail by the laws of the brethren. We all know

what is involved, sir—and we're all behind you to a man.'

Justin hesitated, then, 'Very well. The men will wait for my signal. Do we know who is with us amongst the officers?'

'The bosun will side with the captain, and perhaps Mr Hendry—all the others are as sick of their brutality as the rest of us.'

'Mr Hendry has the keys to the arsenal. We shall need that if we are to succeed.'

'He may resist, sir.'

'Leave him to me,' Justin's eyes gleamed with excitement. A life of piracy was not one he would have chosen, but now that it had been thrust upon him he saw that it was his only chance. If he refused, the men would butcher the captain, officers and midshipmen, and he would receive a knife in the back. Besides, it offered an adventure and freedom from the tyrant who had made all their lives a misery. 'When Hendry comes on late watch I shall offer him the chance to join us. If he refuses, he will be made captive until we have the ship—and then we shall put the men ashore. We are not far from the coast of Venice. The captain and officers can stay there until an English ship makes port and takes them home.'

'They will tell their tales of us, sir—we shall be hunted across the seas.'

'We shall be the hunters, Higgins. We'll head for Cyprus and refit and rename the ship. She needs trimming down to make her faster. We might sell her and buy something more in keeping with our trade. Trust me, I have learned much these past months and my mathematics are good; I know what is needed to improve her speed.'

'Aye, sir, we all know it. You will make a good captain—and you'll have the men behind you. Willing hands make light work.'

Justin smiled—he knew that the men often disobeyed orders or deliberately took their time carrying out their tasks as their only means of revenge on a master they hated.

'Tell the men to be ready for my signal.'

'Aye, aye, Captain Sylvester.'

Higgins saluted and left him alone with their patient. Justin smiled. He had given a false name to the bosun when he was first ordered to report for duty. No one knew his true identity and he would never reveal it. He was Sylvester and would now be the captain of a pirate vessel; for he had no doubt that they could take the ship. Justin was not sure that first officer Hendry would be prepared to sail with them as pirates, but he would be given his chance. If he could achieve it, the mutiny would take place with no loss of life, but he accepted that there might be casualties. Facing reality, he understood that he could not ply his trade without some bloodshed, but he would offer a safe passage to the crews of the ships they took. If they refused… Justin's expression hardened. They would do what was necessary and no more.

He had not asked to be brought on board this ship.

Injustice and prejudice had forced him to flee from England, and a press gang had robbed him of his liberty. In time he would part company from the ship and its crew and make his way to France, as he'd planned, but for the moment he was committed to leading the men to the fortunes they all hoped to make.

'I have had word that Lord Roberts is to send his cousin to escort you to England, daughter,' Don Miguel Sabatini said. 'You have had time enough to grieve. Captain Hynes will be here within days. You are to have your possessions packed and be ready to leave.'

'But am I to have no choice? Supposing I do not like him?' Maribel's head went up, her expression defiant.

'You will obey your husband, as you obey me. I have made my decision, Maribel.'

'What of my lands here in Spain?' Maribel had hoped that he had forgotten his plans for her marriage these past six months, but it seemed he had not.

'You may trust me to administer them for you. Once you are married, they will belong to your husband. He may wish to sell them and I shall await his instructions.'

'They belong to me. Pablo left them to my care. I do not wish to sell them.'

'Pablo has no son to inherit. Your new husband will instruct you in his wishes. Perhaps if you please him he will allow you to keep them and send his agents to inspect them.'

Maribel stared at him, mutiny flaring. She was angry that he refused to listen to her plea, but uncertain what she could do. Had Pablo's father lived, she might have applied to him for help, but her young husband had had no family. She was quite alone and had no influence with anyone; instead, she was at the mercy of her father's will.

As she left him and went out, wandering to the crest of the hill to look out over the sea, her thoughts were heavy. Even if she denied her father he might send her to England. There was little she could do; her fortune was in her father's hands. The lawyers had told her it was for the best and she had foolishly signed—but Juanita had been living then and her father had not been so stern…so unforgiving.

Hearing a muffled sound out to sea, Maribel shaded her eyes. The ships were too far out for her to see them properly, but she believed that one was firing on the other. What was going on? She had heard her father complain of the pirates that often attacked merchant ships in Spanish waters. Could it be a pirate vessel— and whose ship was being attacked?

'We found a rich haul in the holds.' Higgins grinned at Justin as he swung aboard the *Defiance*. 'The captain would not tell us from whence he came, but we found chests of unrefined silver…'

'From the New World, you think?'

'It would seem so, Cap'n.'

Justin nodded. Since he had taken command of the ship, putting its master and most of the officers ashore, they had been fortunate and had already taken three rich merchant ships, all of whom had surrendered when the first shot was fired across their bows.

'They surrendered the ship without a fight. Johnson told me that the crew have no love for the owner of this vessel. They were ordered to kill the slaves who mined the silver for them before they took it aboard and it hath sickened some of them.'

'That is beyond forgiveness!' Justin was angry. 'By God, the man responsible deserves to be taught a lesson!'

'Don Miguel Sabatini is the owner of the *Juanita*. He has men whose job it is to run the mines and they do not treat the slaves well. I have heard of him before from crew I met when we went ashore at Cyprus. His name is feared. Once he knows we have attacked his ships we shall be marked men.'

'We are faster than any Spanish ship, be it man of war or merchantmen,' Justin said. 'I do not fear Don Miguel nor yet any Spanish merchant. Only an English fighting ship can challenge us—and thus far we have outrun them all.'

'Aye, the luck has been with us,' Higgins agreed. 'The men think you are their lucky charm, sir.'

'We have been fortunate so far.' Justin laughed, feeling a surge of elation. 'This is the third rich prize we have taken. One more and we shall sail for Cyprus to re-provision and give the men a chance to spend some of their booty.'

'On wine and women,' Higgins agreed. 'For myself I'll be saving it to invest, perhaps in land in the New

World. I had a wife once, but when I returned from a long voyage I found her in bed with her new lover. She wanted a man who was content to live ashore. I needed to feel the wind in my face and the waves beneath me so I left her to it and signed on for a decent master. I'm in no hurry to retire, but when I do I'll find me a good woman and become a man of property.'

'A goodly ambition.' Justin's eyes revealed no secrets. The austere life at sea had hardened him in body and in mind. Thoughts of his quarrel with his father no longer tortured him. Though he'd not chosen his new life he had become accustomed to it and even relished it at times. 'Make secure the ship, Higgins. We'll find shelter in a quiet cove for the night. The look of that sky tells me that there will be a storm before long…'

As the first mate went out, Justin looked at the small chest he had taken from the captain of the captured ship. It was locked, but he prised it open with his knife and looked at the contents. Realising just what he had found, Justin hid the parchment inside his jerkin. If this fell into the wrong hands, it might cause mutiny and endless arguments, even some bloodshed. The map might be worth a fortune, but it would be more trouble than a little. He would keep it hidden for the moment while he decided what he ought to do with the unexpected discovery.

'Will you not relent and let me stay in Spain, Father?' Maribel asked one last time before she departed for the ship. 'I could go to my husband's house and you need not see me again.'

'To draw back now would cause offence to Lord Roberts and default on our contract,' her father said. 'Go with Captain Hynes. Your future husband has entrusted you to his care and you must forget all that you knew here. Your husband is a man of some stature in England. You should thank me on your knees for arranging such a marriage for you.'

Maribel understood that there was to be no reprieve for her. 'Very well, sir. I shall obey you.'

She turned away, her face proud and cold. Since there was no help for it she must accept her fate. Samuel Hynes was in the courtyard, waiting for her with the horses. He approached, offering his hand as if he would help her, but she gave her hand to her groom, Rodrigo, and let him put her up on her horse. There was something about Lord Roberts's cousin that made her distrust him; he had a sly, lascivious gleam in his eyes that made her uncomfortable and she would not have him touch her.

She saw him frown as he turned away. Her maid, Anna, who was to accompany her to England, was taken up behind the groom. They had both chosen to accompany her to her new home for they loved her dearly. It was Anna who had held her when she wept after Juanita's death, and Rodrigo who had taught her to ride as a child. Knowing that they were with her gave Maribel courage. She was not completely alone. She had people who cared for her—and perhaps in time she would learn to love the man she was to marry.

It was but a short ride to the cove where the ship had anchored. Maribel knew that her father had received bad news about one of his ships recently. The *Juanita,* which was his flagship, had been attacked and robbed of its cargo by pirates. Having sustained damage, it was in port being repaired. She was to travel on an English ship belonging to Samuel Hynes and understood that the *Mistress Susanna* was not as large or as well armed as the *Juanita.*

'Welcome aboard my ship,' Samuel Hynes said as he helped her step on deck. 'I am honoured to have you as a passenger, Donna Maribel. My cousin is a fortunate man. Had I been in his shoes, I would have made the journey myself.'

'I dare say Lord Roberts has much to concern him with the welfare of his estate and people.'

'Yes, perhaps. He is often at court. Yet I believe I should have spared the time for a bride as lovely as you, Madonna.'

Maribel lifted her head proudly, her eyes conveying her feeling of scorn. She would not accept his compliments for she did not like or trust him.

'I believe I shall go to my cabin, sir.'

'As you wish. I have given up my own so that you may be comfortable, Donna Maribel.'

'You will address me as Donna Sanchez, if you please.' Maribel said coldly. 'I have not yet married Lord Roberts and am still the widow of Don Pablo Sanchez.'

'Indeed you are, lady.' Samuel inclined his head respectfully, but there was a glitter of anger in his eyes. 'Forgive me. One of my men will show you the way.'

He signalled to a cabin boy, who came at a run. He grinned at Maribel and beckoned to her.

'Come, lady, I will take you to your cabin.' He hesitated as Maribel did not immediately follow. 'I don't speak Spanish, *señorita*…but you must come or he will be angry…'

Maribel smiled at him, because she sensed his concern. 'I understand English very well. My mother was English and Juanita thought it right I should speak it as well as my father's language. As a child I had an English nurse.'

The lad looked at her, but said nothing, glancing back at Captain Hynes as if he feared him. Only when they were in the cabin did he speak again.

'He would punish me if he heard me say it, lady— but be careful of the captain. I don't trust him. If what I've heard is true, he has tricked you and your father…'

'What do you mean? How hath he tricked us?'

'I heard as Lord Roberts lay close to death when this voyage was begun. If 'tis true, Captain Hynes will inherit the estate from his cousin—and you mayhap?'

Maribel turned pale, her head swimming for one terrible moment as she realised what this might mean. She had seen the look of lust in Samuel Hynes's eyes and felt sick, because she knew that she would be alone in England, apart from her servants, and at the mercy of an unscrupulous man. Hearing the sounds on deck, she understood that they had already begun to cast off.

It was too late to go back, and even if she were to return to her home she was not sure that her father would believe her.

As the cabin boy left, Maribel fell to her knees. She began to pull her rosary through her hands, her lips moving in prayer.

'Save me from this wicked man,' she whispered. 'Please God, do not allow me to fall into the hands of such a man—for I believe I should prefer to lie in my grave…'

'She is an English ship,' Justin said as they saw the flag flying proudly. 'We do not attack English ships.'

'The *Mistress Susanna* belongs to Samuel Hynes.' Higgins growled. 'I've served him and he was a worse devil than Captain Smythe knew how to be. He is a merchant and fair game. We've seen no Spanish ships for three days and the men are restless. I think we should take this prize. Besides—look at the second flag. That is Sabatini's pennant…'

'Why would an English ship fly the pennant of a Spanish Don?' Justin's gaze narrowed. Since discovering what kind of a man Don Sabatini was, he had determined to single his ships out whenever possible. 'There is something odd here. Mayhap Sabatini thinks to fool us into believing it is an English ship. Put a shot across their bows and run up the skull and crossbones. I would discover what kind of trick the Spaniard plays here.'

Justin was thoughtful as his men sprang into action. He knew they were restless and eager to return to their island to turn some of the booty they had taken into gold so they could spend it in the taverns and with the whores that plied their trade on the waterfront. His instincts had been to let the ship pass, but seeing Sabatini's pennant had changed his mind. The Spaniard was obviously trying to sneak one of his ships through under an English flag, and was possibly carrying a rich prize.

The men he commanded were loyal to a point, but wild and reckless. If he denied them such a prize, they might turn against him as easily as they had Smythe. Justin did not intend to continue as a pirate for longer than necessary. Once he had amassed enough gold, he could buy his own ship and become a merchant adventurer, which would suit him better than his present trade. Perhaps one day he might be able to return to England. He was not certain of his welcome, for his father would feel that he had disgraced the family by becoming a pirate, but his mother would always welcome him with open arms.

Justin had sent no word to his home. Better that his family think him lost than that his gentle mother should know what trade her son followed. Before he could return he must redeem himself in some way.

The *Mistress Susanna* was lowering her flag in surrender. She had given in without a fight—why? What cargo was so precious that the master was willing to surrender rather than risk being sunk?

Maribel rushed to the porthole as she heard the first shots fired. She could see that another ship was closing in on them fast—and it was flying the skull and cross-bones. They were going to be boarded by pirates!

'Donna Maribel, you must hurry…' Anna came bustling into the cabin. 'The captain bid me tell you to hide somewhere. He says he did not dare to fire back lest the ship was badly damaged and harm came to you—but he would have you hide for he says these men are scum and they will kill us or worse.'

Maribel's face drained of colour. Her knees felt weak and she was frightened by all the shouting and noise on deck. The ship's captain had surrendered, but it seemed that not all the crew were willing to obey him. Some were putting up a fight and there were screams as men were injured.

'I shall not hide,' she said. 'There would be no point for they will search the cabins and I will not be dragged from beneath the bed. It would not be dignified. I am the wife of Don Pablo Sanchez!'

'You could hide in your trunk, lady.'

'Do you think that would stop them?' Maribel's head went up proudly. 'These men only want money. If I tell them who I am, they will hold me for a ransom. My father is in charge of my fortune and he will pay if my life is in danger.'

Maribel's face was white, but she was proud and stubborn. She was the widow of Don Pablo Sanchez and a rich heiress. Her father would surely pay to have her returned to him safely. He had forced her to take this voyage, but he would not allow her to die at the hands of pirates for what could that gain him?

He had arranged the marriage because he wanted an alliance with Lord Roberts. Nothing had changed. He would pay the price these rogues demanded.

Maribel resisted her maidservant's attempt to make her hide and stood proudly in the centre of the cabin. When the door was suddenly thrown open, she looked at the man who stood on the threshold, facing him angrily.

'Who are you, sir? How dare you enter a lady's cabin without permission?'

The man stared at her for a moment. He was tall, handsome, with long pale hair that looked windblown; his was a strong face, arrogant and bold. His blue eyes seemed to burn her flesh as he stared at her in a way that challenged her. His gaze made her flush and tremble inside, but she did not allow her fear to show. She was a proud Spanish lady and would not show fear in front of a pirate dog!

'A thousand pardons, my lady,' the pirate said and swept her a bow to rival any courtier. A smile played about a mouth that looked sensuous, one eyebrow arched in inquiry. 'And who might you be, Madonna?'

'I am Donna Maribel Sanchez, widow of Don Pablo and daughter of Don Sabatini—and soon to be the wife of Lord Roberts of Helbourne.'

'That old roué? He was on his last legs before I left England,' the pirate said and grinned. His smile made her heart leap in her breast and insensibly some of her fear evaporated. 'Nay, lady, you are wasted on such a husband. I believe we have rescued you from a fate worse than death—the man is riddled with pox and steeped in vice. We shall take you with us to save you from this evil.'

'No!' Maribel stepped back as he approached her. She raised her head, her ringlets tossing as she trembled with indignation. 'My father will pay a ransom. I am wealthy in my own right…' A little gasp escaped her as she saw the gleam of mockery in his eyes.

'Indeed? Then Fate was with us this day, for we have a richer prize than we thought. A cargo of wine is one thing—but the widow of a rich man and daughter of Sabatini is another. Your father hath much to atone for, Madonna—and now we have the means to make him pay.'

'What do you mean? My father is a good man…' Maribel caught her breath as she saw his stern look. 'What is it? Why do you look at me that way?'

'I shall not offend you, lady, for I believe you may be innocent.'

'Tell me! I command it!'

'You command?' The pirate's teeth were white against the tan of his skin as he smiled and then bowed to her. 'Very well, I shall obey you, lady. Your father is a thief and a murderer. He allows his captains to mistreat the crews that sail for him—and he forces the natives of the New World to mine their silver for him and then has them murdered so that they cannot reveal the whereabouts of the silver to anyone else.'

'No! I do not believe you! You are lying!'

Maribel flew at him as he tried to take her arm to drag her from the cabin. She raised her hand to hit him, but he pulled her arm behind her back, catching her against his body, and holding her pressed hard to him. Maribel stared up at him fearfully, sucking in her breath as he lowered his head and took possession of her mouth. His lips demanded where Pablo's had softly whispered; his arms were strong, his body like iron and the heat of his manhood burned her. She felt the press of his desire through the silk of her simple gown and her heart raced. No man had ever treated her thus, and she did not understand why her heart was beating so fast. She should despise him, yet her body felt as if it were drowning in pleasure and a part of her wanted to stay in his arms. It took all her control not to moan and press herself against him for she had never felt such sweet sensation.

What was she thinking? He was a pirate, a barbaric rogue! She placed her hands against his chest and pushed; his strength was such that he could have taken full advantage, but to her surprise he let her go.

As he drew back, she saw the hot glow fade from his eyes and a cold disdain replace the lust that had for a moment seemed to have him in its grip.

'You are proud lady and lashed out in temper. Perhaps that will show you the error of your ways. Attempt to strike me again and I shall not stop at a kiss.'

'You are a pirate and an ignorant barbarian.' Maribel had recovered her senses. Perhaps because she felt ashamed of her weakness in not fighting him sooner, her voice was laced with scorn and she was every inch the haughty lady.

'The barbarians were not as ignorant as you might imagine, Madonna. In some ways their culture out-strips our own.' Justin grinned, more amused than angry. 'Think yourself fortunate that I am not what you think me. Had I been the ruthless devil you would have me, you would this night be warming my bed before I gave you to my men for their sport.'

Maribel drew back in shock, her eyes wide with horror.

A smile touched his mouth. 'Nay, I shall not treat you so ill. You may be a shrew, but you are a lady and I shall treat you as such. You will not be harmed while we hold you for ransom.'

'How can I trust your word?' She would be a fool to believe him for an instant, but something inside her responded despite herself.

'Because I give it. Behave yourself, lady, and I shall restrain my hand—but cause me trouble and I may just put you across my knee and teach you a lesson.'

'You would not dare!' Maribel stared at him. She saw that he was laughing and realised that he was mocking her. Her cheeks flushed; she knew that he might have done exactly as he wished with her, yet she could not accept her fate so easily. Her tone was more moderate, but still cool as she said, 'You are a rogue and a thief and—and no gentleman, sir.'

'I believe you are right. I was once a gentleman of sorts, but life has taught me that I must take what I can from it.'

'Do you give me your word that I shall not be… ravished and despoiled if I come with you?'

'If any man lays a finger on you I shall hang him. You have my word on it.'

'And my servants? My maid and groom?'

'Your maid may attend you and she is also safe from my men—but your groom returns to Spain with the ship, unless he cares to join us and become one of the brethren.'

'You do not intend to keep the ship? Surely it is your prize?'

'We have the cargo and you. The captain will deliver my message to your father. If he sends the gold we demand, you will be returned to him.'

'And if he does not?'

'Then he will never see you again.'

Chapter Two

Could this pirate truly mean his threat? Maribel's heart was beating wildly. She hardly knew how to breathe as he took her arm and steered her from the cabin. Yet firm as his grip was, he was not hurting her and he seemed to mean her no harm, at least for the moment. As they went on deck she saw that his men had surrounded and disarmed the crew. Some of the men were bringing up wine from the hold and transferring it to the pirate ship, which she saw was called *the Defiance*. As far as she could tell only a few men had resisted, but there had been some fighting and one or two men had been wounded, but it appeared that none had been killed. She saw Samuel Hynes on his knees, a knife being held at his throat; it was obvious that he had not surrendered immediately.

'What do you intend to do with Captain Hynes?'

'My men are of a mind to hang him, but I think we may send him back to Spain this time.'

Maribel did not like Captain Hynes but she hated brutality. 'You should not treat him so disgracefully.'

'Why, pray, should we not?'

'He deserves your respect.'

'Indeed? You have known the man a long time, perhaps?'

She flinched beneath the pirate's dark mockery. 'I know little of him—but I believe that all men should be treated with dignity.'

'Then perhaps you should know that Captain Hynes has men flogged for being in the wrong place at the wrong moment and sometimes just because it amuses him.'

Maribel gasped and lowered her eyes, because against her will she believed him. She had always felt something was not right when Samuel Hynes smiled and bowed to her, sensing that he was hiding his true nature.

'He may be a cruel man—but if you allow your men to ill treat him you are his equal.'

'You think so?' Justin arched his brow, his manner icy cold. 'I shall remember your words, lady. Now you must go aboard with your woman and those of the crew that have chosen to serve with us.'

'Are there many?'

'A cabin boy and a few others…'

Maribel turned to Anna as she joined her. The pirate captain had moved away. He was talking to the pirate who had a knife at Samuel Hynes's throat. Another man, older, with a scar on his cheek and a red band around his brow, had come to help them cross the plank that had been placed between the two ships to make it easier for the women to cross from one to the other.

'Give me your hand, lady,' Higgins said gruffly. 'You, lad, help the lady down there.'

Maribel felt a hand on her arm steadying her. She looked round to thank whoever it was and saw the cabin boy who had spoken to her when she first came aboard the *Mistress Susanna*.

'They have taken you too?'

'I came willingly, lady,' he said and smiled at her. 'It can't be worse than my last berth. 'Sides, I've never had more than a few silver coins in wages, and if I do my work well for the brethren I shall be rich.'

Maribel looked at him doubtfully. 'Do you not know what could happen to you if the ship is taken? You might be hung as a pirate.'

'I'd as soon hang as starve on the streets of London, lady—and the life at sea is hard for every man jack of us. I could die of the typhoid or the pox any day.'

Was life so harsh for a young lad? Reared to the privileges of birth and wealth, she had not realised what others suffered. She felt humbled and a little ashamed.

'What is your name?'

'I'm called Tom, lady. 'Tis as good a name as any for I know not my own. I was born in prison. Me ma died and I was brought up by the parish until I ran away to sea.'

'Why did you run away?'

'Because they made me work for nothing and gave

me scraps to eat. I was better off at sea, and if I'd stayed with my last berth I shouldn't have left the captain—but this one is a monster.'

Maribel reached out to touch his hand, her heart moved to pity by his plight. She had not realised there was so much suffering, for as unhappy as she had been after her stepmother's death, she had never known what it was like to go hungry or go in fear of a cruel master.

'If I am ransomed, I shall ask to take you with me. As my servant you would be fed and paid a wage—and I should not beat you.'

'I thank you, lady,' Tom said and lifted his head with a touch of pride. 'Here on this ship all men are equal. We sail by the laws of the brethren and share in the spoils. I reckon I'll be a servant to no man or woman in future—though if I were I could not want a better mistress.'

Maribel inclined her head, uncertain whether she had been rebuffed. Did servants dislike working for their masters? She had never considered it before. For the first time, Maribel was aware of the sheltered life she had led, protected, kept apart—but not loved, at least by her father.

The older man with the scar on his face was ushering her below deck. She obeyed, moving towards the hatch, but lingered for a moment looking about her. Tom seemed to think he had made a change for the better and somehow her fear had evaporated.

Of course their captain was a wicked, arrogant rogue and she disliked him, even though she had felt something very odd when he kissed her. She would do her best to avoid his company, but it would appear that for the moment she had little to fear from the pirates. They were not as wild as she had feared, and, as she looked back and saw that the captain was coming aboard, she understood that he was in complete command of his ship. The men jumped to obey his orders as he indicated they should disengage with the other ship, but they did so willingly. She had seen no sign of fear or resentment in their faces.

Her gaze went beyond him to the deck of the *Mistress Susanna*. She saw that Samuel Hynes was tied to a mast and that his men were beginning to cut the ropes that bound him…but they were taking their time. She had seen both fear and resentment on board that ship—as she had seen it in some of the men who served her father. Why was it different here?

'You should not linger on deck, lady.'

Maribel jumped guiltily as she heard the pirate captain's voice.

'I see that you have allowed Captain Hynes to live.'

'Against the will of some of my men.' Justin's gaze narrowed. 'Have you some affection for this man?'

'None, sir. I merely regret any bloodshed.'

'It is necessary at times, but we are not monsters. We kill only when we must.'

'Then why are you pirates? Could you not find an honest trade?'

'You ask too many questions, Donna Maribel.'

'You know my name—may I not at least know yours, sir?'

'Captain Sylvester, at your service.'

'Do not mock me. If you were at my service, you would not have kidnapped me.'

'I saw no force used, lady. You walked aboard my ship willingly.'

'Because I was given no choice! What would you have done had I refused?'

'Ah…' His eyes gleamed with mockery. 'I should then have had to carry you on board myself, for I would have no other lay their hands on you. As Captain I have first choice of the spoils—and you are my share, lady.'

'You promised to ransom me…' Maribel's heart raced as she looked into his eyes. They were so blue that she thought of a summer sky and for a moment she was drawn to him, but there was ice at their centre and she shivered, sensing his anger.

'Perhaps I shall…' Justin did not smile. 'Yet there is something about you that I think might be worth more than mere gold. So perhaps you should not tarry; I have work to do and you will be safe in your cabin.'

What did he mean? Her heart jerked with fright and yet her body tingled, making her feel more alive than she had for a long, long time. He might be a pirate and a rogue, but there was something compelling about Captain Sylvester—something that made her heart beat faster.

She turned and hastened towards the open hatch. Her pulses were racing as she climbed down the ladder taking her to the cabins below. She squashed the feeling that she might like him if she allowed herself to judge him fairly. No, she would not give in to weakness. The pirate captain was a devil! An arrogant, wicked, mocking devil and she hated him! Yet at the back of her mind a little voice was telling her that he had saved her from a fate that might have been far worse than her present situation.

Maribel stared out of the porthole at the calm sea. They had been at sea for two days and she had not left her cabin. She turned her head as her maid entered. Anna brought her food and wine each day and already knew her way about the ship.

'The captain says you may come on deck for some air, my lady—but that you should keep your head covered for the sun is hot and he would not have you take harm.'

'You may tell Captain Sylvester that I have no wish to come on deck or to mix with rogues.'

Anna looked at her oddly. 'Do you think it wise to send such a message, my lady?'

'How would you have me address him—as a friend?' Maribel knew that her maid's counsel was wise, but something inside her would not allow her to give in so easily.

'We have not been treated ill…'

'Indeed?' Maribel's dark eyes flashed. 'If you do not think it *ill* to be abducted and forced aboard a pirate ship, I do. Sylvester had no right to take us captive.'

'He had the right—'tis the law of the sea. He might have sunk the vessel and all with it, but only those that resisted were harmed, and I think none killed. It is not always the case with pirates. Had we been taken by corsairs we should be dead or on our way to a slave market, where we should be sold to the highest bidder.'

Maribel wrinkled her brow. She knew that her maid spoke the truth; they could have fared worse. However, she had no intention of relenting towards the pirate.

'You will please give my message to the captain, as I bid you.'

'Yes, my lady—but should you not like to go on deck for some air?'

'Not with rogues!'

Maribel turned back to her view of the sea. She was longing for some fresh air, tired of being cooped up in her cabin, and yet her pride would not let her give in.

After Anna had left her, Maribel ate a piece of bread and a mouthful of cheese. The bread was coarse and harder than she was used to, but the cheese tasted good. She sipped her wine, then put it down and began to pace the cabin. How long would it be before they made land? Where was the pirate taking her—and what would happen next?

'Forgive me, sir. My mistress is proud and bid me answer you in her own words. She is angry because she was forced to come aboard your ship.'

'Do not look anxious, Anna,' Justin said, a wry smile on his mouth. 'I shall not blame you for your mistress's words. I shall leave her to her own devices for a few days and then we shall see.'

'She needs to come up for some air or she will be ill.'

'Is she unwell? Does she suffer from sickness?'

'She is well enough, but I know she is fretting.'

Justin inclined his head. 'I shall speak to the foolish woman myself.'

He spoke to his first officer and then left the bridge. The Spanish woman was proud and ill tempered. When he first saw her she had taken his breath with her exotic beauty. Her hair was dressed across her forehead and caught in ringlets at either side of her face in the Spanish style, her clothes heavy and ugly compared with the gowns his mother had worn, for Lady Devere's gowns had come from France. Donna Maribel Sanchez was proud, cold and disdainful, as were most of her kind. Clearly she considered no one but herself and was furious at finding herself a captive. Her maid was concerned for her and would bear the brunt of her sickness if she fell ill. She deserved to be taught a lesson and yet he had seen spirit in her, something fine and lovely. He would not have her become sickly from lack of fresh air.

Outside her cabin door, he paused and then knocked. There was a moment's hesitation and then the word 'enter' spoken in a way that made him smile inwardly.

'Donna Maribel,' he said as he entered the cabin, 'I understand you are frightened to come on deck because you think us rogues and murderers.'

'I am not afraid, sir!' Maribel's head came up with a flash of pride. 'I simply do not wish to consort with murdering rogues…pirates.'

'I shall not deny that we are pirates, for 'tis clearly our trade. However, my men are not wicked rogues.

They were driven to mutiny by a cruel master and must now earn their living by roaming the seas in search of rich merchant ships to plunder.'

'You do not consider that makes you rogues?' She looked at him scornfully.

'Did you see anyone murdered aboard Captain Hynes's ship?'

'No…' She looked at him uncertainly. 'You said your men wished to hang him.'

'Yet I did not allow it. Some men in my position would have taken the ship as well as the cargo and hung or marooned those who would not join us.'

She was forced to acknowledge that he spoke the truth. When he spoke softly to her, she found herself drawn to him against her will, but she was not ready to admit defeat.

'Very well, not murderers, but still thieves, for you took what was not yours.'

'We are adventurers. We take what we need, but we do not harm innocent women and children; men are given the chance to surrender and join us or go on their way. Your maidservant has not been harmed and you may walk safely on our decks. I give you my word that not one member of my crew will lay a finger on you.'

'The word of a pirate?'

'My word is as good as any man's.' Justin moved towards her. She gasped and stepped back, her eyes widening as if she thought he would repeat the punishing kiss he had given her before. 'You are quite safe, as long as you behave yourself, lady. I have never yet taken an unwilling woman…' He laughed mockingly. 'Most come willingly enough to my bed.' His voice had a deep, sensual timbre that sent shivers down her spine. 'I shall not deny that I think you desirable, but I shall never force you to lie with me. You must come to me of your own free will…as you may one day.'

'If you imagine that I would lie with you willingly…' Maribel's manner was one of disdain, but underneath her heart was hammering wildly in her breast; the picture his words conjured up was disturbing. She suddenly saw him bending over her as she lay in silken sheets, his mouth soft and loose with desire, his breath warm on her face, and her throat closed as she was pierced with desire. She gripped her hands at her sides, controlling her feelings, as she had been taught from childhood. A high-born lady did not allow herself to be seduced by a pirate, despite his undoubted charm. It was a picture too shocking to be contemplated. Turning away, she used anger to hide her confusion. This was madness! She was beginning to like him and she must not. 'You are a mocking rogue, Captain Sylvester. I shall never come to you in that way.'

'So be it…but still you are free to take the air every day for an hour or so. If you stay here in your cabin you may become ill and we have no time to spare for nursing a sick woman. I shall not force you to come up, but if you are not sensible I may have to persuade you.'

'What do you mean?' Maribel's heart raced and she caught her breath as her senses whirled and she imagined what he might do. 'You wouldn't dare…'

Justin moved in closer, towering over her. 'I dare anything, lady—but I mean you no harm. We shall soon reach a secluded cove on the island of Mallorca, where I mean to go ashore and replenish our water supplies before we set sail for Cyprus.'

His words banished the foolish thoughts, making her angry once more. 'Cyprus? No, I shall not go with you, sir. You promised you would ransom me to my family! How dare you take me to Cyprus? I demand to be returned to Spain!'

'I believe I made no promises.' Justin's gaze narrowed. 'I have learned that you know nothing of your affianced husband—or his cousin. You would not go so gladly to your wedding if you knew what manner of men they were, believe me.'

'I do not go gladly, but I must obey my father. He controls the fortune my husband left to me and I have no choice…' Her throat closed and the tears stood on her lashes. She looked at him with an unconscious appeal in her eyes. Could she trust him? If he spoke the truth, it seemed her father had betrayed her. She had never felt more alone in her life. 'Is Lord Roberts truly the monster you told me?'

'When I knew of him he was steeped in vice and, I believe, riddled with the pox. I would not have expected him to live long enough to take a bride. If you lie with him, he will infect you with some foul disease—a disease that will cause you great suffering, perhaps even your death.'

Maribel's face was ashen. 'My father could not have

known he was so evil…' Her voice broke on a sob. 'My first husband loved me. He loved me…' The tears slid down her cheeks, her pride forgotten for the moment. 'I would rather die than become the wife of such a monster.'

Justin moved in closer. 'Do not weep, lady. I would not see you break your heart. Perhaps the future holds more than you might think.' His hand moved out to touch her, but fell without doing so. 'For your own sake, come on deck for some air—or I may have to fetch you!'

Maribel looked up at him. Something about him then made her long to trust him. For some foolish reason she wanted to go to his arms, lay her head against his shoulder and weep, but pride made her raise her head once more. She was so alone and he seemed to offer comfort, yet how could she trust a pirate?

'You swore none of your men would lay a hand on me,' she said and even as she spoke saw his frown and regretted that her words broke the tiny thread that had held them.

'Aye, I did—but I said nothing of myself.' Justin glared at her. ''Pon my soul, lady, you could do with a lesson in manners—and I've a mind to give it! Think yourself fortunate that I have much to do on deck.'

He went out, letting the cabin door close behind him with a bang. Maribel caught her breath—she knew that she had pushed him hard. If he lost patience with her, he could make her very sorry for daring to challenge him. She sat down on the edge of the bed, her thoughts whirling in confusion. Her upbringing had taught her that men of his kind were not to be trusted, and yet her instincts told her that he was a man she could turn to in times of trouble. There was no reason why he should help her, and yet a little voice in her head told her that if she asked for help he might give it.

Maribel knew that the ship was no longer moving. She could see the coast of an island a short distance away and understood that they had anchored in the bay. Although she had never been there, she believed they were close to the island of Mallorca. Don Sabatini had estates here, brought to him by his second wife Juanita, who had come from the island. Maribel wondered if there might be cousins or relatives of her stepmother living here. Would they know her if she managed to get ashore? Would they help her to escape from the pirates who had captured her?

Yet if she did escape, what would happen to her? Would her father still force her to marry Lord Roberts? She doubted that he would believe her if she told him that the man was a disease-ridden monster. He would never take the word of a pirate captain, and perhaps she should ignore it—and yet why should Captain Sylvester lie about such a thing? How could it benefit him?

Maribel jumped as the cabin door opened. She swung round, half-expecting another visit from the captain since she had ignored his advice to go on deck, but it was only Anna.

'We are to go ashore this evening,' Anna told her. 'The pirates will provision the ship ready for the voyage to Cyprus and it is the last chance for us to go ashore before we reach our destination.'

'We must try to escape,' Maribel said. 'Juanita came from Mallorca. My father has estates here. If we could reach them…'

'I have given my promise not to try to escape in return for being allowed ashore, and you must do the same. It is the only way, my lady.'

'A promise to a pirate? Would you put that above your duty to me?' Maribel asked, feeling piqued that her maid had seemingly given her allegiance to the enemy.

Anna looked uncomfortable. 'Please do not ask me to break my word. I swore that you would not try to run off, my lady. I think they would punish us both if you did—I might be beaten…'

'No! I should not allow that,' Maribel said. 'If we were caught, I should take the blame.'

'We have not been treated ill, my lady. Why do you not simply wait for the ransom? It might be dangerous to escape. We could fare worse at the hands of others. Remember we have no money to buy a passage home.'

'I am not sure I wish my father to ransom me.' Maribel frowned. 'If my stepmother's relatives would take me in, I might recover control of my fortune—and then I should not have to obey my father. I could marry when I chose.'

'Do you think Don Sabatini would allow that? Do you not know why he is sending you to England?'

'What do you mean?' Maribel's gaze narrowed.

'Your father covets Don Pablo's estates. It was the

reason he allowed you to marry him. I have heard it whispered that it is the reason your husband was killed.'

'That was bandits…' Maribel felt sick and shaken. She moved her head negatively. 'No! You cannot believe that my father…would have had Pablo killed.'

'I do not know, my lady. I have heard these whispers. But why would he send you to such a man if it were not so? Perhaps he anticipates your death…'

Maribel turned away from her, unable to look into her servant's face. She thought of her sweet young husband. She had always believed he was killed by bandits, but if her father… No, she could not believe that of him, even though he had disregarded her wishes in the matter of her marriage. Yet if the servants were talking of these things, there must be some truth in them. Her determination to escape hardened. If she could reach Juanita's family, they would surely take her in and help her…

'I am pleased that you have decided to be sensible,' Justin said, a wry smile playing about his mouth as she came on deck later that day. 'We shall sleep under the stars this night, lady, but a bed shall be prepared for you so that you may lie comfortably.'

'How long do you intend to remain here?'

'A day or two to replenish the supplies of fresh fruit and wine, also meat and water. We have taken on supplies here before and the people are friendly. They do not condemn us, as your people do, as heretics and pirates, but trade with us for gold and silver.'

'When will you send word to my father that you wish to ransom me?'

'Captain Hynes will have carried the tale to him. I said that he might arrange a meeting through an agent in Cyprus. We shall do the exchange there…if one is made…'

'What do you mean—if?' Maribel studied his face, trying to read what was in his mind. She was not sure why his nearness made her feel so odd, as if her chest was constricted and she could scarcely breathe. She drew away, suppressing her feelings. She must not begin to like him. If she once let down her guard… Impossible thoughts filled her mind but she banished them.

'I thought you might prefer your freedom?'

'You would let me go without ransom?'

'I might take the ransom and still keep you.' Justin's teeth flashed white as he smiled in the moonlight.

'You do not mean it?' She was not sure if he was teasing her.

'Would you prefer me to hand you over to a man who would sell you to the devil?'

'I should prefer it if—' Maribel stopped. She had been about to tell him of her stepmother's family and beg him to let her go to them, but something held her tongue. He was persuasive, but she must not trust him. She had only his word that Lord Roberts was diseased and evil, though she could see no reason why he should lie to her.

'What would you prefer, lady? Tell me. Perhaps I might grant your wish.'

Maribel hesitated. His voice was soft; it seemed to promise much and a part of her longed to confide in him. He was so strong and she wanted someone to help and protect her from the things she feared, but he was a pirate. How could she believe the man who had abducted her? Her mind told her it would be foolish and yet her instincts were telling her something very different. Despite herself she was beginning to like him.

'No…' She shook her head, because she could not be sure he would help her. 'I should prefer it if you had never taken me captive.'

'Would you, Madonna?' He smiled at her and her heart missed a beat. 'I am not sure that I believe you. Come…' He held out his hand. 'You must climb down to the boat and be rowed ashore.' She gave him her hand and his fingers closed about it, strong, cool and somehow comforting. 'I have your word that you will not try to run away?'

'I believe Anna already gave you surety?'

'Yes, she did, but I would have it from you.'

'Very well, you have it.' Maribel glowered at him. She looked down at the rope ladder. 'I am not sure I can manage that.'

'Fear not. I shall go before you. I shall steady your feet so that you do not miss a rung—and if you fall I shall catch you.'

'I shall not fall!'

Maribel did not miss the gleam in his eyes. She watched as he went on to the ladder. Tom came forwards to help her place one foot on the ladder and then she was over the side and seeking the next. A strong hand caught her ankle and placed her foot on the next rung, sending a shock running through her that made her gasp and almost lose her balance. How dare he touch her in such an intimate manner? She had almost begun to trust him, but this was too much! She would have liked to vent her fury on him, but it would be undignified to rage at him in this position. She glanced down indignantly and saw the gleam of mischief in his eyes.

'Thank you, but I need no help of that kind.'

'I would not have you fall on me, lady.'

Maribel caught the mockery in his voice and fumed inside. Oh, what a rogue he was! How dare he laugh at her? She would have liked to reprimand him, but all her concentration was on negotiating the ladder without treading on her skirts or lifting them high enough to give him a view of her thighs.

As she reached the bottom he helped her to step down into the boat, steadying her as she found a seat and sat down. She sent him a look of scorn, but refused to speak, because the expression on his face told her that he had enjoyed her predicament.

Maribel watched Anna descend nimbly into the boat and scowled. Her maid had managed easily alone and she might too if that oaf had not grabbed her ankles every time she took a step. How he must have enjoyed that!

She would not look at either of them, sitting stony-faced and staring at the shore as they were rowed closer.

When she realised that she would have to wade through water to get to the beach, she was dismayed. She must either lift her skirts high enough to avoid getting them wet and thus reveal her legs in front of the pirates or suffer a wet gown for hours.

She stood hesitating, unsure of how best to go about it, but then became aware that Captain Sylvester was in the water beside the boat.

'Come, lady, let me carry you.' He held out his hand.

'I can manage…'

'You will get your gown wet and it will not be pleasant.'

'I can manage.' Maribel tried to put one leg over the side of the boat, but he grabbed her waist, swinging her up and over his shoulder. She gave a scream of anger, beating at his back.

'Put me down, you brute! Put me down at once.'

'You tempt me, lady. You sorely tempt me to dump you in the water,' Justin said but carried her up the beach and then set her on her feet. Maribel immediately took a swing at him, but he caught her wrist in an iron vice, his expression stern and forbidding. 'Be careful, Madonna. Try my patience too often and you will regret it.'

'You are arrogant and I hate you!'

'Arrogant? Yes, perhaps I am,' Justin said. 'But I do not believe that you hate me. Tell me you are sorry.'

'No. I shall—' Maribel caught her breath as he suddenly crushed her against him. She lifted her gaze and something in his face made her gasp. He was so powerful and strong and she was playing with fire. 'I take it back. You are arrogant, but I do not hate you.'

The strong feeling he aroused in her was not hate, but a mixture of annoyance and frustration, because he seemed to enjoy provoking her. She was used to politeness and respect and this man—this man had cut through the layers, stripping away all that she had known and accepted as her due.

'That is better.' Justin laughed and let her go. 'Forgive me, lady, but you tempt me almost past bearing. I have seldom seen such delicious ankles and beautiful legs. I could not help myself. You are a siren sent to lure me to my death, I dare say.'

Maribel tossed her head, protecting herself in the only way she knew. 'You are impossible. Would that I were a man! I would run you through with my sword.'

'You might try.' His eyes seemed to flash blue fire, making her hold her breath. 'Tantrums will avail you nothing. We of the brethren are equals. You will be required to work, as is everyone else. You may help Tom fill the barrels with water from the well at the hacienda. It is a job for boys and women.'

Maribel threw him a look of disgust, but held her breath. He had made her very aware of his strength and power over her. She could only obey him for the moment—but when everyone was sleeping she would rouse Anna and together they would escape into the interior of the island. Someone would tell her where she could find Juanita's family.

Justin watched the woman struggle with the heavy pail, tipping it into the barrel, which would be loaded

on to the ship with others for their journey. She had
made her dislike of him plain enough, but she had not
shirked from the job he had given her, even though she
must find it hard after the life she had led.

He frowned as he wondered just what kind of life she
had led as Don Sabatini's daughter. Everything he knew
of the man had led him to feel nothing but disgust and
anger, but the girl was different. Yes, she was proud and
arrogant, but anyone might react that way when taken
captive by pirates. No doubt she had feared for her life
or worse at the start, and indeed if it had been one of
the other pirate vessels that roamed the seas in search
of ships to prey on she might have fared much worse.
Had Corsairs taken the ship she could have been sold
as a slave in the markets of Algiers.

She was proud and spoiled, and at first he had
thought she might in truth be her father's daughter and
not to be trusted, but he had realised almost at once that
she was innocent. Indeed, had he not known she had
been widowed, he would have thought her still an un-
touched girl.

Her beauty stirred his senses, and had he been another
kind of man he would have taken her when she defied him
in her cabin, but her courage in defying him had amused
him. She was Sabatini's daughter and as such could mean
nothing to him save for the ransom she would bring, but
there was something about her that made him smile.

Maribel's teeth sank into the soft meat of the suckling
pig that had been slow roasted over a fire for hours. It

was very strange, but she had never eaten anything quite as delicious. At first she had been inclined to refuse such fare when the succulent thigh was offered her, but the smell was so good and she was hungry after her work.

She wiped the grease from her mouth, then hesitated before rubbing it into her hands. The water buckets had been heavy and her hands felt sore from carrying them from the well to the barrels that the men had then transported to the ship; the grease would act like a salve and ease the stiffness.

The owner of the hacienda had come to greet them. He seemed on friendly terms with Captain Sylvester and more than ready to supply them with all the food they needed for their journey. It was he and his wife who had supplied the feast they had just eaten. Maribel wondered if he might know of her stepmother's relatives.

Getting up from the bench where she had sat to eat her meal, she wandered over to where the farmer's wife was ladling soup into wooden bowls.

'Good evening, *señora.*'

'Would you care for some wine, Donna Maribel?'

'Thank you, but I have eaten well of your suckling pig. I was wondering if you might know some friends of mine who live on the island?'

'I know everyone who lives on Mallorca, lady.'

'Would you know the family of Donna Juanita Sabatini? Her family name is Mendoza.'

'I knew Donna Juanita, a lovely lady.' The woman smiled at her. 'I worked for her family as a young woman. There is only an elderly cousin left now and he lives alone.'

'Where can I find him?'

'At the other side of the island, a journey of some hours on foot—but I would not go there if I were you.'

'Why?'

'He is a peculiar, lonely man. He might not welcome strangers.'

'Juanita was very dear to me…' Maribel hesitated. 'Could I borrow a horse from your stable? I would return it.'

'You will have to ask my husband, lady. Perhaps if Captain Sylvester stood surety for you…'

Maribel hesitated. It seemed these people trusted her captor, but not her. She might have to make her journey on foot—and she could not be sure of a welcome. She had hoped that Juanita might have a sister or female cousin, but when she thought it over, her stepmother had never talked of her family.

It was a risk, but one she must take. She could not go with the pirates to Cyprus and she would not return to her father to be sent to England like a package he had sold.

One thing the pirate captain had done for her was to make her question her father's motives. It seemed that there might be more behind his determination to marry her to an English lord than met the eye—but surely Juanita's cousin would help her? She would pay him once she had control of the fortune left to her by her husband.

Surely someone somewhere would be willing to help her?

* * *

The crew had been drinking and singing for a long time. They were obviously enjoying their time on shore, but at last they had quietened. She believed that most were asleep now.

Maribel sat up and looked about her. She could see no sign of movement. It seemed that the pirates felt secure enough not to set a guard. She reached out and shook Anna's shoulder. The woman snorted and grunted, but would not wake.

'Anna!' Maribel whispered, bending close to her ear. 'It is time for us to leave!'

Anna snored on, giving no sign that she had heard. Maribel hesitated. If she shouted at the girl, someone else might wake. Perhaps it was best to leave her and go alone. Beneath Maribel's gown was concealed a pouch containing all the gold and jewellery she possessed; her clothes and other valuables remained on board the pirate ship, but she must leave them behind if she wanted to escape. She could only pray that Juanita's cousin would be prepared to take her in and help her recover her fortune. If he would not…

Maribel was not certain what she would do then. She only knew that she did not want to remain as the pirate's captive, nor did she wish to return home.

Anna could stay where she was; it seemed she was happy enough under the pirate's rule. Maribel stood up, taking her blanket with her. It was cooler now, though during the day it would be hot. The blanket would keep her warm and if she had to spend more than one day in the open she would have something to lie on at night.

She deliberately put the farmer's wife's warning from her mind. Juanita's cousin would surely help her. Why should he not?

Creeping from the campsite, Maribel slipped away into the trees that fringed the beach. She had only a vague idea of where to find Juanita's family, but she could ask someone. The people at the hacienda had been friendly and she had money to ease her way.

She had been walking for only a few minutes when she heard a twig snap behind her. Her heart beating wildly, she turned but could not see anything.

'Who is it?'

No answer came. Maribel took a deep breath and walked on. She began to climb the ridge that led away from the beach. She could hear rustling sounds behind her and her pulses raced. It must be some kind of animal. Perhaps a pig turned loose in the woods to forage…

Suddenly, the noise came from a different direction. Spinning round, she saw a man's figure through the trees and caught her breath.

'I thought it was you. Where do you think you are going?'

Maribel hesitated. He had followed her! She might have known that escape would not be as easy as it seemed!

'I needed to relieve myself.'

'So far from the camp? Why did you bring a blanket with you? Are you sure you were not trying to escape?'

'Why should I? Where could I go?'

'To the house of Don Vittorio Mendoza, perhaps?'

'She told you…' The farmer's wife had betrayed her!

'Señora Gonzales told her husband and he told me. He warned me that I should not let you go there for Mendoza is not a good man—he is bitter and lives alone since his family died of a fever.'

'He is the only one I can turn to. He will help me because of Juanita.' Tears stung her eyes. 'You must let me go. You must…'

His manner was stern. 'I have given my word that you will not be harmed, but I cannot let you go there.'

'Why? My father will probably refuse to pay the ransom. Why should he pay for my return if he wants my fortune?'

'I think he will pay, for his pride's sake, and because if you married your estates would belong to your husband. Under the law, he could not keep them from you then. Unless your future husband agreed to give them up…'

'Do you think Lord Roberts agreed to give them up? Why…?' Her gaze narrowed. 'Why would he agree to such a bargain?'

'Perhaps because he has little chance of finding a young and beautiful bride of good birth in England. Besides, once you were his wife, he could have reneged on the deal had he wished.'

'Then my father knew what kind of a man he was sending me to.' Maribel felt sickened. 'I will not marry him. I shall never marry, for who could I trust if even my own father would use me thus?'

'You may not have a choice.' Justin's eyes were on her. 'Would you rather go to England with Captain Hynes or take your chance with me? I promise that I will help you find freedom. I shall not let your father sell you to that man or anyone else.'

He was asking her to trust him. It was a huge step, but she was not sure she had a choice, and there was something about him that reassured her…something that made her insides melt and she longed to feel safe and secure within his arms. Her father would call him a rogue and hang him if he had the chance, but her father had sold her to a man she must despise and fear. This man seemed honest and something was telling her to give him her trust for all he was a pirate. Once again she experienced a desire to be held in his arms, to give up the struggle to be free and let him dictate her life.

'Do you swear it?'

'I swear on all I hold sacred.'

'Then I shall believe you.' She felt close to swooning; if he had taken her into his arms then, she would not have resisted.

'Come back to the camp—and give me your word that you will not try to run away again?'

Maribel stared at him for a moment, then inclined her head. 'Very well. I give you my word.' Her eyes sparkled with tears. 'I do not know why I have resisted you. You have been kinder to me than my own father.'

'Maribel…' Justin moved towards her, gazing down at her face in the dawning light. Her heart pounded in her breast and she found it difficult to breathe as she caught the fresh masculine scent of him. She swayed towards him, her will to fight almost gone. 'Will you give yourself into my care? I promise I shall not force you to do anything against your will.'

'I believe you. I think that I…' Maribel hesitated, looking into his eyes. Even as she would have spoken, they heard a booming sound from out at sea. Looking down at the beach, she saw the pirates were awake and yelling something as they dashed down to the water's edge. 'What is happening? Are we being attacked?'

'No, the ship is mine—one that I took captive some weeks ago. It is bringing a message from your father.'

'But you told me you were to meet on Cyprus…' Her eyes widened and she drew away from him, feeling hurt. 'You lied to me. You were planning to sell me to my father all the time!'

'At first, yes, I thought of a ransom.' Justin frowned. 'When I spoke to you of Cyprus I planned to leave a message here for my other ship, but it has arrived sooner than I expected.'

'How can I believe you?' Maribel felt betrayed. 'You are the same as my father—you care only for the money I may bring you.'

She turned from him and began to run back down the hill to the beach below, the tears stinging her eyes. He had looked at her in such a way that she had begun to trust him, to believe that he would treat her fairly—but he would use her for his own purpose like every man she had ever met, except her Pablo.

Chapter Three

Maribel sensed that someone was watching her. She turned her head in the direction of Captain Sylvester and the man who had brought the second pirate ship into the cove. He was older, dark of hair and pale complexioned; his eyes had a strange piercing quality.

'Who is that man with the captain?' she asked of Tom as he came up to her. 'There is something about him…' She shook her head, not knowing why the man's gaze made her uncomfortable.

'Higgins told me he is the acting captain of the *Maria*. The ship was taken a few weeks back and is a Portuguese merchantman. His name is Mr Hendry—or Captain Hendry, I suppose. Higgins doesn't like him; he thinks he is sly and not to be trusted, but Captain Sylvester put him in charge of their sister ship, because of his experience. He will sail with us to Cyprus.'

'Are we still to sail for Cyprus?'

'I have heard the men say that we may sail for the

pirates' island instead. There are many islands in the region that are uninhabited, some used by the brethren. We need a safe haven so that we can divide the spoils of the past months. I am to receive a share though I took no part in capturing them.'

'What is the name of this island?' Maribel looked apprehensive. 'I suppose it is a sinful place where pirates congregate to get drunk and frequent the tavern whores.'

'I cannot tell you the name—its location is a secret—but I believe it is much the same in any port, lady,' Tom told her. 'Men will drink and indulge themselves after a long sea voyage. It is natural for men who live as we do to spend their gold in such fashion. At least until the time comes to settle down.'

Maribel was silent. In her heart she knew she had no reason to condemn the pirates or their captain. It was true they had taken her captive, but she had been treated fairly since then. She wanted to believe in their captain, if only she could let go of her preconceived prejudices and accept his word.

She walked towards Captain Sylvester and Mr Hendry, wanting to know what was being decided between them. As he saw her approach, the captain left his companion and came to meet her.

'Your father has sent word that he wants a truce between us,' Justin told her, but there was an odd expression in his eyes. 'He asks that I meet him face to face. He will pay a ransom for your safe return and for safe conduct through these waters. It would mean an end to what has become a feud between us.'

'Do you wish for an end to it?' She held her breath as she waited for his answer.

'If Don Sabatini agrees to pay us for safe passage, we shall leave his ships in peace. There are plenty more vessels we might take and the Portuguese merchantmen are usually the most profitable.'

'So you will sell me to him?' Maribel's face was white and she felt the sickness rise in her throat.

'I thought it was what you wanted?' Justin's gaze narrowed. 'When I took you captive you assured me your father would pay to have you back—and it seems you were right.'

'I did not know then what manner of man he was.' Maribel was close to tears. 'I hate you… Why did you pretend to care what happened to me?'

She turned and fled down the beach, because the tears were close and she did not wish to shame herself before him.

Justin stared after her. He had not told her the whole truth, because he was uncertain what to believe. The Don's message was a little strange. It seemed that there was something he wanted even more than the return of his daughter.

Touching the package inside his jerkin, Justin frowned. Could the map of the silver mines, which he had captured from Don Sabatini's flagship, be the only one in existence? If the Don wanted the map more than his own daughter, it must be that he could not return to the mines without it. Justin had taken some chests of silver from the Don's ships, but the map to the mines might be worth vast sums—if a man were willing to risk all that it entailed.

Had Maribel been sent to sea as bait? Had he walked into some kind of a honeyed trap—and did she know about it? If she did not and her father truly desired the map above her, he must indeed be as evil as rumour would have him. If he were so evil, it would be wrong to send her back for she would be given to a man whose very touch would corrupt her. This was a problem that required some attention and could not be solved in an instant.

Justin was thoughtful as he stared out to sea. He knew that the Don was a brutal man who had murdered slaves—could he ever be justified in returning the map to such a cruel devil? Giving his daughter back was out of the question.

Maribel walked for some time and then found a rock to sit on. She stared out at the sea. Within hours she might be back with her father—and how long would it be before she was once more on her way to England?

She did not want to marry the English lord her father had found for her! Even if she discarded what Captain Sylvester had told her, she would not wish to marry a man she did not know. If the story of his wickedness were true…she could not bear that her father would send her to such a man. Tears trickled down her cheeks. She dashed them away and began to walk slowly back towards the pirate camp. When she saw Captain Sylvester coming towards her, she hesitated, wanting to run away again but knowing she could not avoid him for long.

'I am sorry if I made you cry,' he apologised as he came up to her. 'Forgive me, Madonna. I shall send word that you are not to be ransomed and there will be no truce. The men would be against it—some of the crew have served aboard his ships and they hate him.' His hand reached out to her, wiping her face with his fingertips. 'Will you forgive me?'

'I do not know what to do.' Maribel faltered, her heart pounding as he moved closer. He was so strong and handsome and powerful, his mouth sensuous and strangely compelling. She felt the pull of his magnetism, but still struggled against it. 'If what you told me is true, I can never return to my home. My father controls my fortune. I have nothing but the things I took with me when I left for England.'

'Have you no friends or relatives who would help you?'

'There is only Don Mendoza…and you say he cannot be trusted.'

'What of your own mother's family?'

'She was English and died when I was small. I know my uncle's name but I do not know if they would take me in.'

Justin cupped her chin in his hand, looking down into her face. 'If you will trust me, I shall try to find where your mother's family live—and if any are still alive I will make sure you get safely to them.'

'You would do that for me?' Maribel's eyes widened, her mouth parting slightly. Before she knew what was happening, she swayed towards him and he caught her against him, kissing her softly on the lips. For a moment she tensed, then allowed herself to melt into his body, giving herself up to the unexpected pleasure that flooded through her. For a few moments she floated away in a cloud of sheer ecstasy 'Oh…that was nice…' she said as he let her go.

Justin chuckled deep in his throat. 'Sweet lady, you tempt me to sweep you up and run off to a place where no one will ever find us, but I have given my word. I shall make every effort to find your English family and return you to them.'

'But how will you discover them? I can only tell you my uncle's name.'

'And that is?'

'Fildene…I think that is right. Juanita mentioned my uncle once—Sir Henry Fildene.' She saw his eyes gleam. 'What? Do you know him?'

'I have not met the gentleman personally, but I believe I may know where to find him—and, since my father purchased wine from him, I believe he must be honest.' He smiled at her in a way that made her feel safe and protected. 'There should be no difficulty finding your family, Maribel.'

'I do not have words to thank you.' She lifted her eyes to his. 'Where shall we go next? To Cyprus as you planned?'

'We shall go to our island so that the spoils of previous journeys may be divided between us. I shall ignore your father's request to return his property and forget the truce.'

'Supposing my father sends his ships to attack you?'

'I do not fear Don Sabatini or any other man.'

'But…I do not wish to cause trouble for you.'

Justin touched her mouth with his fingertips. 'Your father and I were born to be enemies, for he is all that I despise. Whatever may happen in the future it will not be your fault, Madonna.'

He smiled down at her, making her heart beat like a drum. When he smiled like that she felt that nothing could ever harm her again.

Maribel stood on deck watching as the ship sailed away from the island of Mallorca. She had come on board willingly this time, though she was still apprehensive about her future.

She turned her head to smile as Captain Sylvester came to stand by her at the rails.

'You look pensive. Are you thinking of your home— or your husband?'

'My husband was kind to me. We were childhood friends. Pablo always told me that he would marry me one day. For a short time we were happy in our way. I think we were still children and thought like children, but we could not have stayed that way for ever.'

'I am not sure I understand you?' Justin lifted his brows.

'Pablo was killed riding in the hills soon after our marriage—I was told by bandits, but I wonder now if my father had something to do with his death. Pablo was young to inherit such rich estates and he would never suspect my father of playing him false.'

'You think your father coveted his wealth even then?'

'Yes, perhaps. I did not suspect it then and when he asked me to return home after my husband died I was lonely and wanted the comfort of being with my stepmother. Juanita loved me. My father was much kinder to me while she lived.'

'He controlled your fortune. Perhaps he had no reason to be unkind.'

'My father is not a poor man. I do not understand, why would he seek to steal what belonged to Pablo?'

'Wealth is power and some men will do anything for power. There are men driven by sheer greed; he may be one of those men.'

'Supposing he tries to take me back by force?'

'He did not demand your return. There was something he wanted more.'

'Something he wants more than his own daughter?' Maribel was intrigued.

'I suspect that I have the only copy of the map leading to his silver mines in the New World.' Justin's eyes were on her face. 'It was the map he demanded in return for a ransom.'

'A map that reveals the location of rich silver mines?' Maribel was stunned. 'How did you come by such a thing?'

'It was in a small chest I took from the captain of the *Juanita*. No one but me knows of its existence. If my men learned of such a map, they might wish to exploit it, for there is a fortune to be made from these mines.'

'You could be rich beyond your wildest dreams.'

She saw his smile and bit her lip. 'Is that why you refused his truce?'

'You must know it was not my main reason for refusing?' Justin laughed softly as her eyes widened. 'Wealth is not my driving ambition. I am not sure what should happen to the map, but I was not willing to send you back to him once I understood what he intended for you.'

'Oh…' Her breath came faster as she gazed into his eyes. Was he telling her that she was more important than the treasure map? 'Will you keep the map?'

'Perhaps…' Justin's eyes were on her face. 'What do you think I should do with such a map? It must be worth a great deal for your father to offer a large sum of gold for its return but some would say the mine is stained with the blood of those that died there.'

'I…do not know what you should do,' she said and shivered at the thought of what had happened at the mine. 'But if my father wants that map, he may try to get it back. He may send ships and men to look for you.'

'He might try. I have refused his offer. I shall not return the map, at least until I have considered more. Captain Hendry was brave enough to say that he would take the message.' Justin suddenly grinned at her. 'I told you once before, I do not fear Don Sabatini.'

'Is there anything you fear—anything that causes you pain?'

His eyes clouded, his manner becoming reserved. 'If there were, I should not tell you, Maribel. Such things are best unspoken.'

She felt a withdrawal in him and was sorry. Did he have a dark secret that he kept hidden?

Justin frowned as he watched her go below. He thought that she had begun to trust him a little, but he was not certain how he felt about the beautiful Spanish woman. It was true that he found her desirable. From the first moment he saw her standing so defiantly in her cabin he had wanted to make love to her. Being close to her was enough to make him burn with the need to kiss and hold her, the need to feel her heart beating next to his, to have her in his bed—but there were so many barriers between them. She thought of him as a pirate and a rogue, and although she had accepted that he was her only hope of reaching England and freedom, he was not certain that she would ever like him.

He had told her about the map to gauge her reaction, but she had no interest in it, and he was sure she thought it should be destroyed—that the blood of the murdered slaves tainted the mine. At first he had looked for something of her father in her, for a sign that she would betray him if she had the chance, but the more he spoke with her the more certain he became that she was innocent. She was certainly proud and wilful, but now that she had stopped fighting him, he found her too attractive for his peace of mind. Something inside him wanted to take away the look of anxiety from her eyes, to hold her and comfort her, and assure her that nothing would ever harm her again.

A rueful smile touched his mouth. Justin had loved once with all his heart, but the girl he would have made his wife had died suddenly of a fever a few days before their wedding. He had vowed that he would never allow himself to feel that kind of love again, to feel the deep dark despair and the pain that had almost torn him apart.

It was because of Angeline's death that he had become involved with the wild friends that had talked of deposing Queen Mary and setting Princess Elizabeth in her place. His despair had led him to drink too much and become careless—and that was what had brought him to his present situation.

Justin could never ask a woman to marry him, because he was a pirate and he had nothing to offer a decent woman…a woman like Maribel Sanchez.

He should put all thought of her from his mind and make arrangements to restore her to her family as soon as he could. In the meantime it would be better to avoid her company. Being close to her made him think of what might have been—what might be in the future if things were different.

Hearing the knock at her cabin door, Maribel looked up in surprise as the captain walked in. For a moment her heart pounded, but in an instant, she saw that he had not come with seduction on his mind.

'I thought you might like this, to help you pass the time,' Justin said, and handed Maribel a small book. It was bound in leather and looked as if it had been much used. 'It is written in English, but I think you understand the language well enough to enjoy it.'

'That is kind of you,' she said. 'Sometimes the days are long on board ship.' Opening the pages, she saw it was a book of poetry and exclaimed with pleasure. 'Oh, how lovely. I shall truly enjoy reading this, Captain Sylvester.'

'I thought you might,' he said and smiled. 'I shall not keep you longer, but finding the book amongst my things made me think that it might please you.'

Maribel stroked the worn leather with her hands reverently. The book contained an anthology of poems by different poets, but as she touched it, she noticed that it fell open at one particular place again and again. Glancing at the poem, she was struck by the title.

'A Lover's Lullaby' by George Cascoigne, she read aloud in wonder, for she would not have thought that such a poem would hold the captain's interest time and again

> *Sing lullaby, as women do*
> *Wherewith they bring their babes to rest;*
> *And Lullaby can I sing too,*
> *As womanly as can the best.*
> *With lullaby they still the child;*
> *And if I be not much beguiled,*
> *For man a wanton babe have I,*
> *Which must be stilled with lullaby.*

Her eyes scanned the following verses, which told a sad but poignant tale, of a woman who, it seemed had borne children out of wedlock, and must pay the price.

It was a beautiful set of verses, and yet Maribel wondered why it had drawn the captain to it so many times.

Maribel had been taking the air on deck. The sun was very warm and she fanned herself lazily, looking out across the water. They had been at sea for several days now and the weather had remained fine all that time.

She saw Captain Sylvester coming to meet her and waited for him to reach her. Although she had decided to trust him, Maribel never sought him out herself. She tried to keep a little distance between them—she was afraid that if she once let down her guard she would not be able to raise it again, and she suspected that he did the same.

'Have we much longer to go until we reach the island?'

'Are you impatient to get there?' Justin raised his brows.

'I am just curious. Where is this island?'

'It is one of a group off the coast of Greece. You may know that there are thousands of islands in the Aegean? Some are inhabited, many are not. We have made it our own and a small community awaits our return.'

'And is your community known to the wider world?'

'The approach is through a channel of dangerous rocks that keep unwanted visitors at bay. One day we may be discovered, but for the moment it is a haven for us and others of our kind.'

'You could not have taken me to England first?'

'I must honour my word to my men. Once we have

settled our business there I shall do as you ask me, Madonna. You have my word that no man will touch you without your permission. You are under my protection until I can get you to your family.'

'I believe you,' she said. 'But I must ask, how long must pass before we can sail for England?'

'There are things I must do at the island. Besides, we must wait until Hendry joins us. He will have given my message to your father—and he will bring his answer back.'

'Are you certain of that?' Maribel gazed into his eyes. 'My father might decide to hang Captain Hendry and keep your ship.'

'Hendry understood the risks, but he volunteered to take the message. I wanted your father to understand that there will be no truce between us.' Justin frowned. 'In return Hendry will own his ship and may sail where he wishes under his own command. Whatever happens, I shall take you to England—and find someone to care for you. You have my word.'

'Why should you do so much for me?'

'My word is my bond,' Justin told her, a harsh note in his voice. 'I think you have had little reason to trust the word of any man, lady—but I have told you you can trust mine.' His eyes glowed with fire as he looked down at her, causing her stomach to spasm with nerves. 'You tempt me more than you will ever know, yet I shall not force you—nor yet persuade you. You are as safe from me as any other man of my crew. Only if you came to me of your own free will would I make you mine.'

'What do you mean?' she whispered, a strange mixture of fear and hope spreading through her.

'I am not in a position to offer marriage to any woman,' he said and a little nerve flicked in his throat. 'Since I do not wish to live alone for the rest of my life I may take a mistress…'

'Why can you not marry? Are you married—is there someone anticipating your return?' Her mouth was dry as she waited for his answer, which was a while in coming. 'Someone you love?'

'There was once a woman I loved.' He frowned and looked into the distance. 'That was long ago, before I became what I am now. No one waits for me and I have no wife. Love is something I cannot afford, Maribel. It softens a man and makes him weak—but I would be generous to any woman I took as my partner in life. She would have to be the right kind of woman, one who could share the hardships of the life I live.'

Maribel drew a deep breath. What was he saying to her—that she could be his mistress if she chose? Or was he telling her that she was the wrong kind of woman? She knew that he desired her, and suspected that it would be heaven to lie with him. Part of her yearned to tell him that she would rather sail the seas as his woman than be wife to any other man, but something held her back. She knew nothing of this man or his hopes and dreams. It would be foolish to imagine that she could be more than a temporary amusement to such a man.

'I accept your word that I shall be safe on the island,'

she said at last. 'It seems that there are some honourable men left. My husband was one such man and perhaps you are another.'

'You told me your husband loved you—but did you love him? Are you still grieving for him?'

'Yes, I loved Pablo. I did not wish to marry again, but my father forced me to agree.'

She had loved Pablo, but she was beginning to understand that perhaps she had only ever loved him as a brother. However, she could not admit the truth to this man.

'And you truly wish to find your mother's family?'

'Yes…' she whispered, though her heart spoke otherwise.

She could not deny the strong attraction he had for her, the way something deep inside called to him, but he had spoken of taking a mistress. He did not need or want a wife. She was sure that he had been warning her to keep her distance, for he felt the attraction too. He would take her as his mistress and treat her well for as long as it pleased him but then, when it was over, she would be truly alone.

At least he had been honest with her and she must respect him for that, but there could be nothing more than a wary friendship between them.

Justin inclined his head. 'You will excuse me, lady. I have much to do.'

'Yes,' she said and smiled at him. 'I must not keep you from your work. I know I must often be in your way when I come on deck…'

'You would never be in my way,' he replied, and for a moment the heat in his eyes seared her.

Maribel went below to her cabin, feeling restless. Sometimes when the pirate captain looked at her that way she had feelings that were hard to ignore. Without his realising it, he had lit a fire inside her and she could not ignore it no matter how hard she tried.

It was merely physical. The result of a marriage that had not satisfied the woman in her. She had not realised then how much she would have missed as Pablo's wife, but she was beginning to understand now. There was something inside her that craved the kind of love she should have known with her husband—but it was the bold pirate who filled her dreams and made her restless, not her gentle husband. Yet it would not be just physical for her, because if she gave herself she would give her heart and he wanted only her body. He had loved a woman once and he did not wish to love again. Could she be content with such an arrangement?

A part of her cried out that she would take what happiness she could, but her mind denied it. She might long for the kind of loving that she had never known with her husband, but to love and not be loved in return would break her heart.

'Forgive me, Pablo,' she whispered, saying goodbye to the memories she had treasured. No longer a child, she felt that she was at the threshold of becoming a woman—if only she had the courage to step over.

* * *

Justin watched the woman as she stood at the prow of the ship, her long hair blowing softly in the breeze. She had abandoned her formal ringlets and the new style suited her. There was pride in every line of her body. She was a true lady and it showed in all she did, in her every movement and her speech. Her smile was an enchantment, though it was seen seldom enough. Sometimes when, as now, she stood staring out to sea, there was an air of sadness about her that wrenched at his heart. He could only guess at the causes. Was she missing her home or her husband?

Justin was aware of a nagging jealousy. Pablo Sanchez must have been a true man to hold her heart beyond the grave. Given the choice she would remain faithful to her dead husband, but for how long? Anger stirred in him. She should not be allowed to waste her life in regret for a man who could no longer hold or love her. Such beauty should be for the living.

Seeing her day by day as they sailed, spending a few moments in her company, explaining the way the sails were worked and the tools that he used for reading the stars to guide them on their journey, had brought him to a closer understanding with her. Her eyes no longer held that faint hint of fear whenever he approached. He believed she was beginning to trust him, to respect his word—but did she like him? Did she feel anything more than respect?

Justin had given his word that she would be safe from him and his crew. He had told her that she must come to him willingly, but he did not believe that it would happen. It would have been better to have taken her to England, given her money and let her find her own family, but the crew might have mutinied.

No, he would not lie to himself. He could have found a way to persuade them, but he had not wanted to part from her too soon. She drew him like a moth to a flame, but he knew that he would be foolish to hope that a woman like Maribel Sanchez would look twice at a pirate. Her world was not the one he had chosen; there was too wide a divide between them and he did not see how it could be crossed, except in a way that would shame her.

His smile was wry. Of late she had spoken softly to him, but at the start there had been such contempt in her voice when she spoke of pirates. She had challenged him so proudly and her contempt stung. He had been born to a proud family. There were times when he thought of his home longingly, but how could he ever return? One day Queen Mary would die and, pray God, Elizabeth would reign in her stead. He knew that the charges of treason would then be dropped, but there might be others in their place. He had incited men to mutiny. He had preyed on merchant ships, and the ships of friendly countries, also the *Mistress Susanna,* which was an English ship. He could not shame his father by returning to a trial and a hanging.

At the start he had been carried along by his sense of fair play and justice. The men had been ill treated and Captain Smythe had deserved what happened, perhaps more. Had he left the men to their own devices and gone to France to his cousins, Justin might have been able to return home, but it was too late. In Maribel's eyes he had seen the disgust and contempt that his mother would feel if she learned what her son had become.

Justin had not sent word to let his parents know he was still alive. Better that they should think him dead than know what trade he followed…

Maribel sighed as she brushed her hair. The weather had been so hot these past days, and the ship had been becalmed for a short time, making a long journey seem endless. She was desperate to go ashore again, though nervous of what awaited her at their journey's end. The atmosphere on board ship had become increasingly excited and tense as the ship drew nearer to its destination. The men could hardly wait for the promised time on shore and the division of spoils.

She had heard that some of the islands in the Caribbean had been for some time the haunt of pirates, and the seas about them were said to be a lawless place, but she had heard nothing of this island in the Aegean. She knew however that Corsairs haunted the Mediterranean seas, many of them from the Ottoman Empire. Her father had dismissed all pirates as thieves and rogues and spoken of a need for the seas to be swept clean by a sufficient force of ships ranged against them.

'While that nest of rats is allowed to survive we shall none of us be safe from these rogues,' she had heard him say more than once.

However, she knew that it was easier to talk of gathering a force to move against the brethren of the seas than to actually do it. Rich merchants cursed the pirates that preyed on them, but to fit out ships for battle was costly and wasted time that might be put to better effect. In truth, it was unlikely that it would happen unless several countries banded together.

Getting to her feet, Maribel gazed out of the window. She could see a dark haze on the horizon and knew that it must be the island they had sailed so far to find. Her heart pounded and she could scarcely breathe. She had been lulled into a sense of peace on the long journey for she had been treated with respect, both the pirate captain and his men seeming to keep a distance between them and her.

It was not so for Anna, who spent most of her time talking with Higgins or Tom on deck. She still did her work, but there was a new attitude in her manner. Now she was less deferential and treated Maribel more as a friend than a mistress.

Maribel was not certain how she felt about the new order. Anna had moved on while she was in limbo, neither a part of the close community that made up the crew or a prisoner. The men looked at her uncertainly, but few of them spoke to her.

'At first they thought you were Sylvester's woman,' Anna had told her once. 'Now they are not sure what you are to him. They keep you at a distance because he has said that any man who lays a finger on you will be hung.'

'That was harsh.' Maribel frowned. 'Surely such words were not necessary?'

'Some of them would respect you as a lady, others would rape you given the chance.' Anna was brutally frank. 'Some of the men are honest enough, but Higgins said that many are scum and not to be trusted. It will be worse when we get to the island and mix with the other crews.'

'I see…' Maribel shivered. Yet Anna had told her nothing she had not sensed from the beginning. She was safe only because she was under Captain Sylvester's protection. 'Perhaps it would be best if I did not go ashore.'

'We shall all go ashore,' Anna told her. 'The ship must be cleaned and refitted. You could not stay on board while that was happening.'

'I see.' Maribel bowed to her superior knowledge. Higgins must have told her what would happen when they reached the island. Anna was one of them. Maribel was still an outsider. 'Then I must wait until Captain Sylvester tells me what I must do.'

Chapter Four

'We shall drop anchor in the bay this evening,' Justin commented as he came to stand by Maribel that afternoon. She nodded, but did not turn her head to look at him.

Her gaze was intent on the island, a feeling of doubt mixed with anticipation in her heart. It had been just a dark smudge for some time, but now she could see the crowded waterfront with its untidy huddle of buildings. Few of them were substantial, most built of wood, and to her eyes of poor quality. Further back there were houses and taverns of a better standard, larger and more what she might have expected in a port anywhere, but it was clear that the community was small.

'It is not what I expected.'

'The accommodation here is not what you are used to, Maribel. I have a friend whose house is further inland. I shall take you there. Peg will look after you while we stay here.'

'Who is he? I do not know the name? Is Peg an English name?'

'It is a nickname, a woman's name. I dare say she was once called Margaret.' Justin frowned. 'Peg was sentenced to hang for murder. She killed a man who tried to rape her. Someone rescued her from the noose; then she found a lover and went to sea with him, dressed as a man. She served before the mast for some months and was involved in a mutiny. Eventually, the crew landed here. She and her man ran the largest tavern on the waterfront. He died of a fever last winter, but she carries on. Everyone respects Peg and they know she would as soon stick a knife in a man as allow him to take liberties. If she takes you under her wing, you will be safe.'

'Thank you.' Maribel hesitated, then, 'Where will you stay?'

'I shall lodge at one of the taverns. I am building a house. I commissioned it when we were last here with what gold I had, not stolen but my own, which I had hidden about me when I was shanghaied aboard my first ship. It is expensive to bring in stone, though we have an abundance of timber, which is why so many buildings are made of it. Once the house is finished, I shall stay there when we visit the island.'

'You were shanghaied—does that mean you were taken on board against your will?'

'Yes. Why do you ask?'

'I know so little of you, where you come from—and how you became a pirate. I do not think that you were always the man you are now?'

'No, I was not always a pirate,' Justin agreed. 'It was never my intention to become one, but sometimes we have little choice in life. Had I not become a pirate, I and others might have died.'

'You are a powerful man. Others obey you. Could you now not go where you wish?'

'Perhaps this is what I wish for.'

Maribel turned to look at him, her eyes wide and intent. 'Is this what you intend for the rest of your life? To roam the seas in search of prey and then come back to this place?'

Justin's expression hardened. 'I know that it must seem a wretched place after your homeland. The cities in Spain are beautiful and your home was no doubt solid and well built, the house of a wealthy man, but you were not happy there. Even a palace may be a prison if it is not a place of freedom. This island has been a refuge for men such as I for a relatively short time. In years to come it will grow larger. As more settlers arrive the town will begin to look more prosperous.'

'It will always be a haven for pirates,' Maribel said and then realised that her words sounded harsh— harsher than she intended.

'Yes, I dare say it will—until someone decides to blow us all from the face of the earth.' Justin's face was expressionless, his thoughts hidden. 'Yet not all the men and women here are scum. Some like Peg were forced to the life by the unjust laws that would have hung her for defending herself against an evil man. Would you condemn her too? Your own father has done many evil things. He is wealthy, but more to blame than some here for they never had a choice.'

Maribel's eyes fell before his anger. 'Yes, I know. I did not mean to insult Peg—or you. I understand that something terrible must have driven you to this life. I suspect that you were once a gentleman…'

'You suspect that I was once a gentleman…' A gleam of humour showed in his face for a moment, then it faded. He made her a mocking bow. 'Thank you, my lady. What makes a gentleman in your eyes—fine clothes and wealth or a large house?'

'No, of course I did not mean…' Maribel's cheeks were on fire. 'I beg you will not mock me, sir. I did not intend to insult you. I believe you would not describe your present position as that of a gentleman?'

'Oh, no, believe me, I should not,' Justin said, his mouth grim. 'I am well aware that I forfeited all right to call myself by that title long ago. Yet still I have some honour. My word is my bond and you may rely on it.'

'I know and I do trust your word.' She lay a hand on his arm, feeling the hardness and strength of muscle and bone through the thin shirt he wore. He was a powerful man, and could, if he wished, break her with his hands. Yet she sensed that somewhere deep inside there was a different man, a man who knew how to be gentle and generous. It was that man she longed to see, that man she caught glimpses of now and then. 'Forgive me if I have offended you, sir. It was an idle question and not my business.'

'No, it was not your business—yet I shall tell you. I

led a mutiny against a man of such brutality that he drove his crew beyond all limits. After that, there was nothing for us but to make a living from piracy. For myself, I intend to pursue the career only until I can make a new life elsewhere.'

'Shall you return to England and your home one day?'

'I think not.' Justin's eyes were shadowed, giving no indication of his feelings. 'Enough questions, lady. 'Tis time to go ashore. Higgins will look after you and Anna. He will find transport and take you to Peg's, where you will stay until I come. Under no circumstances are you to venture on to the waterfront unless I am with you. Do I make myself clear?'

'Yes, sir.' Maribel was silenced. Why did he think it necessary to give her orders? Was he punishing her for what she had said? It was not necessary, she was not a child nor would she dream of straying to the port alone. 'I shall obey you, for I have no wish to mix with pirates or their whores!'

Justin gave her a searing look. 'Have a care, lady! Such language will earn you no friends on shore. Pride is all very well, but for the moment you are a guest in company that you may despise but should fear. I can command my own crew, but there are men on shore who would rape and hurt you if they found you wandering alone. You have been warned, so take care! I cannot always be there to protect you.'

'Then why have you brought me to such a place?' Maribel demanded, provoked by his attitude into retaliation.

Justin looked at her, seeing the pride but underneath the vulnerability. She was trying to hold on to her dignity but she was out of her depth and afraid of things she did not understand. She might no longer have her hair dressed in ringlets and she had left off her heavy panniers, but the pride of a high-born Spanish lady remained. 'You are asking a question I have asked myself a thousand times on the journey, lady. I should have sent most of the crew here and taken the *Defiance* to England—you are a burden we could do without and the sooner we are rid of you the better!'

Maribel felt the cut of his words like the lash of a whip. He was angry with her and it was her own fault. Captain Sylvester had proved himself a man of his word and yet she had done nothing but provoke him—and she did not know why.

Tears stung behind her eyes as she was assisted into the boat taking her and Anna ashore. What a fool she was to quarrel with the only man who could help her. She knew that he had been forced to keep his promise to his crew and sail them here. She was stupid to make so much fuss about being brought to this place. Captain Sylvester had done his best for her and she must endure whatever discomfort there was until he took her to England. She could only hope that she had not pushed him too far, for she shuddered to think what life would be like for her here if he abandoned her.

'So Sylvester sent you to me, did he?' Peg stood with her hands on her hips and looked Maribel over.

'Yer a lady, ain't yer? What are yer doin' in a place like this?'

'It is a long story. Captain Sylvester has agreed to take me to my family in England when we leave here.'

'Well, if he gave yer his word he will.' Peg laughed. She was a buxom woman, but still attractive though past her best years. 'He is a good man. I owe me life to him, but that is another story—and one yer won't hear from me. Yer can stay here if yer like. It may not be ter yer ladyship's liking, but it is sanctuary on this island. All the scum of the earth frequents that waterfront, believe me. There are a few honest men forced to the trade what retain a sense of fair play, but most would slit yer throat for a handful of silver.'

Maribel shivered. 'I have heard that the waterfront can be a terrible place.'

'Aye, it is that and more—but the brethren live by a code and most won't break it. They know what will happen if they do—either a trial and a hanging or cast off on one of the tiny deserted islands in these seas. We've trees, water and food enough here, but some of the islands are little more than bare rock. There's many a sailor been left to die on an island without a drop of water save the sea. It drives 'em mad in the end. Given the choice, most would rather hang than die that way.'

'I suppose it is a kind of justice?'

''Tis the only law we have. If there were none there would be no living at all—and 'tis as fair as many of the laws in England, and Spain, I dare say. I wouldn't like to be a prisoner of the Inquisition.'

'No, nor should I,' Maribel agreed and smiled. She had begun to like Peg even though the woman was coarse spoken and had killed a man in self-defence. 'Shall I be a trouble to you?'

'Lord 'ave mercy!' Peg shouted with laughter. 'Not the least, though yer'll have to give a 'and now and then. Share the chores we all do, for there are no servants here. Yer woman is free to come and go as she pleases. If it suits her to help yer she may, but she can't be forced to it. We are all equal here—though some of them think they can lord it over the rest of us…' Peg scowled. 'I don't mean you, dearie. That black-hearted scum Captain Pike is in port. He is a murdering devil and would split a man in two as soon as spit. My advice is to stay out of his way. If he sees your pretty face, he'll want yer. You may be under the protection of Captain Sylvester, but Pike is no respecter of property. If he wants yer, he'll come for yer and take the consequences after. He has fought and won more duels than any other man I know.'

Maribel felt sick. She shivered despite the heat of the day. It had been bad enough knowing she must marry against her will to an evil man who laid claim to the name of gentleman—but a ruthless pirate who cared for no man would be far worse! If he had taken her captive she would no doubt already be dead, for she would have taken her own life rather than let a man like that touch her.

Peg's words made her reflect on the treatment she had received from Captain Sylvester. He had given her his protection and shown her respect and what had she offered him in return? She regretted her quarrel with him more than ever. Supposing he decided to leave her to her fate? She would be a prisoner in Peg's house, for she would not dare to go anywhere alone while Captain Pike was in port.

Justin frowned. He knew that he had provoked Maribel to a sharp retort, but he had been annoyed with himself for bringing her to this place. He should have known that it was too rough and ready for a woman like her. She could never live happily on the island. He must see to his business here and leave for England as quickly as possible.

'So you're Sylvester…' The bulky pirate placed himself square in Justin's path, his narrow set eyes glinting with malice. Some of his teeth were black and rotten, and his breath foul. He wore a red scarf beneath a battered black hat and an overcoat with several pockets over his shirt; his breeches were salt-stained, his boots had never been polished and his hair hung on his shoulders in greasy rattails. 'I've heard you took a few prizes this trip—bagged yerself a mighty fortune, by all accounts.'

'We have done well enough,' Justin replied, keeping his tone civil though he disliked the man instantly. They had never met, but Pike's reputation had gone before him and Higgins had pointed him out earlier. 'My men are happy with the fruits of their labour. I trust you had similar fortune?'

'Trust, do you?' Pike spat on the ground, snarling in disgust. 'We took nothing but a poxy merchantman with a cargo of wheat and barley. It will fetch a few guineas here for flour is always needed, but we had no rich pickings. Seems that you had all the luck, Sylvester. Tell me, what be your secret?'

'We have no secret, just good fortune,' Justin said. 'Next time we may not fare as well.'

'I heard tell you took at least two of that devil Don Sabatini's ships?'

'We may have done. Excuse me, sir. I have business.'

The pirate made no attempt to move. His hand rested suggestively on his sword hilt. 'I took one of his ships last year…'

'I dare say you will again.' Justin's eyes glittered. His hand moved to the hilt of his sword. 'I believe there are plenty of merchant ships to go round. Perhaps you should try hunting in a different place—in the West Indies, mayhap?'

For a moment Captain Pike's hand hovered above his sword hilt, a snarl on his lips, and then, as Higgins and one or two others came to stand at Justin's back, it dropped to his side.

'As you say, there is plenty for all. It would be better if we do not tread on each other's toes in future, Sylvester.'

'I wish you luck wherever you choose to go.' Justin bared his white teeth in a smile. The other man glared at him, then pushed by and walked off.

'Take care with him,' Higgins warned in a low voice.

'He has a foul temper and picks a quarrel too often. More men have died duelling with him than we lost in a year at sea!'

'Captain Pike does not bother me.' Justin did not smile. 'He may not lay claim to the seas—they are for everyone to roam as they see fit.'

'I agree with you there and, if we meet at sea, we are more than a match for him. He has but the one ship while we have two…'

'Three—I intend to purchase another ship. We shall be strong enough to stand against anything Sabatini or any other man sends against us when we sail again.'

'The men expect to share the spoils of the last voyage. I am not sure they wish to purchase another ship.'

'They will have their share. I have enough put by from other prizes to buy her. My house takes little of what I earn and I need nothing more. The new ship will earn its price many times.'

'I thought you meant to gather what you could and start a new life elsewhere?'

'In time, perhaps.'

Justin dismissed the question. Once he had thought to make a quick profit and start elsewhere, but he could see no real future for himself. He had forfeited his right to the life of a gentleman. His father would rightly disown him if he returned with the profits gained as a pirate in his pocket—and he was not sure that his cousins would welcome him in France.

Maribel's scorn for his trade was proof if he had

needed it that no decent woman would want him as her husband. He had made his choice when he threw in his lot with the mutineers and assumed command of the *Defiance*. There was no point in trying to be something that he could no longer claim to be.

His mouth twisted wryly as he recalled her scathing words when she was first taken captive. Even recently she had told him that she *suspected* that he had once been a gentleman. Well, she was right. He had been once, the son of a respected landowner and cousin to men who stood well at court. Those days were over. He was a pirate and must live and die as one—though he would not compare himself to the scum he had come in conflict with a moment earlier.

Pike was the lowest creature to crawl on this earth. Justin understood that he had made an enemy of the man. He had not provoked the quarrel, but it had happened and he would have to take great care while the pirate remained in port.

He grimaced and put the incident from his mind. They would split the profits from their successful hunting trip once he had sold what he could for gold. Justin already knew what he meant to purchase with some of his share. He was smiling as he went inside the tavern to meet the man with whom he had arranged to do business. There was something he had it in mind to purchase…

Maribel had finished unpacking her trunk. Anna had offered to do it for her, but under Peg's sceptical eye she had refused, asking only that Anna would show her how to wash her undergarments and how to take the creases from her silk petticoats.

''Tis not fitting that you should do such work,' Anna scolded. 'Some of the linens will need to be held over a steaming pot and then spread flat with a heated smoothing iron. I am not sure that such a thing is to be found on this island, my lady. Leave your linens to me and I shall see what I can do.'

'I must learn to do these things for myself, Anna. Peg told me that there are no servants here.'

'She may say what she pleases.' Anna's eyes glinted. 'I know my duty to you, my lady, though it is so hot here that you may care to do as other women do and leave off some of your petticoats.'

'Leave off my petticoats?' Maribel was shocked. It was true that she was feeling the excessive heat, sweat trickling down her back and legs beneath the heavy layers she wore. She had already left off her heavy padded panniers, but she could not dispense with her petticoats! 'No respectable lady would appear in public without her petticoats.'

'You are not in Spain nor yet England,' Anna reminded her. 'I took off my petticoats days ago. Higgins advised me to go without them for comfort and I have felt much better for it.'

'But you—' Maribel stopped, ashamed that she had almost said the word servant. Anna had been a good friend to her, supporting her through the ordeal they had both suffered. She looked down at the stiff skirts that felt so wrong for her present situation. 'You are right, Anna. I have been very uncomfortable. Perhaps I should leave off two of the heavier ones and just wear a thin shift and one silk petticoat.'

'I am sure you will feel more comfortable, Donna Sanchez.'

'You should call me Maribel. It is best not to use my titles here, Anna.'

Anna looked dubious. 'I am not sure I could do that, my...*señorita.*'

'Yes, call me *señorita* if you will not use my name.' Maribel sighed with relief as she shed some of her layers of petticoats, then, feeling how much better it was, she took off the last of them and stood in just a simple shift and the gown she had chosen. 'This is my simplest gown, but still it is too costly for life here. Do you think you could purchase something simpler for me to wear, Anna? I am not permitted to visit the waterfront, but there must be merchants of a sort, I think.'

'I am certain there are, though they do not have shops to trade from, merely a stall or the window of their house. I shall ask Higgins where suitable clothes can be purchased, D—*señorita.*'

'Thank you. I will give you some gold pieces. I do not know how much you will need.'

'One gold piece should buy you at least two gowns of the kind you require,' Anna said. 'Do not give me more, for I might be robbed.'

'Is it too dangerous for you to visit the merchants?'

'I shall not go alone. Higgins will take me if I ask him.'

Maribel looked at her thoughtfully. 'Has he spoken to you—asked you to wed him?'

'We shall not marry in church, but it is agreed between us that we shall live together once he has built us a house.'

'And when the ship leaves? Shall you come with me to England?'

'We've talked about that,' Anna said. 'I shall look after you on the journey, but once you are in England I shall leave you and return with Higgins to the island. He says that when he retires from the sea, we shall set up a little trading station of our own. More people are beginning to settle here and we can buy from the ships that drop anchor and sell to those who live here.'

Maribel felt a pang of regret. 'I shall miss you, Anna. You have been a good friend to me.'

'You were always a fair and generous mistress. In England you will find others to serve you, perhaps better than I ever could.'

'They will not be better than you, Anna.'

'Well, it will be some weeks before we must part,' Anna said. 'I am to stay with you until Higgins has his house built—and there will be the voyage to England. He says we can buy goods there and bring them back to the island. When you leave to join your family, it will be time enough to say our goodbyes.'

'Yes…' Maribel turned away to tidy some of her things. She had set out her own brush, silver combs, perfume flasks, and a small hand mirror on the top of an oak hutch that served her as a dressing chest. Tears stung behind her eyes. She felt very alone. When Anna left her she would have no one in the world that cared for her. Her mother's relatives would be strangers and she was not even sure they would welcome her to their house. Especially if they knew that she had been living with pirates for some weeks.

Maribel spread the wet clothes on bushes to dry in the heat of the scorching sun. The steam immediately began to rise and she knew she must be careful not to let them dry too much or the creases would never come out. She had washed a few of her things while Anna was out buying things they needed from the traders on the waterfront. Her back was trickling with sweat and her hair felt sticky on her neck, falling into her eyes despite all the combs she had used to keep it out of the way. Anna had offered to help her, but Maribel felt that she must learn to manage these things for herself, and she had merely brushed her hair back and fastened it with combs.

'Well, well, what have we here…?'

The man's voice made her swing round. She stared at the tall man in dismay for he was a fearful sight. His clothes were salt-stained and looked as if he had never washed them, his hair long and greasy beneath the red scarf he wore beneath his hat—and when he grinned at her she saw a row of blackened teeth.

'Excuse me, sir? Were you looking for someone? I believe Peg is in the house. Your business must be with her.'

'My business with Peg can wait, sweet doxy. You will suit me for the moment.'

Maribel gasped and stepped back in horror as she read the look in his eyes. 'No, sir, you mistake things. I am not a whore. You have no business with me.'

'She thinks herself a fine lady!' The man laughed, clearly finding it amusing. 'Well, my lady, when Pike says he has business with you, you would do best to heed him.'

'Stay away from me!' Maribel gave a scream of fear as he lunged at her. 'Keep your distance, sir. I will have none of you!'

'You'll do as I bid you and keep your mouth shut…'

Maribel screamed again as he grabbed her arm. 'Let me go! Take your filthy hands off me, you pig!'

'I'll teach you some manners, whore…'

'I suggest you take your hands off my woman,' another man's voice said. 'Otherwise I shall slit your throat, Pike. The choice is yours.'

Pike swung round, his face shocked as he found himself at the wrong end of a wicked-looking sword. 'Sylvester…' he croaked, sweat beading on his brow. 'I didn't realise she was your woman.'

'Well, you do now.' Justin's eyes glittered with fury. 'Lay one finger on her and you are a dead man, Pike. No man touches my woman and lives.'

'I was just having a bit of fun…' Pike held his hands up, moving away from Maribel. 'Why didn't she say she belonged to you? I wouldn't have gone near her if I'd known.'

'She is a lady, unused to the ways of scum like you.' Justin's voice was like the lash of a whip. 'Stay away from her—and from this house until we leave. Do you hear? If you attempt to touch her again, I'll kill you.'

'I hear you. I'm on my way.'

Maribel watched the man slink away. She was trembling and she felt sick, but she managed to hold back the tears.

'Thank you. I do not know what I should have done had you not come.'

'In future tell any man who tries anything on with you that you belong to me. They won't molest my woman.' Justin's eyes went over her. The thin gown she was wearing was sticking to her, revealing the intimate contours of her body. Desire flared and he was tempted to crush her to him, his need intensified by the temptation she offered in such flimsy clothing. His voice was harsh as he rasped, 'I am not surprised he thought you were available in that gown. Where are your petticoats?'

'I took them off. It was so hot. Anna took hers off and I thought…' Maribel flushed as she saw the expression in his eyes. 'I didn't expect to see anyone.'

Justin was angry, because he wanted to do much the same things as Pike had, and he was disgusted with himself. She had given him her trust and he had no right to feel such hunger just because her air of vulnerability tempted him past bearing. So he deliberately chose words to hurt her.

'No lady would come out of the house without her

petticoats. I am surprised you let a servant tell you what to do, Donna Maribel. I am aware the heat is almost unbearable, but you need to keep a certain standard or you will not be given the respect that is your due. Especially amongst men like Pike.'

'I…' A dark flush stained her cheeks. She crossed her arms over her breasts defensively. 'You are right. It will not occur again. I shall wear petticoats if I come outside.'

'I shall not always be around to protect you.' Justin frowned at her. He knew that his words had hurt her and he was already regretting having spoken so harshly. She was not to blame, because he could not control his hunger for her. 'I know how uncomfortable you must feel, but you need to be careful on this island.'

'You are right.' Maribel hung her head. She saw that he was correctly dressed despite the heat and felt untidy and ashamed of her appearance. 'I was careless. Thank you for helping me.'

'I do not mean to be heartless, Madonna. I know this kind of heat can be suffocating. I speak only for your own good.'

'Thank you. You will not need to reprimand me again, sir.'

'Is Peg treating you well? You are comfortable here?'

'Yes, thank you. She has been kind.'

'My own house is almost ready. I am having it furnished. I had thought you safe here, but perhaps you should move in with me.'

Maribel was shocked, her heart hammering against her ribcage as she stared at him. What could he mean? He had told her he would not marry—was he now suggesting that she should be his mistress? A part of her longed to say yes, but a tiny part of her mind still retained its sanity.

'Captain Sylvester! You may have told that vile man that I am your woman to protect me, but it is not so. I cannot live under your roof, sir.'

'I shall provide a chaperon. Anna will live with us and there will be a woman to keep the place tidy.'

'Peg said there were no servants here.'

'I pay well for service and find willing hands. I think Peg was trying to put you in your place, my lady. There are always those willing to work for good wages—but I treat them decently. They are not servants, as you have known them in your father's house. I pay for their service, but I treat them as equals.'

'Then they are not at all like the servants in my father's house. My father's servants feared him. I do not think anyone would fear to work for a man like you.'

An odd smile touched his mouth. 'Thank you, Maribel. I believe you just paid me a compliment. As to the matter of the house, I have arranged for the furniture to be moved in today. I came to bring you a gift, but now I am asking if you will live under my roof— as my guest, no more and no less.'

'Everyone will think I am your woman…'

'And they will leave you alone as a consequence. You will be able to move freely on the island. If you stay here, other men may have the same notion as Pike. It is the only way I can be certain you will be safe.'

Maribel shuddered. 'I should never have come to this terrible place. I do not belong here. I see resentment in the eyes of those I meet. They hate me because of who I was.'

A nerve flicked in his throat. 'It is my fault that you are here, lady. I have put my mark on you for your protection—it is all I could do to protect you. However, when we leave here you will be as you are now. I shall not abuse the situation. I have apologised, but I cannot change what is done. You must accept it and wait patiently until I can take you to your family.'

Maribel hesitated, then inclined her head. 'Yes, I shall trust you to keep your word, sir. Thank you. I shall be happy to live under your protection.'

Justin smiled and moved closer. 'I will make your stay here as pleasant as I can, Madonna. I wish that it had been possible to take you to your family immediately. I was wrong to bring you here, but I thought it best.' A wry smile touched his mouth. 'Your family will never know anything of your stay here. I promise you that when I take you to them they will accept my story that I have merely been your escort.' He arched one eyebrow. 'You suspected that I was once a gentleman. I know how to play the part and will not let you down, Maribel.'

The way he said her name then made Maribel's insides curl with a feeling she knew was desire. His mouth was curving in a mocking smile. She longed to be in his arms and to feel that mouth take possession of hers, as it had once before. It was all she could do to stop herself swaying towards him. She wanted to give herself to him, to tell him that she would be his woman in truth, but pride held her back.

The expression in his eyes told her that he desired her but she knew that he did not love her. He had made it clear that a man such as he had no time for softness or love. Maribel was certain that to give herself to this man would mean loving him—the kind of love that would become a consuming flame. If she gave him her heart, he would crush it beneath his boots.

'You speak my name,' she said. 'But I know you only as Captain Sylvester. I do not think it is your true name.'

'I may not give you my family name—it would shame them.' His eyes were flinty, distant. 'They do not know that I have become a pirate and it would hurt them. However, my Christian name is Justin…'

'Justin…' she breathed. 'Justin…' A smile touched her mouth. 'Yes, I like it very well. It suits you, sir— for you are a just man.'

'Am I?' He moved in closer, gazing down at her. 'I retain some honour, Maribel, but a man may only be tempted so far. Be careful how far you tempt me—and wear your petticoats or I may not be responsible for my action.'

'Justin…' Her stomach clenched as his hot eyes scorched her. 'Forgive me. I did not mean to tempt you or any man. My gowns were so hot…but I shall be more sensible in future.'

'Be careful when out walking,' he said. 'I have purchased some lighter gowns for you with fine petticoats that will not be so heavy. I should have sent them immediately, but I was caught up with other things. I shall have them taken to my house. They will await you in your room—and now I shall take my leave of you before I lose all sense of honour.'

He turned and walked away from her. Maribel watched. She longed with all her heart to call him back, but her pride held. He spoke of honour and yet he mocked her. If he cared for her, he would surely have asked her to be his wife, but he did not want a wife—only a mistress.

She knew that she had only to say the word and she could become his woman in truth, for she had seen desire in his eyes and felt an answering need in herself. Yet if she were so lost to all pride and sense of what was fitting that she gave herself to him it could only bring unhappiness in the end.

A little voice in her head told her that it would be worth the risk to know the sweetness of lying with him, of being safe in his arms—but he did not love her. He had told her that he had once loved a woman and would not give his heart again. She could be his mistress if she chose, but not his wife.

Chapter Five

'Why didn't you tell me that you were Sylvester's woman?' Peg said when Maribel mentioned that he was sending someone to take her to his house and to fetch her trunk later that day. 'You would not have needed to help with the chores if I'd known you were special to him.'

'I did not mind helping,' Maribel said and blushed. 'It is good to understand what other people have to do.'

'Show me your hands.' Maribel held them out and Peg frowned as she saw the red marks on the palms. 'You should have told me that you had never done hard work. I should not have asked you to carry water from the well if I had known. I'll give you some salve for your hands.' Her eyes narrowed. 'It's the first time I've known Sylvester to take a woman under his protection. You must have made an impression on him! There will be some jealous females once 'tis known you've done what none other could.' Peg grinned suddenly. 'What is he like as a lover? I've thought many a time I would be happy to lie with such a man!' She threw back her head and laughed as Maribel flushed. 'I thought not! You have not lain in his bed, have you? He is protecting you from scum like Pike.'

'Why do you say that?' Maribel looked at her.

'You are innocent, child. Anyone with sense can see it in your eyes. Besides, I know his heart is in the grave of the woman he loved.'

'He has told you this?' Maribel felt as if a knife had entered her breast, because to hear it from Peg seemed to make the woman real instead of the shadowy person Justin had mentioned in passing. 'He has spoken to you of this woman—you know who she was?'

'That I cannot reveal without telling his secret,' Peg said. 'Before I came here I was a servant in a big house. When I killed the rat that raped me I should have hanged had it not been for Sylvester. He took me from the hellhole I was locked in and set me free. I escaped to sea with a man I cared for. I know that Sylvester's heart was broken when the woman he was to marry died of a fever a few days before their wedding…and if you tell him that I revealed so much I'll slit your throat myself!'

He had lost his love shortly before his wedding day. It was not surprising that he could never think of putting another woman in her place. Maribel felt a flow of sympathy for him, feeling his hurt and the pain it must have caused him. In that moment she wanted to put her arms about him and kiss away all the grief and pain, to make him whole again. She knew how it felt to lose someone you loved and she had loved Pablo as a brother. How would it feel to lose someone who meant so much more—someone who was a part of you?

'I swear I shall not reveal what you have told me.' Maribel said. Her heartbeat had returned to normal. Peg had told her something so revealing that she thought it had begun to explain the mystery that was Captain Justin Sylvester. Sylvester was not his true name. He had come from a respectable family, from what Peg had hinted, perhaps a great family.

The mystery was deep and she might never reach the bottom of it, but Maribel suspected that she might be falling deeply in love with the man himself. He *was* a gentleman despite his present situation. He was also a man of honour.

Why did he believe he could not return to his homeland? What had he done that was so terrible?

She knew that he could be harsh. It was necessary to discipline the men that served with him. Yet he could also be compassionate and honourable.

Maribel's heart ached as she saw to the packing of her own trunk for the move to Justin's house. Being here on the island had caused her to lose so many inhibitions that she had had before being taken captive. When she first left for England she had been very much the correct Spanish lady. She was not certain who she was any more. Maribel was not sure that she would ever be able to give orders to a servant in the way she once had, taking it for granted that they should obey her every whim, though she would be expected to do so once she was living with her English family.

If only there was another way to live! One that was possible for her. She did not think that she could be happy living on the island, because the pirates were dangerous, coarse men and she would always fear most of them. Yet to return to the kind of life she had known in her father's house would be hard.

She thought that she would like to live simply in a modest house, somewhere in the country—perhaps a farm—but with whom? One face filled her mind, but she struggled to push it away. To dream of such happiness was foolish.

Justin Sylvester was not looking to settle to a quiet life. He might desire Maribel, but he did not love her. He did not wish for a wife, merely a mistress to lie with when it suited him.

Blinking back her tears, Maribel dressed herself in a thin shift, one petticoat and the thinnest gown she possessed. She looked respectable, because her hair was disciplined into the ringlets she had worn at home. She had teased her comb into her tangled hair, curling it about her fingers. The effect was not quite as neat as when Anna dressed her hair, but she did not look like the wanton hoyden Justin had rescued from that vile man.

Lifting her head, Maribel glanced at herself in her tiny silver-backed mirror. She vaguely resembled the formal lady that had first set sail for England, though she knew that inside she was very different. She had been living inside a shell, in a cold dark place and barely alive. Now she was aware of her feelings, aware of pain and love and a need that she scarcely understood.

Maribel glanced round the room she had been given. It was furnished with an impressive tester bed of Spanish hardwood and hung with silken drapes. Other hutches made of a similar wood, a stool, and a cupboard on a carved stand had been provided for her comfort. She wondered where and how Justin had come by such fine items. They must either have been captured from Spanish vessels or brought here at some cost—perhaps both. A trunk with iron bands had been delivered and when Maribel opened the lid she discovered the gowns and undergarments she had been promised. They were of such fine silk that she knew they must have been extremely costly. Because of their light weight she knew that they would be much more comfortable than the heavier gowns she had prepared for her trousseau. She had deliberately chosen heavy materials because she had been told she would need them in the cooler climate of England.

She was finding herself more and more reluctant to complete her journey to the home of her mother's family. Yet what else was there for her? If she gave herself to Justin without marriage, she would indeed be a whore. What if he tired of her? Where would she go and what would she do then?

The questions weighed heavily on her mind. Her

heart was telling her that even a short time as his woman—to lie in his arms and experience his loving—would be worth losing her honour. However, her mind reminded her that she was a lady and gently born. Her father might be a tyrant and a murderer, but her mother was undoubtedly a lady. If she gave up honour for love, she could never return to the life she was meant to live. She would be an outcast and might one day be forced to earn her living on her back. Yet she was not even sure that she had a family who would take her in, though Juanita had told her that she had an uncle in England and named him. She had received no letters from him. Perhaps he would not wish to know her.

Maribel's tortured thoughts were scattered as Anna came into the room bearing clean linen for the bed.

'This is a fine house,' Anna told her. 'True it is built mainly of wood, but the foundations are set on stone. It should withstand the worst of winter storms.'

'Yes, it is stout enough.' Maribel gave a little shiver. 'I should not want to live here all the time. Are you sure you wish to settle here, Anna? If you change your mind, you will have a place with me—if my family can be found and will accept me.'

'I thank you, my lady, but in England I should always be a servant. Here I can be my own person.'

'Surely you and Higgins could have an inn or a shop of your own in England?'

'It would not be the same. You have always been a lady. You do not know what it is like for the people who serve you. The laws are harsh in Spain for such as us, and Higgins says it is the same in England. A man can be hung for stealing game from the woods, even if he only did so to save his family from starvation. Besides, Higgins would be hanged as a mutineer if he returned to his home country. If he cannot live there nor shall I.'

Anna's words struck home. Maribel had been spoiled in some ways, for she had been waited on and given fine clothes and good food, but in other ways she had been poor. She had never known her father's love or felt her mother's arms about her. Juanita had been good to her, but after her death Maribel had felt alone and at times unhappy. She would not wish to return to a life like that—in Spain or England.

She sighed. 'Is there no country on this earth where a man can be free from such harsh laws? I know you say there is freedom on the island, but the men here…' She shook her head. 'I do not care for men like Pike or pirates.' Save one, her heart said, but she would not voice her true feelings for the man she knew would never love her. Peg had told her that his heart belonged to the woman he had meant to marry. Justin had told her himself that he had no intention of taking a wife.

'Well, 'tis what I have chosen,' Anna said. 'The life may not be perfect, but I have no family waiting for me in England. I would not wish to return to Spain—I should have nothing to look forward to there.'

'You must do as you please, but I could not live here—even though this house is well enough for a short visit.'

Maribel said the words carelessly, though it was not

the house that she found lacking, merely the knowledge that she did not belong on this island.

Justin paused outside the open door and listened to the conversation between the two women inside. He had come to ask if Maribel had all that she required, but he had his answer. It had cost him far more than he had intended to spend to furnish the house to a standard he considered suitable for her use. In his foolish desire to please, he had imagined that she would understand that he had provided the best the island had to offer. It seemed that she found it lacking—as she had found him lacking.

He had given her his first name as a proof that he was willing to lower the barriers between them. Yet now he was glad that he had not revealed his other secrets to her. She did not care for pirates—or their captain presumably. It had seemed to him that she was warming towards him…that she felt something of the passion her beauty aroused in him—but it would seem that he had deceived himself.

She was willing to accept his hospitality for a short visit, because she knew that she would be safe beneath his roof. Clearly she could hardly wait for their stay on the island to be over so that she could continue her journey to England and the family that awaited her.

Frowning, Justin walked away. He had business enough to keep him occupied. His crew wanted only gold or silver that they could spend, which meant that he must bargain with the merchants and other captains for the best prices for the goods they had taken. The chests of silver had already been divided according to the rules of the brethren. He had spent much of his captain's share, which was the largest, but still only a portion of that taken. Each man was paid according to his standing, and even Tom the cabin boy now had more money than he could have earned in ten years before the mast. If he took care of his share, he could be a rich man in another year or so—they all could be if they continued to be as lucky as they had been this trip.

Justin had wondered if his share would buy him a new life somewhere. Not here on the island. The money he had spent here could be recouped when he left, or at least a part of it; he might not get back all for he knew he had spent recklessly to buy things of quality for Maribel. Yet where could he go to start this new life?

Maribel had asked where on this earth there was a country where the laws were fair to all men. Not a pirates' haven, but a land where a man could breathe and make a fine life for himself and his family.

Anna had not known how to answer her and Justin did not know either. He had left England under a cloud for speaking his mind. He had neither spoken nor committed treason. However, just for voicing his opinion that it was wrong to send a man to the fire simply because he followed a different religion, he could have been condemned as a traitor and executed. Perhaps if the old queen were dead he might have found a better life…but not with the stain of piracy hanging over him.

His father would not accept him. He would accuse him of bringing shame to their name and it was true.

So if he could not return to England, where would he find the life he craved? Not in Spain and perhaps not in France—his cousins might also think he had brought shame on them. Justin would have to think again. There must surely be a country where he could find the life and the freedom he craved...

Maribel saw him chopping wood in the yard at the back of the house. Justin had taken off his shirt and his skin glistened with sweat. His body was tanned and his strong muscles rippled as he worked. Her eyes fastened on him hungrily and she was aware of heat spreading through her from low in her abdomen. He was beautiful and she wanted to touch him, to run her hands over his back and touch the scars she thought must have come from cruel whips when he served before the mast. No wonder he had taken the law into his own hands. The master of that ship deserved to lose his position! Yet it had made Justin something he had no wish to be, an exile from the law and his home. For the first time Maribel began to understand why a man might become a pirate. She watched him a little longer from her window. Justin was working so hard, attacking the wood as if it were his enemy. She thought he must be angry for his actions seemed those of a man bent on spending his frustration in work and there was surely no need for so much kindling.

Picking up the hat with a wide brim that he had so

thoughtfully provided, Maribel put it on and fastened it to her hair with silver pins. She went out of the house, hearing the rustle of her skirts and relishing the feel of the silky material against her flesh. She had never worn anything as fine as this and thought that even her stepmother had not owned silk as costly as she was wearing now.

Justin looked up as she approached. He scowled at her, reaching for his shirt. 'Forgive me. You should not have come out. I am not properly dressed.'

'I saw you from the house. You were working so hard. I wanted to thank you for my clothes. They are so light and comfortable. I have never worn anything as fine.'

'I am sure you must have…'

'No, sir, I have not. My gowns were always heavier and thicker. Even my stepmother never had such fine silk as you have given me. I am grateful for your thoughtfulness…and for the room you have provided.'

'The furnishings are not what you are used to,' he growled. 'But all I could find here.'

'I thought it very comfortable. I am grateful for all you have done for me, sir.'

'I am aware that my house lacks the comforts you were accustomed to, lady. Well enough for a short stay, but not for long. I shall endeavour to see you safe in the arms of your family as soon as it may be done.'

'You heard me…' Maribel's cheeks burned as she realised she had been overheard. Shame washed over her, for she had been ungrateful and hasty. 'When I spoke to Anna it was not of you or your house, Justin.

It is merely that I do not find the island a pleasant place…' She saw his expression and stopped. 'I would not have offended you for the world, sir. I believe I owe you more than I can ever repay. It is just that I feel uncomfortable because of what happened with Pike—and what could happen if I left your house to go walking or visit the merchants.'

'Do not judge us too harshly, Maribel. It is true that men like Pike are to be avoided, but many of those who live here would not harm you, especially now they believe you belong to me. You have not seen the rest of the island. The port is a shambles, I grant you, but the community is young and the town is not yet built. The island has become a safe haven for pirates and their kind, but one day it may be something more. As people make their homes here it will become a proper community. I think it might be possible to have a good life here—if one were willing to accept it for what it is.'

'I should not have spoken so carelessly to Anna. I have received no harm at your hands, sir.' She turned away, walking back towards the house, her head down. A moment later she felt her arm caught and looked at Justin. He had put on his shirt and his expression had lightened.

'No, do not leave, Maribel. The other side of the island, away from the port, is beautiful…perhaps as paradise must have been before we humans spoiled it.'

'I should like to visit this paradise you speak of…if it may be arranged.'

'The interior of the island is hilly, covered in woods,

and you would not enjoy the walk in this heat. I could arrange for us to be rowed there—perhaps one day soon. There are other things to enjoy here. This evening there will be a feast and then the division of the spoils. Would you care to attend the feasting? I must do so and I would prefer that you be there so that I can watch over you.'

'I think I am a deal of trouble to you, sir.' She hung her head, feeling ashamed that she had given him cause to think her ungrateful. 'You have been generous… more so than I could ever have expected.'

'I have given you my word that I will deliver you safely to your family, lady. I shall endeavour to keep it. If you do not wish to attend the feasting tonight, I shall ask you to stay inside and lock your door.'

'Thank you, I should like to attend. I think I am safe enough if you are there, sir.'

'You know that I would never allow anyone to harm you while I live.' Justin hesitated, then, 'Would it be too much to ask you to call me by my name? I should like to think we had gone beyond the formality of sir…'

'I owe my life to you. If you wish it, I shall call you, Sylvester, as you are known here. You gave me your first name, but I think you may not wish others to know it?'

'I once had hopes of returning to my home, but I doubt it will happen.' Justin's eyes clouded, his mouth thinning. 'You owe me no gratitude, Maribel. Had we not attacked your ship the first time you might have been in England.'

'And perhaps wed to a man I hated.' She shuddered. 'I think I should thank you, Sylvester. I resented being your captive, but I was proud and foolish, and afraid. I misjudged you and I am sorry. Perhaps one day I may do something for you in return.'

'I ask for nothing.' He inclined his head. 'Excuse me, I have things I must do. You need not stay in the house; you are safe enough here in the garden, such as it is. I have been meaning to clear some of the undergrowth at the back so that a fruit garden can be planted, but as yet I have not had time. Be careful if you stray further. I do not think anyone will attempt what Pike did…but, as you know, these men are not always to be trusted.'

Maribel watched as he walked away from her. The barriers had come down as soon as she spoke of his name and reminded him of his home—and the woman he had loved. Clearly such memories pained him. He must have loved her very much…still loved her if it could cause the shadows to fall. He was a man and had a man's needs. He might desire Maribel, but his heart still belonged to a woman he had once loved.

She was foolish to think of him! He had sworn to protect her but that was all. Maribel began to realise something her heart had tried to tell her long ago. Justin was an exceptional man and she was beginning to feel things for him that she could scarcely understand. He had been kind to her, but she had rebuffed him and it would serve her right if he abandoned her to her fate.

Maribel knew that she must make the best of her stay here. She could only hope that it would not be too long before the ship was ready to sail. In the meantime, she would make herself useful in the house. Some large chests had been delivered earlier and she knew they contained things for Justin's house. He was so busy that he had no time to unpack them. She would do it for him.

Maribel spent an hour or more unpacking items of value from the sturdy oak trunks that had been set down in the living room. She discovered porcelain the like of which she had never seen and stared at the markings on the underneath, trying to make out the strange figures. Beautiful blue-and-white designs depicting figures dressed in clothes that seemed different to her. She imagined they must be very costly and thought that they rightly belonged in the chamber destined for the master of the house.

She sought and found Justin's bedroom, discovering that his bed was much plainer than the one he had given her. Here there were no fancy hutches or carved stools, but just his sea chest and a plain stool with three legs. She set the vase down in a corner of the room, looking round as she thought that something more was needed here to make it comfortable. Noticing some stained linen, she picked it up intending to wash it for him. She was about to leave when she heard a sound and turned to find Justin looking at her.

'What are you doing?'

'I unpacked the chest you had sent here. That vase was so beautiful I thought it belonged in your room. I have never seen its like. Where did it come from?'

'I believe China. It was taken from a Portuguese merchant vessel. I have been told that the Portuguese have trading arrangements with China that no other country has and vases such as these are rare—beyond price. It does not belong here and should have been left in the trunk to protect it.'

'Forgive me. I thought you would wish these things unpacked. I shall replace it…'

'No, leave it now. This room is bare. I dare say it will come to no harm.' He frowned as he saw the linen in her arms. 'What are you doing with those shirts?'

'I meant to wash them for you. It is little enough in return for all you have given me and I have time on my hands.'

'You will ruin your hands,' he said and took them from her, tossing them on to the bed. 'Tom will see to them for me. It is one of his tasks as cabin boy to care for the men's clothes.'

'I feel so useless. Everyone else has work to do.'

'If you wish for work, there is some mending. A lady's hands were not meant for menial tasks, but I believe needlework is acceptable?'

'Yes, of course…' Maribel was hesitant. 'I did not think it right that I should do nothing. I am sorry I unpacked the chest if you did not wish it.'

Justin reached out and caught her wrist, as she would have turned away. She raised her head, holding back the tears that would shame her, but he saw them and reached out to touch her cheek with his fingertips.

'Forgive me. It looks very much better in here. I did

not mean to be harsh to you, Maribel. We should try to deal more kindly with each other for the time we spend on the island. I know there are things here that you cannot like, but it is not such a bad place—is it?'

'No…' She blinked away the foolish tears and smiled at him. 'The view to the sea is breathtaking and some of the flowers are lovely. I should have asked before I touched your belongings, but I wanted to be useful. There is no place for a lady here.'

'I should have remembered that you would need some employment. I will purchase silks another day and then you may use your skills to mend or embroider some trifle.'

Maribel turned away. He thought her good for nothing but idleness or some embroidery! At home she had been used to many tasks—she had helped Juanita in the stillroom and with mending, as well as embroidering covers and hangings for the house and the church. There had always been a task of some kind, though she saw now that much of her time had been spent in idleness, either walking in the gardens, riding or playing her viola.

What had she ever done of real use? If her husband had not died, she would have been mistress of his house, but in her father's she had been nothing—just the daughter of a woman it seemed he hated.

What would she be in the house of her English relatives? Perhaps they would give her some tasks to perform for her keep?

Maribel was aware of a growing unease in her mind.

She was not sure of her welcome in England. Even if her mother's family accepted her, she could only be an outsider at best, for she did not truly belong with them.

Where did she belong? The answer was nowhere. Anna would be accepted here, because she shared the work they all did—but Maribel was too much of a lady to do hard physical work and so she could never belong.

Returning to her own room, Maribel spent the rest of the afternoon staring out of the window and watching birds flitting in and out of the trees. She had nothing to occupy her time and wished for some needlework or canvas and paint so that she might have something to make the hours seem shorter.

As dusk began to fall, she saw Anna at the well. She filled one bucket and left the other while she carried that back to the house. Maribel went out and tied the other bucket to the rope, letting it down until she heard the splash of water. She had begun to wind the handle to bring it up when Anna returned.

'You should not be doing that, my lady.'

'I am sick of being told what I should not do,' Maribel told her crossly. 'I have nothing to do but stare at the walls of my room, while you struggle to carry water, clean, wash my clothes and cook. In future I am going to help you with the chores.'

'Captain Sylvester said that you were to be treated with the respect due you as a lady.'

'He is not my father or my husband! He cannot command me. I shall do as I see fit. When I am in

England I shall be a lady for I shall have no choice, but here on the island I must do some work or go mad.'

'It is better to work,' Anna said and smiled. 'Let me carry the bucket, for you have filled it to the brim and it will be heavy. Tomorrow you can help prepare the food.'

'We shall carry the bucket between us,' Maribel said. 'And then I shall change my gown for the evening. It will be cooler when the sun goes down and I think it would be better to wear one of my simpler gowns this evening.'

Maribel looked around the beach. Bonfires had been built at intervals along the shoreline and tables made of rough planks set upon trestles had been set up. Some of them were covered with plates of food: bread and fruit and messes of meat cooked in wine and sauces. She caught the aroma of roasting pig and the smell made her mouth water. Already barrels of ale and sack had been tapped, and the men were drinking heavily.

On some tables goods were displayed for sale. Weapons of many kinds, boots, clothes, all manner of trinkets, from combs for a lady's hair to gentlemen's silk breeches; barrels of wine and ale, goblets and cooking pots were jumbled together to be haggled over.

'That is what is left of what we took,' Higgins told Maribel and Anna. 'The Cap'n sold the best stuff and we'll be dividing the money later. The rest is there for anyone to buy, but it will not bring much.'

'Is this the kind of thing you and Anna mean to trade?'

'Aye, something of the sort. But there are other things that are scarce here, like flour, salt, spices and sugar—and I mean to buy a cargo after our next voyage and bring it back,' Higgins replied. 'But you must be hungry. May I fetch you food, lady—and you, Anna?'

'I shall come with you.' Anna smiled at him. 'I know what my lady likes to eat.'

'You are not to wait on me. I shall come with you and choose for myself.'

Anna made a disapproving face, but did not try to stop her. Maribel followed behind them, taking one of the pewter platters and moving along the table as others were doing. She helped herself to some coarse bread and a yellow cheese, hesitating over the fruit; eventually she selected a peach.

'You should try the suckling pig,' a voice said close behind her and she jumped, swinging round to look at the man who had spoken. That evening Captain Pike was wearing clothes that looked cleaner than those he had worn the first time they met. His beard had been trimmed, but his hair was still greasy and nothing could disguise the foul smell of his breath. Maribel's flesh crawled; she found him repulsive. 'Let me bring you a slice, Maribel.'

She shuddered, feeling her stomach heave. The lascivious look in his eyes robbed her of the desire to eat and she moved away, going to stand by a palm tree, her back against it as she surveyed the scene. A group of men were dancing on the beach, arms crossed as they performed some kind of a jig. Others were eating or squabbling over the goods set out for sale. She saw one draw a knife and threaten another.

'Are you not hungry?'

Maribel turned her head as Justin addressed her. 'In a little while, perhaps.' She was aware that Pike was watching her still and suppressed a desire to run away.

'Has something upset you?'

'No, no, I am not upset.' She took a peach and bit into it. The flesh was perfectly ripe, sweet and delicious, and the juice ran over her chin. Before she could wipe it, Justin reached out and smoothed it away with his fingers. He ran his index finger over her lower lip and then put it to his mouth and sucked it, his eyes on her face. Maribel's appetite fled once again and she could hardly swallow even the small piece of peach in her mouth. She took a deep breath, her voice shaking, 'You must not worry about me, Sylvester. Please attend to your business. I am perfectly well.'

Justin's eyes flashed. 'I did not ask if you were ill. You are distressed. Was it something Pike said to you?'

'No, of course not,' Maribel said a little too quickly. 'He merely asked if I wished for some suckling pig. I said no…'

His mouth tightened. 'You must tell me if he accosts you, Maribel. I would kill him rather than let him sully you with his touch.'

'No…please, do not kill anyone for my sake. I am certain he will not try to touch me; I shall stay out of his way. Please, mix with your men. I am certain you must have more important things to do.'

'Nothing is more important to me than your safety.' Justin reached out to touch her cheek, caressing it and trailing a finger down her throat to the little pulse spot at the base. She swallowed hard, because the look in his eyes set her pulses racing again. His gaze was full of meaning, conveying a message if only she knew what he meant. Perhaps she did and that was why her heart was thudding so violently. He had told her once that he wished for a mistress, not a wife—was he letting her know she was his choice? 'I would kill anyone who tried to harm you. I shall keep you safe until you are with your family if it costs my life.'

Maribel caught her breath, for his voice throbbed with passion. She wished that they were alone at the house. Her body was aching for his touch. She wanted to tell him that she did not want him to fight for her; she wanted him to love her. The moment was broken by the sound of shouting on the beach. Justin turned to look. A fight had broken out, drawing a crowd to watch.

'I must sort out these fools before they kill each other,' he said grimly. 'I shall tell Anna to come to you.'

'No, let her have fun,' Maribel said, but he did not answer her.

However, as he walked away, Peg came towards her. She smiled, feeling relief as the older woman joined her.

'This is the first feast yer have attended,' Peg said. 'Do not be too alarmed, Maribel. Most of this is high spirits. The men will fight, but it is not often anyone is killed; they are like children at play.'

'Children do not have knives.'

'Perhaps not where you lived. On the streets of London children learn to defend themselves early. I carried a knife from the age of eight. Me parents died of the plague, but I survived. I had to steal to eat until I could find work—and the work I wus offered did not please me, for I would be no man's whore. Later, I found work as a servant, but men would not leave me be. When one of them raped me I used me knife to good effect to defend meself—and yer know the rest.'

Maribel saw the defiance in her eyes, but felt only admiration for her courage. 'Would you teach me how to protect myself, Peg?'

Peg's eyes narrowed. 'Yer have Captain Sylvester to protect yer. Besides, yer will not stay here long. Why should yer need a knife?'

'I should feel safer. You know what happened when Pike first saw me. I do not think he has forgiven me. Captain Sylvester cannot always be with me. If I had a knife, I might stand a chance against him.'

'Yer have spirit despite yer fine ways,' Peg said and grinned. 'Yer may be a lady, but I see no fool. I will come tomorrow and begin yer lessons—and I will bring yer a knife.'

'Thank you. I have some money. I can pay for my knife.'

Peg gave her a look of reproof. 'Have I asked for payment?'

'No. Forgive me. I did not mean to offend you.'

'No offence taken, luvvie.' Peg grinned at her. 'I

thought yer wus above yerself when yer first come to me, but I like yer. I wouldn't show everyone me tricks, but I reckon I can teach yer to protect yerself from scum like that Pike. I seen him lookin' at yer and I reckon he may try somethin' if he gets the chance.'

'Yes, I think he may,' Maribel said. 'I did not wish to say anything to Sylvester because I am enough trouble to him already, but that man frightens me. He is evil.'

'Evil he is,' Peg agreed, her eyes blazing, 'but he bleeds like any man. If I show yer how to defend yourself, yer'll be safe enough.'

'Thank you.' Maribel smiled. Someone had started to play a fiddle. The fighting had been stopped and men were dancing, some with their women and others together. 'Do you wish to dance, Peg? You must not stay with me if you do.'

'Aye, I'll dance,' Peg said and seized her hand. 'And you'll dance with me.' She arched her brow as Maribel hung back. 'Don't tell me yer don't know how ter dance?'

Maribel shook her head. Suddenly, she felt better. She was no longer the outsider, watching and feeling apart from the others. Peg was forcing her to join in the fun, and she discovered that she wanted to dance.

It was just a simple joining of hands. The dancers twirled, broke hands and then joined in a line skipping up to meet each other and then breaking off to dance with a partner once more. Maribel discovered that her partner was another woman instead of Peg, because everyone was changing partners. Next she danced with a man who grinned at her, but held her respectfully, clearly remembering that she was Captain Sylvester's woman. After that, she found herself being twirled by Tom and then she was back with Peg again. When she broke from the line again, her hands were taken firmly and she looked up into bold eyes that made her heart race.

'I did not know you liked to dance, Maribel.'

'You hardly know me, Captain,' she replied and laughed softly. 'We sometimes danced at home in the courtyard when the wine harvest was done. I enjoyed dancing in the sunshine with the people of the estate, but when my father held a banquet, Juanita and I did not dance, for he did not approve of it—though others did. My stepmother taught me even though my father would not allow it.'

'Then dance with me, Maribel…like this…'

He pulled her into his arms, directing her body so that she felt as if she were floating, thistledown in his arms. The music had changed, was slower now, and when he twirled her round and round he did not let go of her hand. Others swapped partners, but he kept her with him, gazing into her eyes as they moved.

Maribel hardly noticed they had moved away from the throng of dancers. When he took her hand and led her along the sandy beach her heart was racing, her breast heaving as she caught her breath. What was this feeling between them? Was it only physical passion, the need for release—or was it something more? Maribel felt that she was being drawn into a net from which she could never escape; her heart told her that this was love—but she was afraid that it was only on her side. Justin desired her and he was both generous and kind— but she wanted so much more.

'Are you feeling better now?' he asked, gazing down at her in such a way that she swayed towards him, wanting to be back in his arms, wanting to be kissed. 'I could not resist when I saw you dancing. You seemed to be so happy…'

'I was—I am happy,' she breathed. 'I am looking forward to seeing the other side of the island, away from—' She broke off as his eyes narrowed. 'Forgive me, I do not mean to criticise your men, but there is a wilder element amongst the pirates. I do not like men like Captain Pike.'

'Well, you need not fear him while I am with you. Besides, I believe he means to leave soon. He had little luck last time out and needs to find a good prize.'

'It would be a better place without his sort,' Maribel said. 'Though I have found friends. Peg is a friend. I like her.'

'You know that she was convicted of murder and should have hanged had she not escaped?'

'Yes—but she took revenge for what was done to her. I cannot blame her.'

'Yet some would say that murder is wrong even if the cause be just.' Justin's expression was serious. 'I shall return you to Anna. Higgins will take you back to the house. The serious business is about to begin and there may some fighting as the men drink too much.'

'Yes, we shall leave you to your business.'

Maribel walked away from him to join Anna and Higgins. She had thought as they danced that Justin wanted to make love to her. If he had taken her in his arms and kissed her she would not have denied him, but she had spoken of wanting to see the other side of the island and the spell had been broken.

Justin was keeping his promise not to take advantage of her while she was under his protection. Maribel knew that if she wanted him to make love to her she would have to show him that she was willing to be his.

While a part of her longed for it, her pride ruled her head. To become his woman meant that she could never return to her own world. If he loved her she would give it all up willingly, but she was not sure he felt more than a fleeting desire—and that was not enough for her. She wanted, needed to be loved. There was a lonely place inside her that only love could ease.

He had told her that he could not return to England for he might be hanged as a mutineer. Maribel would be willing to sail with him—or settle in another country if he truly cared for her. She was not sure she wished to be a lady again. The life she had found here was a fulfilling one. She enjoyed helping to prepare the food and other small chores that Anna allowed her to do. Perhaps the life of a country gentlewoman would suit her, with a maid to help her. Juanita had delighted in her stillroom and Maribel had found it interesting to help with the preserves and cures they made from herbs.

To be a fine lady and sit all day at her sewing would

not suit her. It was the life she would have had as the wife of Lord Roberts and perhaps in the house of her mother's kin. Surely there must be another way to live, something more worthwhile?

Here on the island she would always have to be on her guard, but a simple country life mixing with honest folk would be so much more satisfying than the life of a grand lady.

Maribel shook her head, smiling at her foolish thoughts. Captain Sylvester might want her, but he would not be prepared to give up his way of life at sea to pander to her foolish whims. His was a precarious trade but it brought him great wealth. The money he must earn from preying on merchant ships would be far more than he could expect from the existence of a simple farmer.

Her thoughts were nonsense! She must accept what the future had in store for her. She would be restored to her mother's family and then…her thoughts refused to think further; it seemed like a dark tunnel that she must follow with no turning or reward.

How much better it would be if she were like Anna, free to give her heart to a pirate and think nothing of it. Anna was prepared to live on the island and mix with the rough seamen that lived and visited here. Maribel did not think that she could settle for such a life, even though she longed to be with Justin.

She did not even know his true name! Maribel was restless as she lay in her bed that night. Who was he truly? What was his family like and how did they feel about his disappearance? Did they have any idea of what he had become?

It was very late when she heard him come in. His footsteps paused outside her door and her heart raced as she heard the sound of his hand upon the latch. The door was locked. She had turned the key as a precaution lest Pike should attempt to get into her room while Justin was occupied elsewhere. Now she wished that she had left it unlocked.

Would Justin have come to her? Would he have woken her, taken her in his arms to love her?

Her body cried out for him and she longed to feel his arms about her. Had she been less proud she would have left her bed and gone to him, but years of strict upbringing would not allow her to offer herself to a man.

If he loved her, surely he would speak? Maribel longed for him to give her a sign that he cared even a little for her, but her head told her that she could never expect him to love her.

It was no good, she could not sleep. The night was too warm and her mind would not let her rest. Getting out of her bed, Maribel pulled a thin wrap over her night-chemise and went through to the living room. It was still stuffy and warm in here so she unlocked the door and went down the little steps leading to the veranda.

The moon was full, making Maribel feel lonely. She walked a few steps to a position where she could see out over the cliffs to the ocean below. At night it looked dark and mysterious, the water strangely calm, unmoving. She sighed deeply for she longed for something…something she could not name.

'What are you doing out here at night?'

Startled, Maribel turned to face Justin. He was wearing just his breeches. His feet were bare and he had not put on his shirt. She could see a trickle of sweat running over his bare chest and guessed that he too had been unable to sleep.

'I could not rest. It is so hot and…I was thinking…'

'I often come out at night to think. The air is cooler and things seem simpler.'

'You must have many problems…regrets?' Maribel looked at him. 'You told me that you could not return home—do you miss your family?'

'I think of them sometimes. I know my mother must miss me.'

'Do you have brothers or sisters?'

'I had a younger brother, but he died when he was but a child.'

'Then your mother must miss you terribly.'

'Perhaps.' Justin frowned. 'Did you have no brothers or sisters?'

'My mother died giving birth to a stillborn child, at least that is what I have been told—but my father never spoke of her. I think they quarrelled.' She sighed deeply and turned away to look out over the sea.

'Were you sighing because you wished yourself at home?'

'No.' Maribel met his narrowed gaze. 'I do not wish

to return to my home ever. There was a time when I was happy. When my stepmother lived she made things better. I do not know if my father was always the cruel man you claim, but I remember that Juanita loved me. She was kind to me and I was happy then. I was happy when I married…'

'You loved your husband very much?' Justin's voice was sharp suddenly.

'He was my friend. He loved me. Yes, I loved him very much.' Maribel hesitated, then, 'You told me that you once loved someone?'

Justin was silent for a moment, then, 'There was once a lady I would have married. She was young and beautiful. I loved her and I would have married her, but a fever took her before our wedding day.'

'That must have hurt you terribly.' Maribel looked into his face, witnessing the pain he could not quite hide.

'Yes, it hurt me…' His voice grated, as if he found it difficult to speak of his lost love. 'It was a long time ago. I have learned to live again. A man cannot spend all his life in regret.'

'No, that is true.'

Justin moved towards her. She stood absolutely still, waiting. For a moment his eyes held hers, then he reached out and drew her to him. He lowered his head and took her mouth, kissing her softly at first and then hungrily. Maribel melted into his body, realising that this was what she had been longing for…this was what she needed. She was so alone and she needed to be loved.

'You are lovely. The moonlight becomes you, Maribel, but why are you out here alone?'

'I was restless and could not sleep.'

'Nor I,' he murmured, his hand moving to the small of her back. 'I was thinking of you. You haunt my dreams, waking and sleeping.'

'Justin…' she whispered, lifting her face for his kiss.

'Maribel…' Justin said hoarsely. He ran his thumb over her lower lip and she trapped it with her teeth. A shudder went through him and he pressed her closer so that she felt the hardness of his arousal and a thrill of desire shot through her. 'I vowed I would not.'

'I absolve you of your vow,' she said. 'Justin, I…'

What she might have said then was lost as they heard something and then a man came towards them through the gloom. Justin stood back from her, staring into the darkness for a moment, then he recognised the newcomer.

'Hendry,' he said, cursed beneath his breath and left Maribel to greet the newcomer. 'You are back. I thank God for it. I was beginning to wonder where you had got to and to fear that things might have gone wrong—that Sabatini had reneged on the truce.'

'All went well,' Hendry said and took the hand he was offered. 'The exchange was made and I have the packet for you.'

'Thank you,' Justin said. 'Come and have a drink with me. The ship is yours, as I promised. You may sail with us or go your own way.'

'I shall drink with you—unless you have unfinished

business?' Hendry glanced at Maribel, who was watching them.

'I was merely telling Maribel that she should not wander outside alone at night,' Justin said. 'Go in, Madonna. I shall see you in the morning.'

Maribel inclined her head, turning reluctantly towards the house. She shivered, feeling suddenly cool despite the heat. Captain Hendry had looked at her so oddly. She wished that he had not returned. He had brought the information Justin needed to find her mother's family but something in the way he looked at her had made her uneasy.

She had a feeling that something special might have happened with Justin had Hendry not arrived at just that moment. The barriers had come down between them and she had been on the verge of confessing that she was ready to be what everyone on the island already thought her—Sylvester's woman.

'Captain Sylvester asks that you forgive him,' Anna said the next morning. 'He has had to postpone the trip to the other side of the island, because he has business with Captain Hendry.'

'Oh…' Maribel's disappointment swathed through her. She had been looking forward to the pleasure trip and for a moment the day seemed long and empty, then an idea occurred to her and she smiled. 'I am going to clear some of the undergrowth behind the house. Captain Sylvester told me that he wants to create a fruit garden there, but has not yet found the time.'

Anna looked at her doubtfully. 'Do you know how hard that will be, *señora?* Your hands have never done hard work like that and they will blister.'

'I shall wear gloves,' Maribel said, determined not to give up her idea. 'Captain Sylvester has done much for me. I want to do this to thank him for his care of us, Anna.'

'If you must…' Anna sighed. 'I suppose I must help you.'

Maribel smiled at her. 'We can work together as friends, but I am not ordering you to help me, Anna. We shall clear more ground if we work together, but if you have something else to do I can manage alone.'

Anna gave her a look of grudging admiration. 'I would never have thought you could change so much, *señora.* You would not have dreamed of getting your hands dirty once.'

'I was another person then,' Maribel told her. 'I have been changing little by little, though at first I fought it—now I want to discover for myself what it is like to work hard.'

'We must begin by chopping down the grass and weeds, then we can make a start on the digging…'

Maribel's back ached and she was soaked in sweat when they decided that they had done enough for one day. A patch large enough to plant vegetables and soft fruits had been cleared at the back of the house and they had begun to dig a small part of it. The work had been even harder than Anna had warned, but Maribel was filled with a sense of pride as she looked at the results of their labour.

'I think we have made a good start,' she said to Anna as they walked back towards the house. 'I am thirsty and dirty. I must wash away the sweat and change my gown before we begin to make a meal for this evening.'

'You have done enough for one day. Let me bring water for you. You must be weary.'

'No, I am not tired,' Maribel said and smiled. 'My back does ache and I think I may be stiff tomorrow, but I feel so alive. I have enjoyed working with you in the sunshine. I feel as if I have done something useful for perhaps the first time in my life.'

'You used to have such soft hands and your needle-work was so fine,' Anna said. 'Even Donna Juanita said how lovely your work was—do you not remember?'

'Yes…' Maribel sighed. 'The girl who sewed pretty cushions was a different person, Anna. That world seems so far away. I have become someone different— a woman with a heart and mind of her own.'

Anna looked at her and nodded. 'Why do you not tell him how you feel? I have seen a look in your eyes.'

'I am not sure that he would care. I know that he desires me, but I cannot speak first.'

'You must forget your pride,' Anna told her. 'You must decide if you want to stay here with us.'

'I am not sure.' Maribel's throat caught with emotion. 'I would stay, but only if…'

She would stay if Justin loved her, but she knew that he still loved the woman he had once wished to marry, despite what he had said about moving on. She could have him for a while, but in the end he would tire of her and then she would be alone.

Maribel enjoyed the feel of the cool water on her skin. She had been so very sweaty and her hair had collected bits of twig and dirt. Anna had helped her to wash it in the yard, and now she was stripped of her clothes in her room, the shutters closed for privacy. She washed in the water she had brought into the house herself, drying her skin and pulling on a shift to cover her body. Her hair was still wet and she sat down on the edge of the bed to rub it dry on a towel, singing a little song that Juanita had sung to her when she was small. She looked up as the door opened, expecting to see Anna, but was shocked to see Justin standing on the threshold. For a moment he stared at her without saying anything, but she saw the pulse at his throat and the way his eyes fastened on her and became aware that her body was clearly outlined through the thin shift. Her nipples had peaked with the instant response of her body to his presence, aching with the need to be touched and caressed.

'Forgive me. I heard voices and thought Anna was with you.'

'I was singing.' Maribel reached for a silken wrap and drew it on over her shift. His eyes seemed to burn into her, making her breath catch in her throat. 'Did you want something?'

'The garden behind the house…who did all that work?' he asked, but his breathing was ragged, his voice

FREE BOOKS OFFER

To get you started, we'll send you
2 FREE books and a FREE gift

There's no catch, everything is **FREE**

Accepting your 2 **FREE** books and **FREE** mystery gift places you under no obligation to buy anything.

Be part of the Mills & Boon® Book Club™ and receive your favourite Series books up to 2 months before they are in the shops and delivered straight to your door. Plus, enjoy a wide range of **EXCLUSIVE** benefits!

- Best new women's fiction – delivered right to your door with FREE P&P

- Avoid disappointment – get your books up to 2 months before they are in the shops

- No contract – no obligation to buy

We hope that after receiving your free books you'll want to remain a member. But the choice is yours. So why not give us a go? You'll be glad you did!

Visit **millsandboon.co.uk** to stay up to date with offers and to sign-up for our newsletter

2 **FREE** books and a **FREE** gift

H0DIA

Mrs/Miss/Ms/Mr   Initials
BLOCK CAPITALS PLEASE

Surname

Address

Postcode

Email

MILLS & BOON®

NO STAMP NEEDED!

Ⓜ MILLS & BOON®
Book Club

FREE BOOK OFFER
FREEPOST NAT 10298
RICHMOND
TW9 1BR

NO STAMP
NECESSARY
IF POSTED IN
THE U.K. OR N.I.

hoarse. He looked at her like a man dying of thirst when he sees the oasis for the first time, his need writ plain on his face. 'Anna? Or Higgins?'

'Anna and I did it together. You said you had not had time and I wanted to thank you for—'

'Foolish woman!' Justin strode towards her. 'Show me your hands.' Maribel held them out and heard his indrawn breath as he saw the red welts across the palms. 'You should not have done such heavy work. Your hands will be sore in the morning.'

'I enjoyed it,' she replied. 'I shall rub some salve into them. Anna always packs some into my trunks…' She gasped as he caught her hand and carried it to his lips, licking at the redness in a way that made desire shoot through her. 'Justin…'

'Sometimes saliva will help,' he said huskily, but as her eyes met his he groaned and reached out, drawing her close. 'You were made for love, not hard physical work…'

For a moment she melted into his body, wanting his kiss to go on and on, wanting so much more that she could not name. Yet even as his hands held her closer so that she could feel the heat of his manhood pressing against her through the thin robe, she felt tears rise up to choke her. He said that she was made for love, but he did not love her—he only wanted her. As he gathered her up in his arms, her mind refused to work properly. She wanted him to kiss and touch her, to make love to her, but she knew that she might lose everything.

Justin placed her carefully amongst the sheets, bending over her to kiss her throat at the little hollow at the base. His hand moved aside her robe, exposing the open neck of her shift. He bent to kiss her, slipping his hand inside her shift to caress her breasts. His thumb caressed her nipple, making her gasp and tremble, her body arching towards his despite her fears.

'You are very beautiful, Maribel, and I have wanted this for a long time. Deny me now if you will, for I can no longer deny myself.' He raised his head to look down at her and then reached out to brush away the tear on her cheek. 'Crying? Have I mistaken the case? Last night in the moonlight I thought…but I see I was wrong. You do not want this, do you?'

Maribel could not answer, nor could she control the tears. She felt them slide helplessly down her face, staring up at him wordlessly. How could she tell him that she loved him, wanted to be his woman, when she knew he did not love her?

'Forgive me. I came to tell you we shall take our trip tomorrow and seeing you…I forgot myself.'

He turned and walked to the door. Maribel tried to speak, but could not make the words come.

'Do not leave me. Stay and make me yours,' she whispered, but the door had closed behind him.

Chapter Six

That morning was as warm as the one before it. Maribel rose early, dressed in one of her simpler gowns and went out to draw water from the well. She had carried both buckets to the house when Anna came sleepily into the kitchen. Hair was straggling down her back and it was obvious that she found it difficult to rouse herself.

'I stayed out drinking with Higgins after you retired last night,' she told Maribel, her cheeks flushed. 'I did not expect you to wake so early.'

'I was excited by the thought of the visit to the other side of the island.' Maribel smiled. 'It was no trouble to me to fetch the water.'

'I am still your maid—until you dismiss me.'

'I would never dismiss you, but I should like us to be friends, Anna. Now, I must change into one of the gowns Captain Sylvester bought for me.'

'I shall help you,' Anna did not meet her eyes.

Maribel sighed. She knew that Anna could not think of her as a friend, perhaps she never would. They had been mistress and servant and they would be parted when Maribel travelled to her mother's home.

Maribel was trying not to think of the moment when Justin had kissed her the previous night, the moment when her foolish tears had sent him away. What would have happened if she had not allowed herself to think of love? Would he have made love to her? Would he have accepted her as his woman? Did he care for her at all or was it just the sight of her in her shift that had made him take her in his arms?

When Maribel came from her room dressed in one of her best gowns, Justin was waiting for her. He greeted her with a nod, but gave no sign that anything had happened the previous night. She smiled at him shyly, her eyes going over him. He was so handsome clothed in black hose and long leather boots that reached to his thighs, his thin linen shirt open at the neck, revealing a sprinkling of dark hair on his tanned chest. His long hair had been caught back by a ribbon at his nape; he was wearing his sword and a leather belt across his body into which was thrust a long-barrelled pistol and a heavy knife.

'You look prepared for trouble,' she said, because she needed to say something or the silence between them would be unbearable.

'It is always best to be prepared,' he told her coolly. 'Higgins will help to row us to the shore, but he will remain with the boat while we explore.'

'Is Anna to come with us?'

'Would you like her to?'

'She would be company for Higgins while he waits for us.'

'Very well, she may come.' Justin's eyes were on her face. 'You are certain you wish for this outing?'

'Yes, of course. I am looking forward to seeing what Paradise looks like.' She did not add that the best part for her would be that she would be alone with him for a while, that perhaps she might find the courage to tell him what was in her heart.

'We should leave at once,' Justin told her, leading the way outside. 'The day looks fair, but the air is heavy. It is possible that there may be a storm before nightfall.'

'Surely not?' Maribel looked up at the cloudless blue sky and then out to sea. Several ships were anchored in the bay, though she could see no sign of the *Defiance*. It looked as if the *Maria* and Captain Hendry had already sailed, though Justin's third ship, the *Siren Eater*, which had joined them a few days before the feast, was still in port. 'Did you finish your business with Captain Hendry yesterday? I do not see his ship in port?'

'He told me that he had decided to become a merchant adventurer. I wished him well and we parted on good terms. I shall tell you more later, but the news he brought is good, Maribel. Your father seems to have accepted your decision not to return, though he has doubled his offer for the map. He sent you a letter. I intended to give it to you last night, but—' He broke off abruptly. 'You shall have it later.'

'Do not talk about it now,' she begged, suddenly wanting to delay talking of the future. 'It is a beautiful day and I see no sign of a storm.'

'They come suddenly at times. I would not be at sea in a small boat if a storm should strike. If that happens, we may have to stay at the other side of the island until the morning.'

Maribel's stomach caught. If they were stranded alone with no house or walls to separate them, who knew what might happen…?

'I do not think there will be a storm,' she said and smiled at him. 'But if there is we must make the best of it.'

Maribel watched as the two men pulled on the oars. It was a small boat and the blades cut through the water effortlessly as they rounded the point coming at last to a large, deserted cove. Here the beach was entirely fringed with trees that seemed to be thick for some distance inland; the sand was soft, unsullied by human habitation and beautiful as a glistening sea lapped against it. A few strokes more and the boat was beached. Higgins and Justin jumped out and hauled it into shallow water so that the hull scraped against the bottom.

Justin came to take Maribel's hand, then swept her up in his arms, carrying her through the water to where the sand was dry and silvery-soft beneath her feet. Her heart raced as she inhaled the spicy scent of him and felt her stomach spasm with desire. He was more to her than all the world and she must find the courage to tell him.

She looked about her. The sea was a deep turquoise, white crested with foam where the waves broke against the shore, sparkling in the sunshine like precious jewels. To each side of her was a wide expanse of sand, and behind her the dense woods that looked as if they might be difficult to penetrate.

'Why is this part of the island uninhabited?'

'There are dangerous rocks beneath the water and the ships would have to anchor further out. Until a harbour and a pier are built the only way to approach is in small boats, as we came today. In time I dare say the trees may be cut back and the harbour built—but the other side of the island was easier to settle—the water is deeper and the ships can unload much nearer to the beach if need be. As you know, we have built a harbour of sorts, though as yet it is primitive.'

Maribel nodded. She looked towards the trees, hearing the call of a bird and catching sight of its bright colours as it flitted between branches.

'It will be a pity if the woods are cut down to build houses.'

'Yes, perhaps, but men must have somewhere to shelter. If the island is to become a permanent settlement and not just somewhere for pirates to replenish their ships and enjoy some leisure on shore there must be some clearance in time.'

'Yes, I suppose it must happen. I think it would be pleasant to live where there is plenty of land and you could ride for a day and not find another settlement.'

'Would you not miss the company of others?'

'Yes, perhaps,' Maribel said and laughed. 'I am foolish. As you say, land must be settled and trees cut for wood if people are to live here—but I am glad that this place is unspoiled for the moment.'

Justin hesitated, then offered his hand. 'Come, I shall show you a place I discovered some months ago when I first visited this side of the island. I think you will like it. You may find the walk a little arduous but it will be worthwhile when we get there.'

Maribel took his hand. He did not look at her and she knew he was keeping a barrier between them, but her heart beat very fast. She had thought he might be angry after the previous night, but he seemed to have put it from his mind. Glancing back at Anna and Higgins, she saw they appeared engrossed in each other and envied them the uncomplicated nature of their relationship.

It was darker in the trees, but very warm despite the shade. The heat made the sweat run between Maribel's breasts, and her gown felt as if it were sticking to her. She had worn one of her best gowns for Justin's approval, but wished that she had a simple shift and skirt, as Anna was wearing. Long branches brushed against her face and hair. There were insects on the greenery and in the air, some of them settling on her arms and face. She brushed them away, feeling that the density of the trees was overpowering and unpleasant, and wishing they were still on the beautiful beach. Feeling hot and sticky, Maribel was on the point of asking if they could turn back when she heard the sound of water and

her curiosity was aroused. In another moment the trees
thinned out and then they were in a clearing.

The sound of water came from a little waterfall. It
cascaded down over rocks, making a rushing noise.
Clear and cool, it looked inviting and Maribel ran
towards it, bending down to scoop water from the tiny
pool at the base of the fall and splashing it on her face
and neck. A stream wound away from the falls, and
without thinking what she did, she sat on the bank,
slipped off her shoes and dipped her feet into the
stream, relishing the coolness on her flesh.

'This feels so good…' she said, arching back so that
the sun was on her face while her feet dabbled in the
water. 'This is a beautiful place, Justin. What are those
flowers over there? They look like hibiscus but, I am not
sure.'

'They are probably a different variety to those you
have at home,' he said from just behind her. He sat
down on the ground and hunched his knees in front of
him. 'Was it worth the walk?'

'Oh, yes…' She looked round at him, her eyes alight,
mouth slightly parted, an expression of such delight in
her eyes that he caught his breath. 'Thank you so much
for bringing me here. I think it is Paradise, though while
we were in the trees I almost asked to go back. I was
so hot and sticky.' She bent down to scoop water from
the pool and splashed it once more over her face and
neck. It trickled down her throat and disappeared under
her bodice. The thin material clung to her, caressing the
softness of her breasts where the water had soaked

through. 'I did not think anywhere could be this beautiful…' Her eyes followed one of the birds that called from branches high above her. In the distance she could hear a faint booming sound, which she took to be the sound of the sea crashing against the rocky coasts further round the island. She turned her head to look at him and saw that he watched her.

'Last night…' Maribel sought and found the courage to say what must be said. 'I wept because I am a foolish woman, but after you had gone I wanted you to stay. I know you cannot love me, for you told me, but I…' The words caught in her throat as she saw the heat in his eyes.

'You are beautiful,' Justin said huskily. He reached out, taking her hand, pulling her to her feet. For a moment he hesitated, then his arms went round her, crushing her hard against him. His mouth sought hers, hungry and demanding, yet tender. 'You inflame my senses, Maribel. I vowed I would not do this, but you tempt me beyond bearing. Last night you wept and I thought—'

'Do not talk, kiss me,' she whispered and placed her finger against his lips. 'I want you to kiss me.'

'You know what it means if I kiss you?' His gaze was dark, intense as his eyes drank her in. 'I want more than a few kisses. I want…everything…you, your body, your mind, your heart.'

Maribel swayed towards him, her body melting into him as he kissed her, her mouth opening to his inquiring tongue, giving of her sweetness as she felt the desire race through her. This was what she had longed for.

What she wanted more than anything else in the world. His hand found and cupped her breast, his thumb caressing her through the thin material. She whimpered with need and pressed against him, feeling the hot desire curl inside her. As he bent his head and kissed her, sliding her bodice down over her shoulder, his tongue caressing the dark rose nipple, she moaned with need.

'Justin, I want…'

'What do you want, my darling? Say it is everything…say it is me you want, as I want you.'

'Take me, make me yours. Justin, I…'

Her words were lost as they heard the shot. She looked up at him, eyes wide and startled. Higgins had arranged that he would fire one shot if he needed them to return.

'Damn!' Justin let her go immediately. He looked back towards the shore, a pulse throbbing at his temple. 'Higgins would not summon me unless it was important. I am sorry, Maribel. We must go back.'

Maribel inclined her head. She wished that they could stay longer in this beautiful place, but Higgins would not have given the signal had it not been urgent. Taking Justin's hand, she let him hurry her back through the path they had cleared on their way here.

What could possibly be happening? Why had Higgins given the signal? As they heard a second shot, her heart started to pound. Something must be terribly wrong…

As they neared the beach Justin was ahead of her. He glanced back, signalling to her to slow down.

'Wait in the trees until I call you,' he warned. 'Just in case there is trouble.'

Maribel would have argued, but she could not catch up to him as he ran out on to the beach. She hovered at the edge of the trees, watching as Justin spoke to Higgins. The sailor appeared to be pointing agitatedly towards the other side of the island. Maribel turned her head and saw the smoke rising into what had been a cloudless sky. A cry from Justin alerted her and she left the shelter of the trees to join him.

'What is it?' she asked. 'What is happening?'

'Something is on fire in the port. We think there has been an attack of some kind.' Justin frowned. 'We must get back to the settlement, but you and Anna should stay here until someone comes to tell you that it is safe to return.'

'No!' Anna and Maribel spoke together.

'I would rather be with you whatever happens,' Maribel insisted. 'If we stayed here and you did not return, we might never reach the other side of the island. No matter what is happening, I shall come with you.'

'I'm not staying here without Higgins.' Anna said, her mouth set stubbornly.

Justin inclined his head. 'Very well. I have no time to argue. Into the boat with you.'

He was frowning as he assisted Higgins to push the boat into deeper water and then helped Maribel to climb in. She sensed that he was anxious for the crew and friends he had left behind. There were no words of comfort to offer for the smoke did not lie. Something terrible must have happened and she could sense the urgency and frustration in the two men as they pulled on the oars. They must be wondering what they were doing on a pleasure trip when their comrades were in trouble.

Maribel caught her breath as they rounded the point and she saw the ships blazing in the harbour. At least three were on fire and the smoke was thick, blowing across the sea towards the land.

'Damn it!' Justin cried. 'One of the ships burning is the *Sea Siren!* By the look of her she is finished.'

'What of the *Defiance?*' Maribel asked. 'I did not notice it in harbour as we left this morning.'

'Yesterday, I sent *Defiance* and a crew to fetch supplies from another island. We were running short of essentials like meat and milk and I bargained for livestock that can be reared here.'

'Then *she* is safe?' Maribel said, thinking that if he had not sent his best ship for supplies that too might have been destroyed. It was bad enough that he should have lost the *Sea Siren,* because he had given his third ship to Captain Hendry as a reward for bringing the information about her family. Maribel felt relieved for his sake, but he misunderstood her question.

'You need not be concerned. A ship would be found to take you to England even if my ships were all destroyed.' His tone sounded scornful and she knew he believed she had been thinking of herself.

'I did not mean…' Maribel began but her words were lost as Anna cried out and pointed to the island

and they saw that some of the houses had been damaged by what could only be cannon fire. 'Who has done this terrible thing?'

The attack was clearly over; people were working frantically on shore to stop the fires spreading. The burning ships seemed to be done for, blazing too fiercely to be saved, but on land the people seemed to be winning their battle. Maribel's expression was puzzled as she looked at Justin.

'Why have these people been attacked?'

'We are pirates, hunted and hated by many,' Justin told her, white-lipped. 'The attack could have come from anyone. We may discover more when we go ashore. Whoever made the attack did as much damage as possible from the sea and then fled before they could be attacked in return—the cowards! May they rot in hell!'

Maribel flinched. Something in his tone made her feel that he blamed her for what had been done. She could hardly wait to be on shore. Terrible damage had been inflicted and people would be hurt. She wanted to help wherever she could, dousing the fires or tending injured people.

Everywhere was confusion and chaos. Maribel joined a chain passing buckets of water, asking the woman next to her what had happened as she took the bucket and gave it to the next in line.

'Three ships sailed into harbour. At first we took no notice, then we saw that some of our ships were on fire. The intruders worked swiftly and secretly, inflicting the most damage they could. When it was seen, the men manned the cannon that protect the harbour and started firing on the strange ships. That is when they fired on the buildings. Some of the men tried to swim out with pistols and swords, but the strangers fired on them. Then, sensing that the fires they had started might spread to their own ships, they sailed off.'

'I was on the other side of the island. Once or twice I thought I heard a muffled boom, but I thought it was just the sea,' Maribel said. 'Are there many hurt?'

'Several injured and some dead, those that were caught in the first blast—also men who tried to reach the swine that attacked us.'

'Where are the injured housed?'

'In the taproom of the Nag's Head, I heard.'

Maribel saw that the fire was almost out. She left the line and ran towards the inn where she had been told the wounded were housed. As she went into the taproom, she saw men and women lying on the floor. Some had been attended, others were moaning, begging for help. One man seemed to be in charge; by his instruments she guessed that he was a ship's surgeon. He was binding a man's head when she went up to him and asked if she could help.

'Have you treated wounds before?' Maribel shook her head. 'Give water to those that ask for it—and get out of my way.'

Feeling rejected, Maribel moved away. She found a barrel of water and a jug. Filling it, she took a pewter cup from the bar and began to move between the injured men and women, giving those that asked a few sips of water. Never in her life had she felt so useless, especially when she saw that Anna was washing away blood and binding wounds at the surgeon's direction. Why could she not have done that?

Maribel noticed that Anna was having some trouble holding a patient and trying to bandage his arm at the same time. She went to her and asked what she could do and was rewarded by a fleeting smile.

'Hold him for me. He keeps flopping over and I cannot bind him and hold him.'

'Like this?' Maribel put her arm about the injured man, supporting him while Anna bound his shoulder with clean linen. 'Let me help you with the others—please? I feel so useless.'

Anna looked at her for a moment, then nodded. 'You can give him a little of this mixture to ease his pain. Support him on your lap and spoon a few drops into his mouth, and then come to me. We need all the help we can get.'

'Yes, whatever you say. You are the mistress here, Anna.'

Maribel managed to spoon a little mixture into the man's mouth, then laid him gently down and made sure he was comfortable before moving on to help Anna with the next injury. She waited for Anna's directions and obeyed them implicitly, never asking why or deviating from her instructions. They worked together quietly and efficiently until all the wounded had been treated.

Maribel did not care that her beautiful gown had bloodstains on the skirt or that her face was smeared with it. She was moved to tears by the suffering of men, women and even one child who had received burns, but she held them back, knowing that she could not give way to sentiment.

At last Anna stood up and looked about her. 'We have done all we can here for the moment,' she said. 'We should go back to the house. I shall come back later to see what else may be done for them.'

'Then I shall come with you.'

'You are tired and hungry. We must prepare food for the men when they come back.'

Maribel followed Anna from the inn. She could see that the fires were out, but two buildings were burned to a shell and others were blackened and badly damaged by the fire. The stink of burning and thick smoke was in the air, as the two women left the waterfront and walked through the row of houses behind.

Maribel was too tired to notice the way people looked at them. She was thirsty and anxious now to be at home so that she could help prepare the food for Justin and Higgins when they had time to eat.

It was an hour or so later that Justin and his first mate came back to the house. Maribel had washed her face and hands, changing into one of her simple gowns before helping Anna to prepare food. The men were grim-faced and silent as they came in, both of them drinking water before seating themselves at the table.

'How bad is it?' Maribel asked. 'I know several were hurt—were many killed?'

'Three men and two women,' Justin replied. 'Two ships were lost, another damaged but not beyond repair. It might have been worse.'

'Was one of the ships lost yours?'

'Yes. Pike's was damaged, but it will sail again.'

'So you have only the *Defiance?*'

'I am fortunate to have that.' A nerve flicked in his cheek. 'It seems that my ships were what they were after. Pike's vessel and another caught the flames, but the fires were meant for us.'

'Meant for us?' Maribel's eyes widened. For a moment she did not understand, then the colour drained from her face. 'Are you saying…no, how could it be?'

'The ships that attacked us were Spanish. Pike saw the attack. He says that the pennant belonged to Sabatini…your father…'

'No! How could my father know where to find you?'

'Word of this place may have spread. I do not know that they came looking for us, but it was not mere chance that made them attack my ship.'

Her throat tightened. 'You think…you blame my father…and me?'

'No, I do not blame you,' he said, his voice hoarse. 'But I fear others will, Maribel. They will blame you— and me for bringing you here.' He frowned. 'It may be that I am to blame…'

'Why? I do not know what you mean.'

'If it was your father's ships, then I may have brought them here.'

'Surely not? My father could not have known you would come here—he could not!'

'You forget Mr Hendry. He had knowledge of our plans. It may be that he passed on his knowledge.'

'You think he betrayed the location of the island?' Her eyes widened. 'He sailed away before the attack. You think that he brought them here? Why would he do that? He took your message to my father and you gave him the ship, as you promised. Why would he betray you—all of you?'

'He may not have had a choice. Your father may have hoped to trap me. When I did not walk into the trap or send back the map, he decided to take another kind of revenge. I was told that he had doubled his offer, but that may have been just to lull me into a sense of security. Hendry may have agreed to show them the way here to save his own life…and a cowardly attack is something your father might try. He knows that our ships will beat his when we meet at sea, but with the ships anchored and a skeleton crew aboard…'

'What happened to those men?'

'Some managed to swim for the shore, some died.' Justin's mouth settled into a hard line. 'I care little for the ships. We began with one and we can rebuild our fleet, but…' His eyes were flinty. 'Tom was one of the crew on watch. He did not make it to the shore.'

'Tom is dead?' Tears welled in her eyes. 'No! Oh, no, I cannot bear it. He was so happy to be a part of all this and he was so young.'

'He knew the risks when he threw in his lot with us.'

'How can you say that?' Maribel was too distressed to think clearly or to notice that he was strained and tense. 'Tom was little more than a child.'

She ran from the room, feeling close to tears. In her own bedchamber she sat on the bed, covering her face with her hands. The tears she had held back as she helped with the wounded fell thick and fast. She had known that the pirates led precarious lives, but the cabin boy's death was shocking and painful. She looked up as her door opened and saw Justin standing on the threshold.

'You should not weep for him,' he said. 'We all run the risk of a violent death. It could have happened at sea. Ours is a precarious trade and death is common amongst us.'

'You speak so lightly of death.' Maribel's face was white as she stood up. 'I cannot help but weep for Tom. He was like a young brother to me.'

'Weep then, but accept it.' Justin moved towards her, looking down at her face. She believed she saw something like regret in his eyes. 'I thought perhaps we might have something, you and I—but this is no life for you, Maribel. You do not belong here. The life is too harsh for a woman of your breeding and you would sicken and die of a broken heart. The sooner I get you to England the better for all concerned.'

'I thought…' She choked back the words. Earlier that day he had held her in his arms and kissed her until she melted for love, but that was a different man, a man she could love and respect, the man he had been before he became a pirate perhaps. This man with the cold eyes looked at her as if he despised her, thought her weak and useless. 'Yes, you are right. Yet even if I do not belong, I can do something to help. Anna and I tended the wounded and we shall return to see what more we can do in the morning.'

'No! You are not to go down to the waterfront. I forbid it.'

'You forbid it? I do not understand. I am capable of helping to nurse the wounded.'

'Now that the fires are out there will be plenty to help the wounded. You are not needed—and Anna would do well to stay away too. These people can look after their own.'

His words struck her like the lash of a whip. 'You are cruel, sir. I wished only to help.'

'You will do more harm than good. People are blaming you for this attack—and me. They do not want your help. Even I must watch my back when I walk there—you would be too vulnerable.'

Maribel was silenced. He was so harsh and his words were like a knife in her heart. He spoke of others blaming her—but he blamed her too. The ships that had wreaked so much damage on the island and its inhabitants were part of her father's fleet. She had tried to change, to become like Anna and the others, but she had never belonged here—and now she was hated.

'I would not have had this happen…' Her eyes were wide, filled with tears. 'You know I would not…'

'What I know is nothing to the point. For your own safety stay away from the waterfront. The *Defiance* should return in a few days. As soon as it has unloaded its cargo and provisioned we shall leave the island.'

Maribel inclined her head. 'Very well, I shall be ready. As you said, the sooner I am on my way to England the better.'

Maribel slept little that night. She had wept until there were no more tears, but then she tossed restlessly, going over and over all the events of the past weeks in her mind. What could she have done differently? People believed that she had brought this cruel attack on them, but even if her father's ships had been responsible it did not mean that she had brought them here. Had they been looking for her they would surely have brought a party ashore and demanded her return? No, she could only think that the ships had come at this time by chance—and seeing so many pirate ships assembled had taken a swift revenge before retreating.

It was unfair for Justin to blame her!

In the morning she rose early and went out to fetch water. Anna came into the kitchen as she was washing some clothes. She looked tired and her hair was hanging down her back, as if she had not bothered with it.

'Did you not sleep last night either?'

'I went to the inn to see if I could help but I was told to stay away.' Anna looked at her sulkily. 'They are blaming us for bringing the trouble here. Higgins says that we may not be able to return to the island.'

'I am sorry. I know that you wished to make your home here.'

'Higgins says we may have to find somewhere else to set up our trading store. Some of the men told me that we are no longer welcome on the island. I think we must be careful, Maribel. There could be trouble.'

'Surely we are safe enough here?'

'Perhaps—but we must not go to the waterfront alone.'

'Captain Sylvester forbade it. Yet you still went last night—why?'

'I thought the resentment would not be for me, but it seems I am tarred with the same brush as you.'

'Do not hate me, Anna. Please. You know that I would not have had this happen. Besides, I do not think they came to look for me, because no one came ashore—though it seems they were my father's ships.'

'Perhaps they thought you were not here since the *Defiance* was not in the harbour.' Anna frowned. 'Higgins says people are wondering why it was not here.'

'They cannot think that Sylvester knew the attack would happen? If he had, he would have warned others and sent all his ships away.'

'When people are hurt and angry they do not think clearly.'

'This is so foolish,' Maribel shook her head. 'We were not even here when the attack happened.'

'That makes it all the worse… Do you not see what people think?'

'They believe he deliberately chose to be absent?

How foolish can people be? We rushed back as soon as we saw the smoke…we all helped as best we could!'

'Higgins says someone is stirring them up, making trouble.'

'Why? Who would do that?'

Anna shook her head. 'I do not know. I only know that things have changed. We must leave this island and the sooner the better.'

Maribel was about to reply when she heard a noise behind her. Swinging round, she saw Peg watching them.

'I did not hear you come in?'

'I wanted to creep up on yer,' Peg told her, unsmiling. 'Yer asked me for lessons to defend yerself and yer will need them. Folk are saying yer brought the trouble on us and they want yer gone—one way or the other. Some are fer hanging yer.'

'Anna has told me what people are saying. I knew nothing of this, Peg. I swear I would not have had it happen for the world.'

Peg looked at her in silence for a moment and then nodded. 'Aye, I believe yer, but others will not. They won't listen. Especially with Pike stirring them up. He says Sylvester sent his ship away to save it.'

'That is nonsense! You know he would not do that, don't you? He could have sent all his ships if that had been the case—so why didn't he?'

'Yer need not try to convince me, lass—but others will listen to Pike. Sylvester has been too successful. Some are jealous of him and need only a grievance to make them turn against him. He brought yer here and that's good enough for most.'

'Is he in danger?' Maribel asked. 'I have not seen him this morning. I do not know where he is.'

'It's yerself they hate most. Come outside now, and I'll show yer a few of me tricks with a knife so that yer can defend yerself, but it will be best fer yer all if yer leave as soon as yer can.'

'It is getting late,' Maribel said as the sun began to dip on the horizon that evening. 'Sylvester has been gone all day and Higgins with him. I fear that something has happened to them.'

'Someone would have told us,' Anna said, but was clearly worried. 'They are not all against us despite what happened. Sylvester's crew would stand behind him whatever others thought.'

'Would they?' Maribel eyed her uncertainly. 'Supposing they have been hurt? The crew might be afraid to send for us…Sylvester might forbid it if it meant danger for us.'

'There is little we can do. They might be anywhere.' Anna frowned. 'I do not think they would leave the island without us.'

'Of course they would not. Captain Sylvester would never desert us.'

Chapter Seven

$\mathcal{O} \! \! \! \diamond \! \! \! \mathcal{O}$

Maribel's anxiety grew with every minute that passed. Justin must know that they would be worried. Why was he so late? It was almost dark and he had still not returned. Her instincts were to go and look for him, but he had forbidden her to go down to the waterfront.

She could not sit and wait. The house felt too small and confined to contain her and she needed some air. Anna called to her as she moved towards the door.

'Where are you going? It is nearly dark and too dangerous to go looking for them now.'

'I just need some—' Maribel broke off as she heard sounds outside. She rushed to the door and threw it open, staring in dismay as she saw Higgins and two of Justin's crew she recognised. They were carrying something between them—Justin's body. She saw blood on his shirt and clapped a hand to her mouth to stop herself screaming. 'What happened?'

'He was set upon by some ruffians.' Higgins

scowled. 'It was Pike's crew, ordered to it by him no doubt. The captain had been to see some of the wounded. He had promised to make good their losses and explained why our ship was not in the harbour. They listened to him and he left believing all was settled—then this gang attacked him. He fought them off and wounded or killed three, but they were too many for him. Had I and some of the crew not arrived in time he might have been finished.'

'Carry him through to his room,' Maribel said, hovering as they brought Justin's unconscious body into the house. Her heart was hammering and she felt sick with worry, but would not give way to her fear. 'He has lost blood—where is his wound?'

'He has a wound to his thigh and another to his shoulder—but he was knocked unconscious by a blow from one of those murdering devils. Fortunately, we drove them off before they could finish him, but he will need nursing. I've sent word to the surgeon and he'll be here soon.'

'Thank you for all you have done. I am so grateful.'

In the bedchamber, Anna had pulled back the sheets. Justin was deposited gently on his bed by the men; they then drew back to look at him in silence, not sure what to do next. Anna brought a knife and slit his breeches at the side so that they could see the wound to his thigh. She examined it and then looked at Maribel.

'It has bled a lot, but is not too deep. He should mend without too much help from the surgeon,' she said on a note of relief. She then slit open the sleeve of his shirt all the way to the shoulder. 'This is a little deeper, but I think neither wound will kill him—providing he does not take a fever.'

'It seems you were in time to save his life. Thank you,' Maribel said to Higgins. Tears trickled down her cheeks, but she brushed them away. She turned to Anna, an appealing expression in her eyes. 'Please tell me what to do. You know better than I how to help him.'

'We must cleanse and bind the wounds,' Anna told her. 'I do not know what more we can do, but the surgeon will tell us when he comes. It may be that he will cauterise the wound to Sylvester's shoulder.'

Maribel's face turned white and she swayed, clutching at a bedpost to steady herself. She had never been present when it was done, but she knew that to apply a hot iron to open flesh must be fearful and would cause terrible pain.

'I pray God that it will not be needed,' she whispered. 'I shall fetch water and clean linen.'

She was praying and crying at the same time, for she was afraid that whatever they did Justin might die.

The surgeon had closed Justin's wounds without cauterising them, cleansing the skin with a mixture of his own that smelled like alcohol to Maribel and binding him tightly to stop further bleeding. When he had finished, he turned to Maribel.

'Fortunately, they are both little more than flesh wounds. He should heal within a week or two if he rests, but you must watch for a fever. That blow to the head has rendered him unconscious. Such wounds can kill a man, but sometimes the victim recovers without serious harm. You must watch over him and wait. I will leave something to help him with the pain. If a fever develops, you must keep him cool, and if necessary send for me again.'

'Thank you.' Maribel's throat was tight as she held back her tears. 'Anna is very good. She will help me to nurse him and she knows how to prepare mixtures that help with a fever, if she has the herbs.'

'Send to me if you need anything and I will bring whatever Anna requires. It is best that she does not go looking for her herbs alone—the mood here is still uncertain.' He wrinkled his brow in thought. 'I do not blame you or Sylvester. I dare say the ships found us by chance, as was bound to happen one day. Had they been prepared for an attack, they would have done much more damage and probably sent a party ashore to look for you.'

'I think much as you do,' Maribel said. 'My father would have sent men ashore to look for me if he had planned this attack; I believe they must have found the island by chance. However, they may return with more ships and more men; my father is a vengeful man.'

'There is talk of setting up cannon on shore in case we are attacked from the sea again, though others talk of leaving the island, giving up the attempt to settle here. Most of the captains neglected to protect their ships; they felt safe here, but this attack will make them take measures to make sure next time we can at least fight back. However, some feel the island is no longer safe for us.'

He smiled as he took his leave. Maribel thanked him. She stayed by Justin's side, watching as he lay unconscious. He was breathing still, but had given no sign of coming to himself, though he had moaned once or twice as the surgeon treated his wounds.

'Please live,' she whispered. Her tears came freely now for she could no longer hold them back. One or two fell on his face as she bent over him, pressing her cheek to his. 'I love you, my own dear pirate. I would not tell you if you could hear me—but I love you as I have never loved anyone else.'

Bending over him, she bathed his forehead with a cloth wrung out in cool water, then slid it over his shoulders and arms. His body was so hot and he had been throwing his arms out of the bed.

'I love you so,' she said as the tears trickled down her cheeks. 'I know so little of you, but you are brave and generous, and I was luckier than I knew when you took me captive. Please get better, my dearest. If you died I should not want to live.'

Justin did not stir. She looked for a flicker of his eyelids, but there was none. Please God he would wake soon…she could not think of a future without this man.

As the night wore on he began to moan and move restlessly in his bed, calling out a name she could not quite catch. She lay a hand on his forehead and thought he felt too warm. The surgeon had told her to keep him cool. Maribel hesitated and then fetched water in a bowl; it was cold from the well and she dipped a cloth into the cool water bathing his face and neck once more. He was still hot, so she stroked her cloth down his arms, then drew back the covers to his waist and bathed his chest. He seemed to settle then and she replaced the covers.

His breathing was easier now and she thought that he seemed more comfortable than before. She settled down on a blanket beside the bed and after a little fell asleep.

When a sound awoke her light was beginning to creep into the room. She started up, giving a little moan as she felt the stiffness in her back from lying on the floor. Getting to her feet, she looked at her patient and saw that he was now awake and staring at her.

'That was foolish of you, Maribel,' he said, looking stern. 'You should have gone to your own bed—or had someone else watch me. Where is Anna?'

'Anna has enough to do. She helped the surgeon when he tended you—and she stopped the bleeding when you were brought back. It did not hurt me to watch over you for a while.' She reached out to touch his forehead, but he caught her wrist. 'You were hot last night. I thought you might have a fever.'

'I have a damnable soreness in my thigh and left shoulder.' His gaze narrowed. 'I remember fighting the rogues off, but then something hit me from the side.' He scowled. 'There were too many of them. It is impossible to guard against such a cowardly blow. What happened after that—how did I get here?'

'Fortunately, Higgins and some of your men arrived to drive the wretches off. You were unconscious when they brought you home. Anna tended you first and then the surgeon came.'

His eyes were on her face. 'You know what is being said of you?'

'That the attack was because of me. Do you believe that? Do you think I would want that to happen?

'I know you would not. That it was your father's ships is not in question. However, it may have been chance that brought them here—unless Hendry revealed the secret of the island and how to enter its waters. One reason this island was chosen from so many others is that there is chain of rocks guarding it. Only those that have visited know how to navigate the channel. If your father's ships got close enough to inflict so much damage, they must have known the secret—but if they came for you, why was there no attempt to rescue you?'

'I do not know—perhaps I was not important.'

Justin frowned and was silent for a moment. He knew, but would not tell her that her father cared so little for her that he had been willing to give her up for the return of his map. Sabatini was evil and it made him wonder if the man was truly her father. 'I think he came to show me what could happen to me if I do not return his map.'

'You think the attack was planned merely for revenge? Because you refused to give up the map?' She was silent for a moment. 'What will you do? Shall you send it to him?'

'The way he so callously destroyed property and life here tells me that he should never have that map. With it he will become even more powerful and I cannot condone what he did. He is an evil man.'

'But if you keep the map he may attack you again.'

'Do you think I should be safe from his vengeful spite if I sent him his map? He would see it as a sign of weakness.' Justin looked thoughtful. 'I had considered trying to find the silver mine myself, but it has cost too many lives already. I think it is cursed and I shall destroy the map. Better it is never found again than it should cost more lives.'

'My father will always be your enemy.'

'You need not worry yourself over my safety. In two or three days I shall be able to get up. As soon as the *Defiance* returns she will be provisioned and we shall sail to England. Once you are with your family you will be safe.'

'The surgeon said you need to rest.' Maribel felt that he was dismissing her once more and her eyes stung with tears she would not shed.

'I shall be well enough to leave when the *Defiance* is ready to sail.'

'What will you do next? Will you return to the island? You've built a fine house and furnished it—but you have lost one of your ships and people may turn against you because of what happened.'

'It can be of little interest to you what I do. I promised to keep you safe until you are with your family. After that you should forget me.'

How could he speak to her so? Was he deliberately trying to drive a wedge between them?

'I think you must be thirsty. I shall draw some fresh water from the well.'

She walked away from him, her throat closing with choking emotion. He was still determined to take her to her family and leave her. Did he blame her for the loss of his ships and the destruction here? She blinked away her tears. Maribel had wept when she believed he might die, but she would not weep now!

'If your father saw you now he would not know you,' Anna said as Maribel was drawing water from the well three days later. 'Your skin used to be a pale olive and was much admired, but now…you are as brown as a gypsy.'

'I cannot stay in the shade all the time here. There has been more work to do since Justin was injured. It would not be fair to expect you to do everything. You chopped the wood so that we can cook, so I draw the water and help with the washing and other chores.'

Anna stared at her in silence for a moment, then smiled a little reluctantly. 'You have learned to make yourself useful. Sometimes I almost forget that you are a lady and I am your servant.'

'You are my friend, Anna. The old ways are forgotten here.'

'But when you go to England you will be a lady again, and if I came with you I should be a servant.' She shook her head as Maribel was silent. 'No, do not deny it. That is the way of your world, the way it has always been. You cannot change it if you would, which is why I shall not stay in England.'

Anna was right, but Maribel did not want to admit it. Here on the island she had found a measure of freedom and she did not want to return to her old life—but what else could she do?

'Where will you go if you cannot return to the island?'

'Higgins thinks he shall go to the New World and I shall go with him. There is plenty of land there for settlement. If you have money for sufficient supplies to get you through the first year or two until the land begins to grow enough crops, it could be a good place to live.'

'The New World…' Maribel wrinkled her brow. 'I have heard it said that it is a land of savages. My father and men like him take silver from the mines, but to live there…I am not sure…'

'At first our people, men like your father, sought to conquer and take only silver and gold, but other people have begun to settle further to the north. Higgins has heard from men who have taken settlers to the New World. The savages are called Red Indians, because of the colour of their skins, and it is thought that there are many tribes. Some of them are thought to be friendly to the white man.'

'It sounds dangerous and the living will be primitive at first,' Maribel said, but she felt a tingle of excitement at the nape of her neck. 'Even here on the island there are often shortages of food, which is why Justin sent the *Defiance* to bring pigs and chickens here from one of the larger islands.'

'In the New World they say there is an abundance of game. Ships taking settlers to a new life will carry seed corn and other supplies to tide them over. A ship bringing in fresh supplies to be sold at a trading station could do well.'

'Yes, I see.' Maribel nodded. 'You would set up your trading station there instead of on the island as you planned, but—' She had questions concerning such trading, but she broke off as she saw a man coming towards them. Chills ran down her spine as she saw the look of hatred on his face. 'Go inside, Anna.'

'And leave you alone with that pig? I shall stay with you.'

Maribel faced the pirate. One hand moved to the place in her skirts where she had created a pouch to keep the knife that Peg had given her. Her heart was pounding wildly as he came closer.

'Why have you come here?' she asked. 'You tried to have Sylvester murdered. You are not wanted here.'

Pike's eyes narrowed to menacing slits, his mouth curved back in a sneer. 'I came only to tell you that the *Defiance* is back in the harbour. People are demanding that you leave immediately. I have some business with Sylvester that he might want to hear.'

'Do you imagine I shall let you near him after what you tried to do?'

'You?' He laughed harshly. 'What will you do, my lady? Kick me, perhaps, or scratch my eyes out—if you can?'

'Go away. If you have business, you may return

when Higgins is here…' Maribel gasped because she had revealed their vulnerability.

Pike grinned evilly. 'Oh, do not distress yourself for betraying your weakness. I saw Higgins on the waterfront not twenty minutes ago. I know he is not around to save you or your precious Sylvester, whore.'

'I am no man's whore.' Maribel flashed.

'Are you not? Then I might as well amuse myself a little before I complete my business with…'

Maribel moved back a step as he came towards her. Then she stopped, determined to stand her ground. If she ran or showed fear, he would have the advantage. She could not let him into the house because Justin was not yet strong enough to fight him off.

Pike laughed mockingly and reached out to grab her. Whipping her knife out, Maribel struck his right arm, making him yell out in shock. His left hand moved to cover his wound. He stared in disbelief at the blood running between his fingers.

'You bitch! I'll teach you a lesson—and then I'll pay your lover a visit.'

'You will have to get past me first.'

Maribel held her knife in front of her the way Peg had taught her. She circled him warily, her eyes never leaving his face. He made a move to grab her once more and she flicked her wrist, stabbing him swiftly on his hand and darting back. He swore, looking at his hand as if he did not know what had happened.

'You asked for this,' he grunted and drew his cutlass. The sunlight glinted on the wicked blade as he advanced on her. 'I thought to have a little fun before you died, but it is not worth the bother. I'll be rid of you once and for all!'

Maribel held the knife in front of her, but she knew a knife could not compete with a cutlass. Peg had told her to keep the knife secret and wait until her target was close enough to stab him in the stomach, but she had struck too soon, inflicting only superficial wounds. The element of surprise had gone. She had wounded him, but not sufficiently to stop him. He would kill her and then Justin.

Maribel was vaguely aware that Anna had run into the house. She retreated slowly towards the house, her gaze holding his as he advanced on her, knowing that it was only a matter of time before he killed her.

'Stay away from her!'

Hearing Anna's voice, Maribel glanced round. Even as she saw the pistol in her hand, Anna fired. Her shot hit Pike in the chest and he fell, clutching himself. For what seemed like an eternity, he writhed in agony on the ground, his eyes wide and staring at them. Anna came towards them, her hand shaking. She looked sick and shaken as she watched the man twitching on the ground.

'Have I killed him?'

The twitching had stopped at last. Pike lay still. 'Yes, I think so,' Maribel said. Anna dropped the pistol. She was shaking, clearly upset by what she had done. 'Do not look so guilty. You had no choice. If you had not shot him, he would have killed us all.'

'I meant to stop him, not to kill him.' Anna looked

frightened. She turned away to vomit on the ground, then wiped her mouth on the back of her hand. 'Will they hang me?'

'No, they won't hang you.' Justin's voice spoke from the doorway. 'It was in self-defence, Anna—but no one will know, because we shall bury him out there.' He jerked his head towards the back of the house. 'I can't do much to help you. There is a spade in the lean-to at the rear. You will have to drag him there between you. I'll help to dig the hole.'

'No, you will not,' Maribel spoke decisively. 'You have told us what to do. Go back to your room and rest. We can do this between us.'

Justin set his mouth stubbornly. He took a step towards them, then hesitated, his face white.

'Go on, then. I will make sure there is no sign of the blood here—and I'll keep watch and warn you if anyone comes.'

'Yes,' Maribel agreed, because she knew that he would only follow them if she refused his help. 'As soon as it is done you must go back to bed and rest. Pike told us that the *Defiance* is in the harbour. When it is provisioned we shall leave as intended.'

Justin nodded, his mouth set in a grim line.

'Come, Anna,' Maribel said. 'You have to help me drag him. I can't do it alone. Take one leg and I'll take the other.'

Anna shuddered, then did as she was told. Pike was heavy and it took both of them to drag his body across the front yard and out behind the house.

Maribel chose a spot where the earth looked softer. A tree had been cleared to supply timber for the house and the earth had been disturbed, making it easier to dig. When Anna fetched the spade, Maribel started the digging. She dug out an oblong large enough to hide the body. After the first few cuts were made, Anna went to the lean-to and came back with a chopper. She used it to dig down into the earth and then scraped the dry earth out with her hands.

The women worked in silence for what seemed like an eternity. At last the hole was deep enough and between them they placed Pike in his grave and then started to scrape the earth over him. When they had finished Maribel looked at Anna.

'He was a wicked man, but I think we should say a prayer for him.'

'Yes…' Anna was pale and penitent. 'You are right, Maribel. I did not mean to murder him, only to stop him.'

'You did what you had to do—we both did,' Maribel said. She felt sick and a little faint, but forced herself to continue. 'God keep and forgive this man. He was not a good man, but we pray that his soul will find peace.'

'You can see the earth has been disturbed,' Anna said when the prayer was done. 'We should lay branches over it to hide it for a while. The grave may be found, but it will not matter once we are gone.'

'You will not be able to return here now.' Maribel remarked as they finished their work and returned to the house. 'But you should not feel guilty, Anna. You saved my life—and Captain Sylvester's.'

'And my own. He would not have let me live to tell the tale.'

'No, he could not have risked it, for Higgins would have demanded justice.' Maribel saw that Anna was still pale, still shocked by what she had done. She reached out and kissed her cheek. 'Forget what happened, Anna. You must put it behind you.'

'He was a bad man.' Anna met her eyes, seeking re-assurance. 'I do not believe I shall burn in hell for what I did, do you?'

'No, of course not. It was the only way,' Maribel replied. 'I shall never forget that you saved my life, Anna.'

'I could not let him kill you.' Anna smiled, oddly shy and uncertain. 'We have something in common now, Maribel. We share a bond that can never be broken—it is a secret we must keep to the grave.'

'Yes, it is.' Maribel took her hand. 'We are friends, Anna, truly friends. What has happened here has changed us both for ever. I am no longer the lady you served. I am different and I can never go back to what I once was.'

'We both need to wash and change our gowns,' Anna said, looking at the dirt beneath her fingernails. 'You should speak to Captain Sylvester, ask when we are leaving.'

'Yes, I shall.'

Maribel pushed her hair back from her eyes. She was damp with sweat, her clothes sticking to her. There were blisters on her hands and her back ached. The hard labour had exhausted her, but she had a feeling of satisfaction, because she would never have believed herself capable of doing what she had just done.

A part of her felt ill at ease because a man's life had been lost, but Pike was evil. He had tried to have Justin killed and would have succeeded this time if Anna had not stopped him. Maribel knew that she would not have known how to shoot the pistol. Anna must have learned it from Higgins, just as she had learned to use a knife from Peg. So although she felt uneasy that a man's life had been taken, she believed it was inevitable. Pike had been their enemy from the beginning. It was always his life or theirs.

She went into the house, then knocked at Justin's door. He was sitting on the bed. He invited her to enter, looking at her face as she did so.

'Is it done?'

'Yes. We put branches over the grave. It is not deep enough and it will be found, but perhaps not just yet.'

'We shall leave in the morning with the tide. Higgins has instructions to see the ship provisioned immediately.'

'Anna had no choice but to shoot him. He would have murdered us all.'

'I should have seen to it before it got this far,' Justin said. 'You both did what you had to do, Maribel. Put all this from your mind.'

'I shall try.' She brushed the damp hair from her brow. 'Your shirt has blood on it. I think your wound has opened,' she scolded. 'You have done too much. I saw that you brushed away the marks we left when we dragged Pike into the woods.'

'I wish I could have done it all.' He reached up to trail his fingers over her cheek as she sat beside him. 'You have dirt on your face and your gown is muddy. You must wash and change it for another.' He took her hands and looked at them. 'Rub some ointment into your hands; they will be sore for some days.'

'Let me tend your shoulder first.'

'No!' He caught her hand as she attempted to push his shirt back. 'I can manage for myself. Wash and rest, Maribel. You should drink a little rum or some wine. You have had a shock.'

'We buried a man,' Maribel said. 'Anna is feeling guilty. It will take time to forget.'

'I know. It is something you learn to live with. I've never been able to accept it, which is why I didn't just kill Pike at the start—but it might have been better if I had.'

'Yes, perhaps.'

Maribel turned away. She needed to wash and change. The dress she was wearing would be discarded, because she could never wear it again without remembering.

She had told Anna to forget what had happened, because to dwell on Pike's death would cast a shadow over their lives. She shuddered, because she knew it was something she might never forget. They had done what was necessary and they must put it behind them and move on.

* * *

Maribel could not sleep. The night was hot and stuffy and in the morning they were to leave the island for ever. In a few short weeks they would be in England and she would be with her mother's family. She might never see Justin again.

Rising from her bed, she dressed in a thin gown, pushed her feet into light slippers and went through to the main room and then outside. Here it was a little cooler. Maribel knew that she was taking a risk to leave the house, but Pike was dead and she did not think anyone else was likely to come looking for her. Most of the men on the island respected Justin, even if they blamed her for what had happened here.

Was it her fault? She had done nothing wrong and yet it might be because of her that the island had been attacked. She tried to put all the terrible happenings of the past few days from her mind. Soon now she would leave this place and perhaps…

Maribel heard a twig snap behind her, but before she could turn something thick and heavy was thrown over her head. She screamed, but the sound was muffled and the blanket filled her mouth, making her gag on the coarse wool. Fighting and kicking, she felt herself being tossed over someone's shoulder. She was being carried away. As she realised that she had been kidnapped, panic swept over her.

Justin would think she had run away! He would think she did not care. He would never know that she loved him. She might never see him again; it would break her heart, but she was just another woman to him. He would find someone else and forget her.

It was unbearable beneath the blanket. She found it difficult to breathe and after a while she ceased to struggle because she no longer had the strength to fight. She could only wonder who had captured her and where she was being taken.

After a while, Maribel heard the sound of the sea. She knew that she was in a rowing boat and that she was being taken to a ship. Was it her father's ship? It was the only explanation that occurred to her, because surely no one else would have come to the island to kidnap her. Her father must have sent someone to steal her back. He had sent Captain Hendry to bring the information they needed so that he knew where to find her and now she was a prisoner.

What was going to happen to her now? Justin was angry with her. He would not rescue her a second time—why should he?

When Maribel opened her eyes again she found that she was lying on a bunk. Her mouth tasted dry and she knew that at some time after being brought to this cabin she had fainted. As yet she did not know whose ship she was on or who had captured her.

Hearing a key in the lock, she looked fearfully at the door, her heart pounding. It opened slowly and she saw a man standing in the opening looking at her. When she saw the man's face she shrank back, feeling frightened, but determined not to show it.

'Why have you brought me here?' she demanded. 'Are you taking me to my father?'

'Your father has no more use for you, Donna Sanchez. He has given you to me in return for a contract for his wines—and favours rendered.' An unpleasant smile touched his mouth.

'What do you mean he has given me to you? I was to marry your cousin.'

Samuel Hynes looked at her triumphantly. 'Sadly, news reached us that my cousin is dead. All that he once owned is mine—and that includes you. I knew that he might not live to see his wedding day. Why else do you imagine I agreed to fetch you? I wanted to make sure I had you fast before the news of his death reached your father.'

'I shall never marry you. Never! I would rather die.'

'You speak wildly, Madonna.' His mouth hardened. 'Have I said that I wished to wed you? I might simply use you for my pleasure.'

'I shall fight you. You may force me, but you will never truly have me.'

'I think you will learn to obey me in time,' Hynes said. 'You are too proud. I shall enjoy teaching you your manners, Maribel. However, it will suit me better to have you as a wife. Your father thinks to cheat us both of your fortune, but he has met his match in me. I shall have you and then I shall claim what belongs to me.'

Maribel stared at him, feeling sick and miserable. 'I wish that Pablo had never left me his fortune,' she said.

'It seems that no one cares what I want. No one cares for me. You all want my husband's estates.'

'Beautiful women are easy to find,' Hynes told her with a sneer. 'However, a beautiful rich woman is another matter. I shall leave you to rest and think carefully, Maribel. We could be married almost immediately on board ship and I should treat you fairly—but defy me and you will learn to regret it at your leisure.'

Maribel lay back against the pillows as he left her. Her head was aching and her heart felt as if it had been torn apart. Tears trickled down her cheeks. She had not known how fortunate she was when Justin took her captive. She had called him a pirate and accused him of being a rogue, but he was a true gentleman—and she loved him. The time spent at the island had taught her many lessons and she knew that she had been offered something true and special.

The tears fell faster as she realised that she would probably never see him again. She was now at the mercy of a ruthless devil; if she lived, her life would be unbearable.

'Do you know where Maribel is?' Justin demanded of Anna when he realised that she had gone that morning. 'Has she taken anything with her?'

'Only the gown she meant to wear today.' Anna looked at him tearfully. 'Surely she would not run away? She had nowhere to go.'

'She must be somewhere.'

Justin strode into Maribel's room, looking for

evidence that she had taken something with her. Her combs and perfume bottles were still there, as were her jewels. He whirled round as he heard a step behind him.

'Maribel…' Seeing Higgins, he frowned. 'What is it? Have you found her?'

'I have found signs of a struggle. What looks like the marks of several pairs of boots in the dust outside the house—and I have heard that a strange ship was seen at anchor outside the reef.'

'You think someone snatched her last night?'

'I've never trusted Hendry,' Higgins said sourly. 'Did you not wonder why Sabatini let him return? Or why he bothered to come back at all? He already had the ship. Why should he have come back to the island merely to bring you another message?'

'You believe Hendry brought Sabatini's ships here in return for his freedom? That the intention was to snatch Maribel all the time?' Justin frowned. 'There was a map that showed the way to some silver mines… I destroyed it because a man like that should not be allowed to have such power. He is evil.'

'You destroyed a map showing the location of silver mines?' Higgins looked at him intently. 'Those mines are worth a king's ransom.'

'I considered trying to find the mine, but decided it was cursed.'

'Sabatini must think you still have the map. Do you think that is why he has snatched her?'

'If it is, then I am at fault,' Justin said. 'I do not

know where they are taking her—but we must try to find them. I shall go to her father. He may hate me and he may take my life, but, it is the risk I must take.'

'Do you think that is wise?'

'I do not care whether or not it is wise,' Justin replied. 'I shall not ask anyone else to risk their life for me. You will drop me on shore and then go back to sea. I will meet you on the beach at midnight. If I am not there, come again the next night, but after that you must go and leave me to my fate.'

'Let me go in your stead?'

'No. You have been a good friend to me, but if I do not come the second night leave me and seek your own fortune.'

'Will you not take the air on deck, Madonna?' Samuel Hynes looked at her, his eyes narrowed. 'We are forced to put into port for repairs to the mainmast and it may be some weeks before we reach England.'

Maribel sighed. It was hot in the cabin and since the third night after leaving the island, when a storm had badly damaged their mainmast, they had been forced to drift aimlessly. Now that the ship had at last managed to limp to the nearest port, which was Gibraltar, the carpenters could make repairs while the stores were replenished. Under Moorish domination for many years, Gibraltar had briefly achieved independent status until the beginning of the century, when it was taken under Spanish rule. Although in no hurry to reach England, Maribel did not wish to spend more time than need be on board ship with this man. The looks he gave her made her skin creep and the thought of being his wife filled her with revulsion. Perhaps if she reached England she might find a way to escape him.

'You do not answer.' His face clouded with anger. 'Your father warned me of your pride and stubbornness, lady.' He moved closer, menacing, angry. 'He told me you are mine, and I would have you as my wife, but I have a mind not to wait. You are here and there is nothing to stop me taking my pleasure of you.'

'If you touch me, I shall kill myself.'

'Damn you!' He struck her once across the face and she fell backwards against a table, hurting her back, but she gave no sign of her pain. Lifting her head, she looked at him defiantly.

'If you force me, I shall never reach England alive.'

Samuel looked at her and hesitated. He wanted the girl, had wanted her since the first time he saw her. But he wanted the money as much or more. His cousin's estate was heavily encumbered, leaving him little but an empty house. He needed a fortune to restore it to the great house it had once been, and this girl was his means of achieving his aim. Her threat to take her own life had given him pause for thought. If he forced her to yield, she might find a way to kill herself and he would lose the rich prize that could be his for the taking.

He must be patient and wait a little longer. A ship-board marriage might be contested. It would be better to wait until they were in England and he could be certain of her. Once the repairs were made, the ship would get under way once more and he could be sure that that damned pirate was not lurking somewhere in these waters!

Chapter Eight

Justin was in his cabin, lying on his bed, when Higgins knocked at the door and then entered. He rubbed at his shoulder, which was still sore, looking at his friend with raised brows; it was less than an hour since he had left the bridge to take a much-needed rest.

'Is something wrong?'

'Look-out has just spotted a ship not far ahead of us. It is the *Mistress Susanna*—Samuel Hynes's ship. Shall we go after it or let it be?'

'The *Mistress Susanna* was one of the ships that attacked the island. We cannot let this chance for retribution pass.' Justin frowned. 'My meeting with Sabatini will keep another day for if she is not there…'

His words died away unspoken, because he would not let himself think of what might happen to Maribel if she was not at her father's house. Samuel Hynes was no better than his cousin had been and would treat her badly.

He would find her even if he had to follow her to England!

'We shall take the ship. We need to replace the *Siren Eater* and the men must be itching for a fight. It might be better if Hynes resists.'

'After what happened on the island you will need to crack the whip, Cap'n, for the men's blood is up. And you cannot blame them.'

'We will have no brutality, no wanton killing. Tell the men to chase and attack Hynes's ship, but when we board her any man caught using unnecessary violence will answer to me.'

Maribel turned as her cabin door opened. They had left Gibraltar that morning and were once more under sail. She was expecting the cabin boy with food and water. He was a Spanish lad named Pedro. He had helped her after she was hurt by Captain Hynes and treated her with respect, but instead of the friendly boy, she saw the man she both feared and hated. Her heart sank; he had a purposeful gleam in his eyes and she knew why he had come.

'Stay away from me!' she warned, brandishing her dagger. 'Come near me and I shall slash my wrists. I would rather die than be your whore.'

'I thought I had taught you a lesson?' Samuel moved nearer, watching her warily. 'If you take your own life, you will burn in hell—is that not your belief?'

'I do not care!'

'Oh, but I think you do.' He took another step closer.

Maribel held out her left arm, placing the blade against her white skin. Samuel halted. 'Do it, then,' he challenged. 'Kill yourself.'

'Do not think I should hesitate…' She touched the knife to her breast as he moved towards her, then a booming sound from above made him halt. He looked round as the cabin door was flung back and the cabin boy entered.

'We are being attacked,' he said, looking frightened. 'I was sent to fetch you.'

'Curses! Out of my way, imbecile,' Samuel growled and pushed past the lad, who looked at Maribel with scared eyes.

'Is it pirates?' Maribel asked, her heart thumping. She had prayed that Justin would come after her, but had not believed it would happen 'Did you see the name of the ship?'

'I could not see, but the look-out said it was named the *Defiance*. I was told that we were forced to surrender to these pirates before. The men are nervous and talking of surrender; they fear what may happen if they resist after what was done at the island.'

Maribel's heart raced as the lad went away. She felt the shudder as the two ships came together and heard the shouting and noise on deck as the pirates boarded. However, she could not hear sounds of fighting and she realised that the crew must have surrendered immediately, hoping that they would be allowed to go free, as they had been once before. She did not know if there was a cargo on board—she had remained in her cabin while they were in port and had no idea what had been loaded in the holds.

She sat on the edge of her bed and waited, and after a little while Pedro came to her. He grinned at her and she realised that he was no longer frightened.

'Is all well?' she asked.

'I was asked if a lady was on board and told to fetch you. The pirates have given quarter to all who surrender and will sail with them; the captain and those who refuse are to be put into a boat with food and water for six days and set adrift. If they return to Gibraltar, they will make land soon enough.'

'So the ship is not to be returned to its master?'

'Not this time. It has been taken as a prize and all those who sail with Captain Sylvester will receive their share.'

Maribel nodded. The crew set adrift in a longboat should make shore within the day, for they were not many hours out of Gibraltar. She followed the cabin boy on deck and discovered that some trunks were being taken aboard the *Defiance,* though it seemed there was no cargo, which was perhaps why the ship was being kept as their prize. She could see no sign of Justin or Captain Hynes, but Higgins was directing the transfer of trunks and men. He smiled as he saw her and came towards her.

'We were on our way to look for you at Don Sabatini's house, lady. It was touch and go whether we attacked the ship. I think Providence must have been watching over us.'

'Yes, I believe you are right.' Maribel felt her eyes sting with tears. 'Thank you for rescuing me once more. I am truly grateful—and I am sorry if I have caused you more trouble.'

'The captain will be glad to get you back,' Higgins told her with a gentle smile. 'Just don't expect him to admit it. He thought you might have run away.'

'With Captain Hynes?' Maribel shuddered. 'I would rather die than live as that man's whore!'

'Go below to your own cabin, lady. Anna is waiting for you. She has been worried sick.'

'Welcome back, lady,' Anna said as Maribel went to her cabin. 'I was worried about you. Captain Sylvester was so angry. He thought that you had run away, until Higgins told him you had been kidnapped. I told him you would not run away, but he would not listen to me.'

'It was so hot in my room and I was restless. I could not sleep and I went outside to get some air. Someone— I think there was more than one—crept up behind me and threw a blanket over me. I struggled and tried to escape, but they were too strong for me.'

'Have you been harmed?' Anna looked at her oddly. 'You were taken captive some days ago…'

'If you are asking if I was raped, the answer is that Hynes had it in mind to force me, but I defended myself with the knife Peg gave me. I have a bruise on my back where he hit me and I fell.'

'Let me see. Take off that gown. You will need to wash and change into fresh clothes. I shall—' She broke off, giving a cry of distress as she saw the bruise on Maribel's back. 'Oh, my lady, that looks so sore. That brute deserves to hang for what he has done to you! If Captain Sylvester knew…'

'You will please not tell him,' Maribel said. 'I do not want Hynes's death on my conscience.' She saw Anna's face pale and reached out to her. 'I did not mean to remind you, my good friend. I shall never forget what you did for me on the island.'

'I shall fetch you some water,' Anna said. 'It may be best to use salt water for that will ease the sting from your bruises.'

Maribel sighed as Anna went away. She felt tired and anxious and her eyes were gritty with the tears she was trying not to shed.

After she had washed all over in the salty water, Maribel rubbed a little of the salve into her back. Her cheek felt tender where Hynes had struck her when she fell and Anna had told her she had a bruise there as well.

She was still in her shift when the cabin door opened abruptly. Giving a little cry, she grabbed her shawl and held it against her as the man came in.

'Oh…it is you…' She stared at Justin, feeling vulnerable and unsure of him. She had been told he was very angry with her. 'I was just about to dress.'

'Your pardon, Madonna.' Justin's eyes were on her bare arms. Her soft olive-toned flesh was firm and sweet, her hair loose on her shoulders. He felt a rush of desire and it took all his strength of will not to grab her and take her to the bed. 'I did not think…forgive me. I shall turn my back while you put on your gown.'

'Thank you.' Maribel reached for a loose wrapping gown, tying the sash about her waist. Her heart was racing wildly, her head raised proudly. 'I am decent now, sir.'

Justin turned and looked at her. 'I came to see if you had all you needed. We have a long voyage ahead of us. I believe all your things were brought across from the island, but you must tell me if something is missing—it may be in the hold.'

'I have not looked, but I believe I have all I need, thank you,' Maribel said. She frowned. 'You took the ship captive this time and set her captain adrift?'

'The ship is the price for the crew's freedom, lady. My men were angry because of what happened on the island. I persuaded them to let Hynes and his officers go, but it went against the grain with some of them. I have given Hynes a message for your father.'

'Yes, of course. I understand. What happened on the island was wicked and unpardonable. I regret that I was the cause of so much pain and suffering.'

'It was not your fault, Maribel. I told you of the treasure map?' She nodded, looking at him enquiringly. 'I have destroyed it. Hynes told me that your father threatened to hang Hendry unless he led your father's ships to the island. But the *Defiance* was not there and he thought I was with the ship, so he destroyed what he could in revenge for what I had stolen from him.'

'Then it was for the map. Do you think it was the only one in existence?'

'I thought at first that there must be other copies. However, when we were at Mallorca, your father sent word that he would trade for the map...' Justin frowned. 'Hendry did not know where I intended to go next. He thought I might head for Cyprus. When I told him to rendezvous at the island I gave away my plans...and that was what your father wanted all the time...the map and revenge.'

'Yes, he wanted revenge.' Maribel shuddered, her throat tight. 'I know now that he never cared what became of me. He told Captain Hynes he could have me and do as he would with me. I think he hoped for my death, but...Hynes wanted to marry me for my fortune. He...would have raped me, but I managed to stop him...' She caught back a sob.

'The brute. Had I known, I would have hanged him from the yard-arm!' He moved towards her, stopping as she flinched. 'What did he do to you? You did not leave with him willingly?'

'No! How could you even think it?' Maribel hesitated, then untied her wrap and drew it back, lifting her bodice to show him the purple bruise on her back. 'This is what he did to me when I refused him; there are other smaller bruises on my arms.'

'And on your cheek, I think...' Justin took her chin in his hand, turning her face to look at the swelling that had begun to turn dark red. 'Had I known of this, I should not have been so lenient with him. Next time we meet he will not fare so well!' His eyes dwelled on her, hungry and yet oddly tender.

'Cover yourself, Madonna. I am sorry you have been treated so ill.'

'It was not your fault. You warned me not to venture outside at night alone and I ignored your advice.' She caught back the sob that almost broke her. 'Forgive me. When we first met, I called you such terrible names and you never treated me ill.'

'You must not cry.' Justin smiled at her. 'You are safe now. I shall not let harm come to you again. Very soon now you will be in England with your mother's family. You will be a lady again, living as you ought—I believe your uncle is a good man.'

'No, I shall not cry,' Maribel said, blinking back her tears. 'I am being foolish. I am safe now and, as you say, I shall soon be with my mother's family.'

In a few short weeks she would be in England. Perhaps then all the nightmares of the past months would be forgotten. She could return to being the lady she had been before she left Spain for the first time. It was what she had wanted from the start—to be with her mother's family. So why did she feel that her heart was breaking?

'Captain Sylvester says we are sailing under a fair wind and you may come on deck whenever you wish,' Anna said as she entered the cabin the next morning. 'If the weather continues to be good, you will be in England within a week or two.'

'Yes, I expect so.' Maribel got to her feet. She draped a lace shawl about her shoulders and went on deck. Her gown was one of the lightweight ones that Justin had given her. The heavy, elaborate gowns her father had sent as her trousseau lay unused in the chests in which they had been packed. Maribel preferred the simpler style of gown she had become used to on the island. Her Spanish clothes seemed outdated and ugly and she did not enjoy wearing them, though she might have to when she reached England—she had been told it was much colder than Spain.

What would her mother's family be like? Would they welcome her to their home? Justin had given her letters from her uncle to her mother. He spoke in fond terms and asked if she were well many times. It seemed that he had received no answer to his letters, though he had continued to write until her mother's death.

She pushed the fears and doubts concerning her relatives to the back of her mind. In a few days she would part from Justin, never to see him again—and it was breaking her heart. She did not want to leave him, nor did she wish to become a fine lady again; all that had changed on the island and she knew she could never be as she had been before her capture. If her mother's family took her in, she would be forced to live as they directed, behaving as a high-born lady and never knowing the freedom she had tasted on the island. She would never see Justin again. How could she bear it?

Was there any way she could change her destiny? Maribel's thoughts had been going round and round in her mind ever since she had been rescued for the second time. She was no longer the proud and sometimes cold lady she had been when she first sailed for England. Her life had changed the day she was taken captive the first time, and her experiences on the island had moulded her into a different woman. The fear and revulsion she had experienced at Captain Hynes's hands had made her realise how fortunate she had been to be taken captive by a man like Justin. She had called him a pirate, but he was a truly generous and gentle man despite his harsh looks when he was angry. When she had thought she might never see him again she had realised just how much he had come to mean to her. She loved him with all her heart, her mind and body. How could she bear it when the time came to part for ever?

It was fresh and cooler on deck than it had been in her cabin. Maribel took a turn round the deck, then went to the prow, looking out to sea. The sky was blue and appeared endless. Far away in the distance it seemed to end where the sky met the sea on the horizon; it was this strange phenomenon that had made people believe that the earth was flat until brave explorers began to prove that it was not so. She knew that it was a Spanish King who had funded the expedition that found a way to the West Indies and the New World, proving that the world was round and that it was not possible to fall off the edge.

Maribel wrinkled her brow. Anna and Higgins had such exciting plans for the future and they were willing to take risks. Was there really a chance of a better life in the New World? She knew that men like her father had used it only for the silver and precious things to be found there, stealing its resources and ill treating its inhabitants—but were there truly other men who chose to live in this New World? What kind of men were they?

'Why so pensive, Maribel?'

Justin's voice made her swing round to gaze at him.

'You are safe now. Once we are in England you must forget all that happened on the island—and what that beast did to you.'

'Would you have me forget everything that happened on the island?' Her eyes sought his. 'I thought for a moment…that day, on the other side of the island near the falls, before Higgins fired the warning shot…' She stopped, cheeks burning.

'What did you think, Maribel?' Justin's gaze was deep blue like the ocean and it held her fast. 'Tell me.'

'I thought perhaps there might be some other way…' She shook her head and turned from him. His eyes promised so much, but he did not love her. He would have spoken before this if he truly cared what became of her. 'It does not matter.'

'Does it not?' His voice was deep, husky with passion. 'I believe you fought Pike because you were afraid for my life. Anna fetched the pistol because she knew he was too strong for you—but you stood your ground with just a knife. Why did you do that?'

'I could not let him kill you.'

'Why?'

She whirled round to face him. 'Will you have it all? Will you shame me? I could not bear that you should die because—'

Justin reached for her, pulling her close. His mouth stopped her from confessing it all, his kiss so demanding that she melted into his body, almost swooning with pleasure. Heat pooled inside her, making her moan with wanting. When he let her go at last, she looked at him, touching her fingers to her lips, eyes wide and searching.

'Why did you do that?'

'Because I want you more than you will ever know. I am not worthy of you, Maribel. I have no right to ask you to be mine. You are a lady and you will make a good marriage to a man whose hands are not stained with blood, a man who does not live under the shadow of crimes that are punishable by death.'

'Supposing I do not wish to marry this man whose hands are white and soft because he has never lifted one finger for himself?'

Justin laughed softly. 'Is this the proud Spanish lady I first captured? I think you have changed, Maribel.'

'Of course I have changed.' She held out her hands, showing him the ridges that had been caused by hard work. 'I have learned what it is to work if I want to eat—and I should not want to become the lady I was.'

'But you must.' His expression was serious. 'What else can you do?'

Maribel stared at him. Tears were brimming and she felt like screaming. Why could he not see? Why would he not love her as she loved him?

'You are impossible! An arrogant, stupid…pirate!'

She ran from him, not heeding his cry. He called her name, but she would not look back. Her heart was breaking, because she knew there was nothing she could do but return to England and hope that her family would take her in.

Rushing down the iron ladder that led below decks, she entered her cabin and flung herself down on the bed, covering her face with her hands as the tears broke. Her life was ruined and all because he had stolen her heart with his kisses and his bold looks. Why had he kissed her so if he did not love her?

'Maribel. You must not weep for me. I am not worthy of you.'

'Go away. I hate you!' she cried without looking round.

'It would be much better if you did hate me.'

'Do you imagine I love you?' She raised her tear stained face, blazing with anger. 'You are an arrogant, stupid—'

'Pirate,' he finished for her and laughed. 'You have told me so many times that you do not like pirates. How can you love a pirate, Maribel?'

The softness in his voice broke her. She rolled over and got to her feet, flying at him in a temper. Her fists beat against his chest until he caught them, his eyes gleaming with humour as he looked down at her. She wanted to weep and scream, but most of all she wanted to be kissed.

'I don't love you. I hate you.'

'Liar…' Justin bent his head, his lips caressing hers softly. 'You know you want me, my sweet, beautiful temptress. You know that you have driven me to the edge with your smiles and your beauty, but I swore that I would not take you unwillingly.' His fingers brushed against her breasts and her flesh tingled beneath the silken material. Her body swayed towards him, heat building deep inside her as she felt the need sweep through her.

'Justin…' Her lips parted on a sigh. 'I am not unwilling. You must know it. You took me captive, but for a long, long time I have been your willing captive. Surely you knew?'

'Perhaps…' His hand caressed her cheek, his voice husky, throbbing with desire. 'I want you so much, but I am not worthy of you, my love.'

'You are a wicked pirate,' she said, her breath catching on a sob or a laugh. 'But I want you…I love you. Make love to me, Justin, for I cannot bear it if you do not. Your kisses lit a fire in me, but you did nothing more.'

'Only because I gave my word. You must know that I burn for you? You have kept me restless in my bed many a night.'

'Justin…' she breathed, moving closer, offering herself. 'Make me yours. I am asking you. Please, make me your own…love me.'

Justin gave a little moan; reaching for her hand, he led her back to the bed and sat down, pulling her down beside him. For a moment he sat looking into her lovely face, then he reached out and drew a finger over her lips, tracing their fullness.

'You have such a sensuous mouth. It begs for kisses.'

He leaned towards her, bending his head so that their

mouths touched. His kiss was soft at first, setting little butterflies of sensation winging down her spine; then, he pulled her to him, holding her so that her sensitised breasts pressed against his chest, his kiss intensifying, becoming hungry and demanding.

'My love,' he murmured in a voice made deep by passion. 'Let me look at you without these clothes, pretty as they are.' His fingers pulled at the lacings at the back of her gown, loosening them. As the bodice came free he pushed it down over her shoulders. Maribel unfastened the hooks that held her skirts in place and let them slide down over her hips. Now she was clad only in a shift made of such fine material that the pale tones of her flesh showed through. He touched the bruises, which had begun to fade. 'Do these still hurt you?'

'A little, but I do not mind them. Do not fear to touch me. I have longed for this moment so many nights.'

Justin smiled down at her. 'So beautiful, but I want to see you.'

With a swift upward movement, he tugged the shift over her head, his eyes feasting on the glorious body revealed to his eyes. Maribel was slender but full breasted, her nipples pink and pert as he leaned towards her, stroking first one and then the other with his tongue. She sighed with pleasure as his hands cupped her breasts and he buried his face against them, breathing in her scent and using his tongue to give her pleasure. Her body was melting in the heat of his desire, no longer her own to control. She gave a cry of intense pleasure as he licked his way between her breasts, down her navel to the damp moist hair that covered her femininity.

'You smell gorgeous…' he murmured huskily, his hands on her buttocks, pulling her in closer so that he could inhale her. His tongue seemed to set off little explosions of sensation within her, making her weak with desire so that she moaned, her fingers tangling in his hair and working at the back of his neck.

'Let me see you,' she said urgently, and reached for his shirt, ripping at the ties so urgently that it tore and he laughed at her impatience. He took it in his hands and ripped it apart, shrugging it off. Maribel drew a shuddering breath. 'I thought you were beautiful when I saw you chopping the wood. I should have liked to do this…' Her hands smoothed over his back, making him shudder and cry out. She pressed her mouth to his shoulder, sucking at him and then nipping him with her sharp white teeth. 'I want to taste you…' she murmured.

'Little witch…' he muttered hoarse with desire.

He bent to tug off his long boots, then stood and released his breeches. Maribel reached out, pushing them down over his hips so that they fell to the floor and he kicked them away. Now they were both naked. Her eyes feasted on his slim hips and strong thighs, then moved to the male glory that was fully erect and ready for her. She reached out to touch him, her hand stroking that part of him with tentative fingers. His manhood seemed to move and pulsate beneath her touch and she laughed as she heard his indrawn breath of rapture.

'Does that please you?' she asked, her eyes holding an appeal she was not aware of. 'I want to please you, Justin, but I am not sure…'

'But you were married?' His eyebrows arched. 'What are you telling me…have you not been with a man this way?' She shook her head and he frowned.

'My husband was a boy. He did not love me in this way, but as his childhood friend.'

'You should have told me. I thought…but you are virgin…'

Maribel reached out, catching his wrist, as he would have moved away. 'No, do not leave me now, I beg you. I want to be yours, Justin. I want to know how to please you, but you must teach me.'

'You are certain?' His eyes glowed with blue fire, searing her, his gaze searching deep into her soul. 'You want this truly?'

'I love you,' she said and lay down on the bed, gazing up at him trustingly. 'Show me how to be the woman you need.'

Justin hesitated, then sat down on the bed. He bent his head to kiss her, his mouth trailing kisses down her smooth navel. His tongue flicked at the inside of her thighs as he parted her legs, then moved to the moist heat of her femininity. He flicked at her delicately so that she whimpered and arched her back towards him, her body begging for more of the exquisite pleasure he gave her.

His hand caressed her throat and then her breasts. He lay beside her, pressing his flesh to hers so that their mutual heat flared as they kissed, tongues touching, flicking, tasting each other's sweetness. Maribel was quivering, her back arching at each touch as she whimpered and moaned, crying his name as he moved to cover her with his body.

She felt the heat of his manhood pressing against her and instinctively opened wide to accommodate the thick, thrusting shaft that pushed up inside her with sudden urgency. The pain was sharp as he broke through her hymen, but her cry of pain was smothered by kisses so sweet that she almost swooned with love for him. When he withdrew she reached for him, wanting him back inside her, wanting to feel him thrust deeper and deeper into her moist centre. Her body moved with his, her nails unconsciously scoring the smooth flesh on his shoulders as she lost all control and screamed his name aloud over and over again.

She felt his fluids come inside her and then his face was buried against her neck. His body was slick with sweat, as was hers. She stroked the back of his neck, tears trickling down her cheeks as she held him. For a few moments he lay still, his face pressed against her, then he raised his head and looked at her.

'Why are you crying?'

'Because you made me feel so wonderful.'

'I didn't hurt you?' He looked contrite. 'Your bruises still pain you. I was too impatient.'

'No, no, I wanted you as much as you wanted me.'

'Yet I hurt you?'

'A little just at first. I suspect it is always that way.'

'I have never taken a virgin before,' Justin said and touched her face. He looked regretful. 'I did not think you virgin when I teased you so unmercifully, Maribel. Forgive me?'

'There is nothing to forgive. You were as gentle with me as you could be. Besides, it was what I wanted.'

Justin rolled on to his back. 'Your husband must have been very young.'

'My own age, sixteen when we wed, barely seventeen when he died. Why do you ask that?' She turned her head on the pillow to look at him.

'I cannot imagine why a man of any age would not want to lie with you, Maribel. Even Tom was in love with you—the poor lad.'

'Poor Tom.' Maribel raised herself on one arm to gaze down at him. 'I think Pablo was perhaps not as other men—not as you are, Justin. I loved him dearly but I see now that we were friends, or close like sister and brother perhaps.'

'Yes, perhaps.' Justin sat up and reached for his breeches, pulling them on and then his boots. His shirt was too torn to wear and he grinned as he tossed it to her. 'Perhaps you would mend this for me?'

'Of course…' She sat up, her long hair falling forward over her breasts. 'I am yours to command, Justin. Your woman, your—'

'No! Not whore, never that,' he said and frowned. 'When we reach England I shall take you to your mother's family, Maribel… Nay, do not look so. I mean not to abandon you, my love. I must discover how the land lies. I shall wed you, Maribel, but things have altered now.'

'You will wed me? But you said…you wished only for a mistress.'

'I said many foolish things in my pride. I can never let you go. You must be my wife, but I cannot expect you to live as we have lived these past months. You must have a home worthy of you.'

'Surely you know that I would live anywhere with you?'

'We can never return to the island, nor would I wish that kind of a life for you. You are a lady, gently born. You deserve the life you were born for. I shall strive to give you all that you should have by rights. It may take some time—I must clear my name if I can, though I fear it may not be possible.' His expression was serious. 'If I am not welcome at my home it may be that we shall have to live elsewhere. I have money despite the loss of two ships. There is money held by the goldsmiths in London that was left for me by my great-grandfather, who died just after I was born. We may have to live in France or Italy, but I promise I will make a home worthy of you, my darling.'

'I shall be content to be with you wherever we live.'

'Yet I know that I can never be worthy of you. I wish…' He shook his head and smiled oddly. 'The past is gone. We may both regret things that were, but we shall have no regrets. We shall look to the future and it will be good for us.'

'Yes…it will be good for us.'

Something in his eyes caused a shiver to run down her spine. He was so urgent, so grim. What wasn't he telling her?

Chapter Nine

Justin went straight to his cabin to find a fresh shirt. He did not wish what had just happened to be whispered of by the crew. They might suspect it, but there was no need to confirm their suspicions. His conscience had begun to bother him from the moment he learned of Maribel's virginity. He could scarcely believe that she had been married for almost a year and remained a virgin. What kind of a man had her husband been? Perhaps the kind that preferred to lie with his own sex.

Justin knew that something had changed in him once he learned the truth. Until that moment he had fought the little voice in his head that told him she was special to him. He had tried to convince himself that she was just a beautiful woman and that all he felt for her was desire. Having had her in his arms, known her absolute surrender, he felt humbled and guilty for having destroyed her innocence. She was a lovely, loving woman and she deserved so much more than he could give her.

He must and would find a better life for them both. When he became a pirate he had had no choice, but now he must take his fate into his own hands.

How could he ask her to share the kind of life that might well be his in the future? Justin knew that his life would be forfeit if Queen Mary still lived. She would not listen to anything he had to say excusing the mutiny—in the eyes of her council he was already guilty of treason.

Only if Elizabeth had succeeded her sister would Justin have a chance of returning to his home. He believed that his mother would forgive anything, but his father might not wish to receive him. His great-grandfather's legacy was lodged with the goldsmiths in London. Justin could collect the gold and take Maribel to France or Italy; there they could mix with people of her own class, but would it be enough for her? Neither of them would have family about them. Would she come to resent him for taking her away from her family?

It might have been better if he had resisted her invitation, but the appeal in her eyes had broken his will, an overwhelming desire to make love to her sweeping all else from his mind. He knew that he would never have enough of her. Just the thought of her, of her scent and the softness of her body as she yielded to him was enough to make him hard again.

He couldn't give her up! He might not be worthy of her, but she was imprinted into his mind and his body and to lose her now would tear him apart.

Justin decided that he would take Maribel to her relatives and then visit his father. If the situation were favourable, he would journey to court to plead for his freedom and forgiveness. He thought of the chest of Spanish silver in his cabin. Perhaps if he presented that to Elizabeth as a gift—pray God she was now Queen!— she would find it in her heart to forgive him.

Later that evening Maribel glanced at Justin as he stood on the bridge. He was at the wheel as the order to bring down the sails and anchor was given. They had chosen to anchor just off the white cliffs of Dover, the plan being to use the rowing boats to take her and Justin and some of the crew ashore the next morning. Most of the men had voted to stay on board, because they feared they might hang if they set foot in England. She knew that Justin had promised he would secure pardons for them all if he could.

'I shall take you to your mother's family, Maribel,' he had told her the previous night when he came to her cabin. 'Once I know you are safe with them I shall journey to my home and then, if Elizabeth is Queen, to London. I shall ask her to pardon us all for the mutiny.'

'Will she grant you a pardon?' Maribel's eyes widened in fear. 'Supposing she refuses?'

'I shall hang and my men will sail away without me.'

'What of me?'

'You will be safe with your family.'

Maribel felt sick with fear. 'Why must you risk your life after everything we have found together? Turn the

ship about. Let us sail for Italy or France. I beg you not
to do this, Justin.'

'I have to do it.' His mouth set into a hard line. 'I
have money with the goldsmiths and I must claim it if
we are to live as a gentleman and his wife should. I owe
it to my family to explain what happened when I disappeared—and I owe it to myself to at least try to clear
my name, Maribel. Please try to understand how I feel.'

She looked into his eyes, then shook her head. 'Our
love is more important than all the rest. You have your
ship. You could earn enough money for us to live on
without this foolishness.'

Justin reached out, taking her chin in his hand,
tipping it so that he forced her to look at him. 'Will you
scold me, lady? Have I found myself a nagging wife?'

Maribel shook her head. 'You make fun of me! I do
not find this amusing, sir. If they hang you it will break
my heart. I shall have nothing to live for.' Tears hung
on her lashes and then slipped down her cheeks.
'Please, I beg you, let us go now while we may.'

'But I cannot claim you as my wife unless I have
made some effort to throw off the shadow that hangs
over me. I am a pirate, Maribel, and as such I am not
worthy. I must see my family and receive my father's
blessing if he will give it—and hope for mercy from my
Queen.'

Maribel was torn between anger and disappointment. How could he imagine that honour was more important than the way they felt about each other? She
turned away from him, holding back the torrent of

anger and despair that welled inside her. If he were willing to throw everything they had away on a whim, he could not feel as she did; he could not truly love her.

Never had she felt such unease. Her love for Pablo and the grief when he died were a pale shadow of her present emotions. She did not know how she would bear it if she lost Justin after what had happened between them. It had been hard enough when she had thought he did not love her; it would be unbearable after their lovemaking.

'Do not be angry, my love,' Justin put his arms about her, nestling his face into the softness of her hair and holding her back pressed against him. 'I do this for you so that you can hold your head high and be proud of the man you call husband.'

She turned in his arms, looking up at him, intense passion in her face. 'Swear to me that you will come for me? Swear that you will not just sail away and leave me with my family!'

'You must know I would not?' His fingers trailed her cheek and her throat. He bent his head to kiss the hollow at the base of her throat. 'If I live, I shall come back to claim you—you have my word.'

Maribel had accepted his promise—what else could she do?

Yet as she watched the boats being lowered, nerves started to jangle. Until this moment she had not truly thought of what it would be like to meet her family— or of what she would tell them.

If she told the whole truth, they would condemn

Justin as a pirate and forbid her to see him again. She must think of some way to explain how and why she had come to them on the ship of a man who was not related to her.

Her cheeks became hot as she thought about how it would seem to her mother's family if they knew she had been a pirate's willing captive. How could she explain that she had lived on his ship and in his house on the island? It was impossible!

She knew that she must speak to Justin, ask him what she ought to say before they arrived at her family's home.

Maribel turned in Justin's arms. Before they made love he had told her that they would be rowing for shore the next morning. The knowledge that they must part so soon had made her cling to him desperately, as his loving took her to new heights. She moaned with pleasure, enjoying the moment of surrender as she gave herself completely to him.

'What shall I say to my uncle?' she asked, her face pressed against his chest, tasting the salt of his sweat and inhaling his scent. 'He will want to know how we met—and what my father had to say.'

'You must leave this to me.' Justin's hand moved down the arch of her back, stroking the soft skin so that she moaned and pressed herself against him. 'I have thought of how it should be handled a great deal and all I ask is that you follow my lead and agree with what I say.'

Maribel raised up to look down at him, her eyes on

his face, trying to read his mind without success. He looked serious, but gave her no hint of what he intended. Instead, he reached up and drew her down to him, rolling her beneath him in the bed and kissing her with such passion that she forgot everything but the need to feel him inside her.

'I shall take care of you,' he promised huskily. 'You belong to me now and nothing shall ever part us. I promise you that everything will be well, my love.'

'Yes…' She smiled up at him, her thighs parting as he moved between them, her hips arching to meet the thrust of his passion. 'I love you. I shall always belong to you.'

They had been riding south along the coast road for some hours and with each mile they covered Maribel's feeling of apprehension had grown.

'What will you say to my aunt and uncle?' she asked when they stopped to rest the horses. 'I fear they will be angry if they know I was your captive.' He had told her to trust him and she did, yet she could not help feeling nervous as the time to meet her family drew closer.

'We shall rest at an inn I know of not far from here. One of my men will take a letter from me to your relatives, telling them that you are coming to visit them. They will be prepared for good news, Maribel—for you are visiting them with your betrothed husband: Justin Devere, son of Lady and Sir John Devere of Devereham House—and great-grandson of Lord Robert Melford, also grandson of the Earl of Rundle.'

'Your name is Devere?' Maribel's eyes widened. 'You are the grandson of an earl? Why have you never told me this?'

'On board the *Defiance* I was a pirate and a mutineer. Here in England I am a gentleman. I did what I thought best to protect my family from the shame of hearing from others what I had become.'

'But why did you…?' She searched his face for the truth. 'Why were you ever a part of that crew, Justin? You have told me that you were shanghaied and something of the mutiny, but not why you were about to board a ship in the first place?'

'I was leaving England under a cloud of suspicion. Queen Mary had sent to arrest me for treason, though I was not guilty. My father thought I should spend time with my cousin in France, but on the waterfront I was knocked on the head from behind as I fought other ruffians. When I regained my senses we were at sea and I was forced to serve behind the mast—but not until I had been given more than fifty lashes to bring me into line. Had it not been for Higgins I should probably have died after the beating. I survived and the crew came to respect me. When a young lad was beaten near to death the crew would not go on with Captain Smythe. I was asked to join the mutiny. Had I refused, they would probably have marooned the officers on a deserted island or simply hanged us. I decided that I would lead them and in that way I saved the lives of Captain Smythe and his officers.'

'So you never wished for a life at sea?' Maribel

arched her fine brows. 'I am glad you have told me this, Justin—but you make a bold pirate.'

'I did what I had to do.'

'If you had not, we should not have met. I should now be wed to Lord Roberts, or, worse, I could have been his cousin's whore.' Maribel shuddered. 'I should prefer to lie in my grave than submit to either man.' She reached out to touch his hand. 'I love you, Justin. Please remember that I would rather wed a pirate than live without you as a fine lady.'

Justin gazed down at her, his eyes seeming to search her face. 'You must not be anxious for my sake. When we landed in England I asked questions of men on the waterfront and I learned that Elizabeth is now England's queen. I shall speak to my father and then ride to London to beg an audience with her Majesty.'

'Will she grant it?'

'I have every hope that she will.' He reached out to touch her face. 'Do not fear for me, my love. I shall return to you and all will be well.'

'I shall pray that it is so.' Tears misted her eyes as he helped her to remount. He had reassured her on many counts, but her apprehension grew as they neared their journey's end.

The house of Sir Henry Fildene sat just above the cliffs some thirty-odd miles on the coast road from Dover. It was a large old house, built of stone in the last century with an undercroft, small-paned windows and a sloping thatched roof. The approach was across an expanse of grass and rock, for it faced square to the ocean and a sandy cove set at the foot of steep cliffs. The house looked slightly forbidding and Maribel guessed that it had once been a fortress or look-out station in case of attack from the sea. In the event of a force of ships sent to invade England, a beacon would be lit on these cliffs, where it could clearly be seen for miles around. Other beacons would then be lit so that the news could swiftly be passed to London.

A stout wall surrounded the house, but at the approach from the land side there was a large iron gate, a moat and a wooden drawbridge, which was down, as if the occupants were expecting visitors. The small party of Justin, Higgins, Anna and Maribel rode over the bridge, their horses' hooves clattering on the thick boards.

'I believe we are expected,' Justin said as he saw a group of men and women gathered in the courtyard. He smiled at her. 'Have courage, Madonna.'

Maribel felt as if her face were frozen though the day was mild enough. She attempted a smile as he dismounted and came to lift her down, but found that she was trembling with nerves.

'Remember you are a lady and my betrothed.'

Maribel's head went up at the reminder. A tall man with greying hair and a lined face moved towards them. He stared at her for a moment and then inclined his head.

'You are Marguerite's daughter. I can see her in you. Indeed, you are very like your mother, my child.'

'Thank you. Forgive me, I do not know you.'

'How should you?' He held out his hand to her. 'I am your Uncle Henry. My sister and I were close when we were young, but my father made a match for her with Don Miguel Sabatini and I lost contact with her. I wrote to her often, but she replied only a few times before she died—and your father wrote only twice to tell me of your birth and her death. I was grieved that she died so young. I would have come to visit, but duty kept me here. My father died and I was forced to repair our fortunes before thinking of my own wishes—but I thought of you often and I am so pleased that you have chosen to come to us until you marry.' His steady gaze went to Justin's face. 'Captain Devere. I believe I once met your father, sir. It was years ago, but he spoke then of his son as being a fine young man.'

'I thank you for your welcome, Sir Henry. Perhaps we may talk again later? I am hoping that you will take my lady into your home while I perform some necessary duties. I shall return for her as soon as I have visited the court.'

'You wish to pay your respects to the new Queen.' Sir Henry nodded. If he wondered why Justin did not wish to take his betrothed with him, he did not ask. 'Please leave your horses to my grooms, sir. My wife is most anxious to greet Maribel. We have sons, but no daughters, and she hath always wished for one.' His gaze returned to Maribel. 'Come and meet Lady Fildene—she is anxious to welcome you to her home.'

Maribel's nerves abated a little as she moved with

him to meet the rather small, plump lady waiting to greet her. Lady Fildene smiled and embraced her warmly, clasping her to her ample bosom.

'How beautiful you are, my dearest child. We are so glad to have you with us if only for a time. I know my husband wrote to your father asking that you might come to us for a while, but he received no answer to his letters.'

'My father was not always kind, ma'am,' Maribel said. 'I think his marriage to my mother was not as happy as it might have been—for either of them.'

'Henry told me that she did not wish to wed him,' the lady said, placing a hand on Maribel's arm and drawing her into the entrance hall of what was clearly a grand house. The ceilings were high; the walls were of stone, but covered with rich tapestries that gave the rooms a warmth and colour not always seen in older homes. 'Your maid will be shown to your apartments, my dear. Everything is being prepared, though we had little notice of your coming.'

'I think it was not possible to let you know sooner,' Maribel told her. She was very conscious of the fact that it had been some time since she had left her home in Spain, and she was most certainly not the same girl. Her skin was no longer the palė olive it had been when she protected it by staying out of the midday sun. On the island she had become careless, allowing her skin to be kissed by the sun to a pale gold, a little freckling appearing across her nose. She was wearing gloves, but she knew her hands had not yet become as soft and smooth as they had once been. 'I am sorry to be a trouble to you.'

'You could never be a trouble to us, dearest girl. We are delighted to have you with us, even if only for a short time.'

'I am happy to be here,' Maribel replied, her fears falling away as she saw the genuine welcome in the lady's eyes. 'I shall enjoy getting to know my mother's family.'

'My sons Beavis and William are married and living in London,' Lady Fildene said. 'However, my son Michael is expected home any day now. He has been to the north on business for his father. We import wines, you know. Mostly from France these days, though it was because of the Spanish wines we once imported that my father-in-law entrusted his daughter to your father. I am sorry to learn that the marriage was not a good one.'

'I think my mother may have been unhappy, but I do not remember her. My stepmother was kind to me and I was happy enough until she died soon after my husband.'

'You were married? We did not know that. How sad to lose a husband at your age.'

'I was sad—but then I met Justin,' Maribel replied, her mouth curving. 'I think I shall be very content as his wife.'

'His family are respected and wealthy,' her aunt said. 'Everyone knows of Lord Robert Melford and the important family he founded. I believe they are all well connected and popular at court, though we do not often visit London ourselves. My husband was never one to seek royal favour, though we have recently been honoured by a royal contract for our fine wines.'

Maribel was not sure whether her aunt sounded regretful or a little jealous of those who had the royal favour. She sensibly kept her silence. Since she had only just learned Justin's true name it would not do to pretend to knowledge about his family that she did not have.

Glancing back, she saw him talking with her uncle. He seemed at ease and gave no sign of being anything other than he claimed to be. Clearly he had put the memory of his time at sea behind him, and she must too. She would have to be careful when answering her aunt's questions—she did not wish to reveal that she had been a pirate's captive.

'I shall return for you as soon as I can,' Justin told Maribel as he took his leave two days later. 'At least I know that you are safe here with your family. Your uncle is truly pleased to have you here, as he has made plain to me—and I believe his wife to be a good woman.'

'Lady Fildene is both kind and generous,' Maribel admitted. 'I like her very well. She is a good chatelaine and she loves her family. Her son Michael is expected home soon and I think he must be her favourite. Even so, I would rather come with you if I could, Justin, but I know I may not for I should only hamper you.'

'I am sorry I must leave you, but I know you are safe here. I shall travel faster alone, my love—but I shall think of you often. As soon as I am free to do so, I shall return and take you to my home, where we shall be wed.'

'I pray that you will return to me safely. You know that I love you.'

'As I love you. Take care of yourself until I come to claim you.'

Maribel went to his arms, clinging to him until he disengaged, pushing her back. 'Be careful, my love. It is not seemly to show such passion. We may be observed and I would not have your aunt lose her good opinion of you.'

Tears crowded in her throat. It was on the tip of her tongue to beg him to take her with him, but she knew that he would refuse. He had decided that she must remain here in safety with her aunt and uncle and she could not make him change his mind. Parting from him would tear her in two, but she must bear it as best she could and pray for his safe return.

Reluctantly she drew away, 'I should not like to shock her. I am very careful how I answer her for she would be shocked if she knew where I had recently been.'

'Be patient for a while. We shall soon be together.'

Justin touched her face lightly and then turned away. Higgins was waiting nearby with his horse.

'Farewell, Justin.'

'Farewell, my dearest one. I shall return.'

Maribel watched as he rode out of the courtyard. A breeze had sprung up suddenly, bringing storm clouds from the sea. The dark sky looked ominous and she shivered as she turned and went into the house. The time would seem long while Justin was gone. She hardly knew how to occupy her time, because the pretty sewing she had once delighted in for hour after hour was not enough to fill her days. She disliked the damp coolness of the English weather, finding the grey skies depressing, and thought wistfully of the time she had spent at the island and the long voyage back to England. Did the sun ever shine in this land? How many days would pass before Justin came to claim her as his bride—and how would she live if for some reason he never came? She thrust the thought away for it was unbearable. She must believe that he would return or she had nothing.

Justin was aware of a shadow hovering at the back of his mind as he rode the last few leagues to his father's home. Higgins had wanted to accompany him, but he would not allow it.

'If I am to be hanged as a mutineer and a pirate I will not take you with me, my friend. Remain near my lady and guard her until my return. I shall bring your pardon if I am spared. If not, you must take the ships and sail away. They will both be yours then.'

'You risk your life for nothing, Justin. I have not found English justice fair in the past. I do not expect it now.'

'You may well be right, which is why I ask you to remain with Maribel until…' Justin shook his head. 'If I do not return, she is safe enough with her uncle.'

'Aye, she is safe enough.'

They clasped hands and then Justin mounted his horse and rode away. He had not looked back—it was costing him a great deal to leave Maribel. If his heart had ruled him, he would have turned back, swept her up on his horse and taken her far away. His head told him that he would never be at peace if he did not at least try to obtain his father's blessing and the Queen's pardon. He could not take her with him, but he had ridden off with a heavy heart.

Now that he was close to his family estate, Justin felt uneasy. What kind of a welcome awaited him in his father's house? John Devere was an honest man. He had taught his son to live with honour. Would he be able to accept Justin for what he was—a mutineer and a pirate?

As Justin dismounted in the courtyard of his home a groom came running towards him. He hesitated as he drew near, stared at Justin in stunned disbelief for a moment, and then grinned.

'God be praised! 'Tis Master Justin home at last.' The groom took the reins of Justin's horse. 'We thought you dead, sir. Your lady mother has been grieving for you these past months.'

'I was lost, Jedruth, but now I am found,' Justin said and clapped him on the shoulder, feeling overcome by the man's obvious delight. 'Tell me, are my parents within?'

'Your lady mother is at home, sir, but the master has gone this day to visit a neighbour. He should be back this evening.'

'Thank you. I shall see my mother immediately.'

Justin went into the house to be greeted by a shriek

from the keeper of the household as she saw him. 'Lord have mercy!' she cried and flung her arms up. 'If it isn't Master Justin—and the mistress crying her heart out for him day after day! Where have you been that you could not send a message to your mother? Wicked boy!'

'Forgive me, Lizzie.' Justin grabbed her in a bear hug. 'There were good reasons why I could not let my family know where I was. Tell me, where is my mother?'

'She is in her stillroom, of course. Where else would she be at this hour of the day?'

'Bless you!' Justin kissed her soundly on the mouth. She pushed him away and frowned at him, but smiled as he turned in the direction of his mother's stillroom and then crossed herself.

'The Lord be praised!'

Justin hurried to the room where Lady Devere prepared all the preserves that ensured they had jams and fruit in the winter, also creams and lotions that she used to cure the ills of the people who served her. He paused outside, almost fearing to enter, and knocked at the door.

'Come in,' her voice called and he opened the door. Lady Devere stood at a bench made of a scrubbed wood board and trestles. In front of her were bundles of leaves, dried herbs and berries, as well as stone jars and pots with squares of cloth, wax and string for sealing them. 'Yes, Lizzie, what is it?'

'It is not Lizzie…' Justin said and saw her shoulders stiffen. She turned slowly with a jar in her hand. When she saw him her eyes widened, she gave a little cry and swayed, dropping the jar she was holding so that it clattered onto the floor. 'Mother…forgive me…' He darted to support her, holding her close until she recovered. She straightened and pushed him away. Her eyes were filled with tears of love and forgiveness as she reached out to touch his face. 'I am so sorry, Mother…so very sorry for distressing you.'

'I thought you must be dead. Justin…my dearest son…' Lady Devere caught back a sob. 'Your father received a visit from a man called Captain Bolton. He told him that you had booked a passage with him to France, but failed to board, though your horse was lodged at the hostelry he told you of. It was months before he came to tell us, because he had been at sea. We were led to believe that you were somehow taken aboard another ship against your will.'

'Yes, that is what happened, Mother. I was shanghaied and forced to work for a cruel master who treated his crew ill. What happened after that is a long story. I had best wait until my father is here, for I would tell you both at the same time. I am not the man I was when I left my home—I have done things you may find impossible to forgive.'

'You could never do anything so wicked that I would not love and forgive you,' Lady Devere said. She put her arms about him, kissing him on the forehead. 'You look well, my son. I am glad to have you home. I care only that you are alive and well.'

'I thank you for your love, Mother. I regret that I did

not let you know I was alive sooner, but…' He shook
his head. 'I shall wait until Father is here. He should
hear my story at the same time, for I would not seek advantage and I know he may not forgive as easily as you.'

'Maribel, my dear. May I speak with you for a
moment, please?'

'Yes, Aunt? Did you need me?'

Maribel had been walking in the walled garden at the
back of the house. Behind the high walls that protected
them from the full force of the sea was a sheer drop to
the beach below. To reach the cove, you had to walk a
little distance along the cliff until you came to a path
cut into the rock by some ancient mariners. Maribel had
been considering whether to walk down to the beach,
but as yet the weather had been too cool to entice her.
She turned at the sound of her hostess's voice and
walked back to meet her.

'There will be a fair in the village tomorrow,
Maribel,' Lady Fildene said as the girl came up to her.
'We may purchase silks and materials for new gowns—
and many trinkets that may please us perhaps.'

'I have little money to spare—most of what I have
is still with the ship. Captain S…Justin said that he
would arrange for my trunks to be sent on, but I have
only what was brought on the pack horses thus far.'

'Which is why I thought we should visit the fair to
buy silks from the merchants. We can sew some gowns
for you between us, Maribel. What you have is
charming, but the Spanish style is heavier than the

English fashion. I believe you would feel more comfortable in something new.'

'I am sure I would. Justin—' Maribel broke off. It was difficult to remember that she must not mention her time on the island. 'I do have some simpler gowns in my trunks, but it would be pleasant to make a new gown.'

'Your uncle would be happy to make you a gift of the gowns,' her aunt told her. 'It has given us such pleasure to have you here, my dear. I hope you will visit us again when you are married to Captain Devere?'

'Yes, I am certain we shall,' Maribel told her. 'You and my uncle are both so kind to me.'

'We love you as your mother's child—and as the daughter we never had.'

Maribel's cheeks felt warm, for she felt uneasy at deceiving these good people. What would they think if they knew the truth? She would feel terrible if her aunt ever discovered that she had been so indiscreet as to become a pirate's mistress, for that was what she was until Justin married her.

Justin would return soon and marry her. Her aunt and uncle need never know the truth! She thrust the uneasy thoughts from her mind.

'Then I should love to visit the fair with you tomorrow, Aunt.'

'Justin!' John Devere came rushing into the parlour where his son and wife sat together. 'I could scarcely believe it when they told me you were here! I thought you lost to us for good.'

Justin stood up. He held out his hand, but his father smiled and embraced him.

'Welcome home, my son. This is a wonderful day!'

'Perhaps you should hear my story first, Father. You may not be so pleased once you know what happened—what I have done.'

John moved back, his gaze narrowed and questing. 'Should this be said before your mother?'

'I would wish Mother to hear it all. I have done things that may shame you, Father—but I ask for your understanding.'

'You mean the mutiny? I have heard that there was a possibility that you led a mutiny against a cruel master—namely Captain Smythe?'

'You knew that and yet you welcomed me home?'

'I heard from Captain Bolton that you might have been shanghaied aboard Smythe's ship. He visited us concerning a horse and told me what conditions aboard such a ship would be like and that he had heard the captain's life had been saved by one of the mutineers. Apparently, the leader forced the others to put the captain and his officers ashore at Venice rather than hanging them as others wanted. Was that what happened, Justin?'

'Yes, Father. I must explain what happened. When a young lad who had done little wrong was beaten half to death I could no longer hold out against the crew. They would have killed Smythe, his officers and me if I had not taken charge. I did not think I had a choice.'

'You did what you had to do,' Sir John agreed.

'Mutiny is a serious offence, but I must tell you that some of Smythe's officers reported him for gross misconduct, blaming him for losing the ship and putting their lives at risk. He has lost his master's ticket and will not sail as the captain of a ship again.'

'I am glad to hear it, sir. It is time that men like Smythe were shown for the bullies they are. However, that is not the end of my story. I fear there is worse to come. Something for which I may not be so easily acquitted.'

'You had best tell us then, Justin.'

'When we took the ship and set the captain ashore, I became its captain in his stead, but we sailed by the rules of the brethren, which make all men equal.'

'Brethren—you mean pirates?' John's eyes narrowed. 'You became a pirate? You preyed on the ships of others and stole what was theirs—you killed men for gain?'

'We took the cargoes we captured and sold them. We did not kill wantonly, Father. If the ship surrendered immediately there was no bloodshed, though a few may have been killed, those that refused the truce and tried to resist. Not by my hand, but by others. I have killed only when forced.'

'But the ships were taken by your order?'

Justin met his gaze. 'Yes, sir. I was the captain. I gave the orders, which my men obeyed. I sold the prizes we took and distributed the gains between them, and kept my share. I have ordered men flogged and I have killed men in fair fight—but I punished the crew only when I had no choice.'

'You are by your own admission a pirate?'

'Yes, Father.'

'Then you have shamed your family and yourself.'

His father stared at him a moment longer, then turned and walked away, leaving the room.

'Father…forgive me…'

'It will take time.' Lady Devere stood up. She placed a gentle hand on her son's arm. 'Do not be hurt or bitter, Justin. Your father is an honest man. This news has shocked and distressed him. He was always so proud of you and now…'

'I have brought shame on him and myself.'

'No, Justin.' Lady Devere's eyes were soft and moist with tears. 'You did what you had to do—what seemed right at the time. You were forced to lead the mutiny and then it must have seemed that you had no choice but to become a pirate. I understand, dearest. Your father will learn to think as I do and to forgive you.'

'You will persuade him, Mother.' Justin's face was fiercely proud. 'You may persuade him to make a show of forgiveness, but in his heart he will never forget what I have done. He will never truly forgive me; he will never be proud to call me son.'

'He is a proud man, Justin—proud of you and his honour. Give him time to think this through.'

'I had to tell him, to tell you both. You must feel that I have let you down, Mother. I did have a choice. I could have put the captain and his officers in chains and sailed back to England to take my chances.'

'Would the crew have accepted your decision?'

'I am not sure. I did not offer them the choice.'

Lady Devere touched his cheek. 'You know that they would not have listened if you had. You would have died with the captain and his officers. They owe their lives to you, my son. You have done the right thing now. Your father will understand in time.'

'I shall leave in the morning, Mother.'

'Why?' She looked at him in alarm. 'Where will you go?'

'To London to beg an audience with the Queen. If I am to live as I was born to live and hold my head high, I must seek a royal pardon. Only then can I build my house and bring honour to the woman I love.'

'The woman you love?' Lady Devere's eyes widened. 'You have said nothing of this, Justin. Please tell me about this lady—she is a lady?'

'A beautiful, innocent, perfect lady. Her father is a Spanish Don. He meant to sell her to a rogue so that he could steal her lands and fortune, but I stole her away from the rogue who would have harmed her. I love Maribel and she loves me.'

'Maribel, that is a beautiful name,' his mother said and smiled. 'You will bring this lady to see me, Justin. Give me your word that you will return once more and bring your bride with you.'

'Maribel is not yet my wife, for I wished to clear the shadow that hangs over me if possible. She is with her mother's family and I shall return to claim her as soon as I am able.'

'Supposing the Queen refuses to see you?'

'If I am at liberty I shall sail away and never return to England.'

'And if you are thrown into the Tower?'

'I must take my chances, Mother. I must pay my respects to Queen Elizabeth. I pray that she will remember me as a loyal supporter at a difficult time. I shall arrange for a gift to be sent to her; if it pleases her, she may grant me a pardon.'

Lady Devere leaned forwards to kiss his cheek. 'My prayers are with you, my son. I shall speak to your father. It may hurt him to know that you were for a short time a pirate, but I believe he will forgive you.'

'Thank you.' Justin smiled. 'At least I know I have your forgiveness and your love.'

'Nothing could ever change that,' she said. 'You are my son.'

Maribel looked about her excitedly. She had never been to a fair such as this, because her father would not have approved. A large field had been set aside to accommodate all the merchants and pedlars that had made their way here for the festival. All kinds of goods were set out, either on blankets set on the ground or on boards and trestles. There were men of several races displaying their wares; men with dark skins and eyes from the east with perfumes and trinkets made of ivory, silver and horn. Also merchants of France and Italy selling materials so fine and beautiful that Maribel could not resist touching them, letting the silk run through her fingers. Some of the merchants had leather belts and jerkins

tooled with gold and vibrant colours, others had slippers
and purses of leather or velvet, still more sold cures
with strange-sounding names and relics from the saints.
One man had a sliver of wood in a silver casket that he
swore came from the Cross of Our Lord Himself.

'Do not buy any of the relics,' Lady Fildene advised.
'Rarely are they true relics and thus have no magical
properties. Many of the baubles you see are merely
glass and cheap metal—but the perfumes are usually
good and the material is quality.'

'I love this green silk and the bronze velvet is beautiful. It would make a wonderful cloak to wear over a
cream gown.'

'Are you thinking of your wedding, Maribel?'

'I am not certain whether I wish to make my
wedding gown just yet. It might be better to wait until
Justin returns—' Maribel broke off as she saw a man
looking at her. He was standing some distance away,
beyond the stalls, in a part of the field where contests
and games of chance were being held. She turned away
immediately, her heart thumping. It could not be! She
must be mistaken. 'I think perhaps I should like to go
home, Aunt. I have a sudden headache.'

'My poor child.' Lady Fildene looked at her with
sympathy. 'You have not bought anything yet. But you
must go back and rest. I shall purchase the silk and
velvets you have chosen and have them sent to us. Go
now, dearest. You look exceeding pale.'

Maribel thanked her in a low voice. She walked
slowly from the field so as to avoid looking as if she

were in a panic, climbing the steep hill towards her uncle's house. Her heart was pumping hard as she increased her pace, wanting to be safe, afraid that *he* had known her and would come after her. Reaching the drawbridge, she glanced back, shading her eyes against the sun that had come out from behind the clouds. She could see the figure of a man some distance away. He was just standing there, staring at her, but making no move to follow.

Perhaps she had been mistaken. Surely it could not have been Samuel Hynes? How could he have been here? Why would he have come to this quiet village? Had he known she was living with her uncle and aunt?

She was almost certain that he had seen her even before she had noticed him. Yet he had made no attempt to speak to her or to accost her. If he had come to abduct her, he would have surely taken his chance. No, he must have visited the fair for purposes of his own. What would he do now that he had seen her?

Maribel felt sick and frightened. Her uncle would protect her from Hynes if she told him that she was in danger, but to do that she must explain everything…tell him that she had hidden the truth from him. She had allowed him to believe that Justin was her betrothed and implied that she had her father's blessing. Sir Henry would have every right to be angry if he knew the whole.

No, she could not tell him! She must keep her secret and make certain that she stayed safe within her uncle's house. Samuel Hynes would not come looking for her there.

* * *

'Your fortune is safe with us, sir,' the goldsmith assured Justin. 'The funds lodged with us by your esteemed great-grandfather, Lord Robert Melford, have grown to almost twice that placed in our care when you were born. The money is available whenever you wish for it, Mr Devere.'

'Thank you. I may wish for a part of my fortune to be transferred to France or perhaps Italy. I have not yet made up my mind. Can you recommend a safe house for my business?'

'I have a cousin in Lombardy. He is well trusted by the most noble of the land, sir. I could write a letter of introduction. He would advance you anything you required against your funds held here and they need never leave England.'

'I shall let you know of my decision in good time, sir. Meanwhile, I have this chest of raw silver. I would like to barter it for a precious jewel—something that might please a noble lady. Something worthy of a queen.'

'Ah, yes, I think I may have the very thing.' The goldsmith smiled. 'Wait there, sir. I shall bring you something I think may please the most discerning lady.'

Justin nodded, glancing round the goldsmith's shop. It was sparsely furnished and nothing of great value was on display, for amongst the common folk there was some dislike of the trade and the goldsmiths, who were often of the Jewish faith. It was not unknown for their shops to be attacked by those who disliked repaying money loaned to them and felt they had been cheated. However, Master Baldini was well known for his honesty.

'This may be what you wish for, sir?'

The goldsmith laid a packet of black velvet on the counter and opened it, displaying a large ruby of such a deep blood red that Justin was struck by its beauty. It had not been mounted, but could easily take pride of place in a necklace or a crown.

'That is magnificent, Master Baldini. Will you accept the silver in return?'

The goldsmith looked at the silver, examined its quality and nodded. 'It is a fair exchange, sir. I shall be pleased to trade with you for the ruby.'

'Thank you. I may return to purchase another trinket—something as precious as the ruby, but simpler, more suitable for the lady I intend to wed.'

'I have many such trinkets, sir. Perhaps pearls might be what you would wish for?'

'Yes, pearls would do very well.' Justin offered his hand. 'My thanks, Master Baldini. I shall visit you again before I leave London.'

'May your business go well, sir.'

'I thank you for your good wishes. I pray it will— my future depends upon it.'

Justin left the shop, the ruby safe inside his inner jerkin. He had asked for an audience with Queen Elizabeth and been told that he might have to wait some weeks before it was granted. He was by no means the only man who desired an audience with England's new Queen. Ambassadors from France, Spain, the Netherlands and Italy were only some of those ahead of him in the queue, along with many English nobles.

It was possible that he would have to kick his heels for weeks before being granted an audience. The enforced separation from Maribel was hard to bear. His thoughts were always with her, for he knew she would be thinking of him, anxious for his return. However, he must attend the court every day and wait as patiently as he could.

At least she was safe in her uncle's house. He hoped that she would not think he had deserted her, but there was little he could do except wait for the moment.

'Michael has sent word that he will arrive by this afternoon at the latest,' Lady Fildene told Maribel that morning when she asked what was going on and why the servants were hurrying about their work with more urgency than usual. 'He says that he is bringing a guest with him—a gentleman who may put some business our way.'

'Oh, that sounds promising,' Maribel replied going to sit beside her on the oaken bench. It had a high carved back and would have been uncomfortable to sit on had her aunt not made thick cushions to make it easier. 'I know my uncle trades in wine, as do other English gentlemen. You said he mostly imports wine from Italy and France, I think?'

'Yes, that is true. We have not bought from Spain for a long time, but we may do so soon, because it is Spanish wine we have been offered—from Don Sabatini's winery, I understand.'

'My father's wine?' Maribel drew her breath in sharply. 'It is not he that your son brings here, Aunt?'

Lady Fildene looked at her. 'You have turned pale, Maribel. Does something bother you? The mention of your father? It is not he that visits with Michael, but a man who imports wine from him. We are to be offered an interest in bringing over a cargo of wine, but my husband may not accept. He would not if he thought it might harm you.' Her gaze narrowed. 'Did your father do something to hurt you, Maribel?'

'Yes…' She shook her head as her aunt's brows rose. 'I cannot speak of it. Forgive me. Will you excuse me, please? I must think.'

Maribel left the room hastily. Her heart was racing. She knew only too well that the man importing her father's wine must be Samuel Hynes.

It *was* he she had seen at the fair. Each day since then she had wondered if he would come to the house and demand to see her…if he would betray her to her uncle. She felt sick at heart and uneasy. Supposing Hynes claimed her for his bride as he'd threatened? Would she be forced to go with him? Would her uncle throw her from his house if he knew what had happened to her— that she had been Justin's captive and then his lover?

Could her father demand that she be returned to him or handed over to the man he had chosen as her husband?

Maribel paced the floor of her bedchamber. She was anxious, afraid of what might happen when the visitor arrived. It might be better to confess all to her aunt, who was kind hearted—but supposing she turned from her? Maribel knew that without Justin to protect her she would not be safe outside her uncle's house. Higgins was around somewhere, but she did not think there was much he could do to help her, especially if her uncle was of a mind to hand her over to her father's agent.

She did not know which way to turn for the best. Justin had left for London more than two weeks previously. How much longer would it be before he returned?

She wished that he was with her. He would tell her what she ought to do or take her away. She had been happy enough here despite missing him every day he stayed away, but now she was on thorns. What ought she to do?

'Maribel, my dear…' She heard the knock at the door and her aunt's voice. 'May I come in, please?'

'Yes, of course.' Maribel opened the door to admit her. 'I was about to come down, Aunt.'

'Something is troubling you, my love. Will you not tell me?'

Maribel hesitated. If she ignored this chance it might be too late. She took a deep breath and then inclined her head.

'I must begin at the very beginning. I beg you will forgive me—I have not been entirely honest with you. When I first came here I did not know you and was afraid that you might turn me away. It is true that I am promised to Captain Devere, but we were not betrothed in the proper manner. My father wished me to marry a man I had never seen—a man called Lord William Roberts of Helbourne.'

'Impossible! That wicked man…' Lady Fildene's face reflected her shock. 'I have heard of him and the very idea offends me. How could your father suggest such a thing?'

'He hated me, as I believe he once hated my mother. I begged to be allowed to wait and perhaps choose a husband for myself, but he would not listen. Lord Roberts sent his cousin to fetch me and I was forced to go with him, but then…I met Captain Devere. We fell in love and he asked me to wed him.'

'How did you meet Captain Devere?' Her aunt's eyes were on her face. 'I have felt there is some mystery, Maribel…something you did not wish to tell me? Will you not be honest with me so that I may protect you from those that would harm you or take advantage of your innocence?'

'Justin attacked the ship and forced Captain Hynes to give me up to him. At first I believe he had some thought of a ransom, but then—' She broke off as she saw her aunt's face. 'No, it is not like that, Aunt. He truly loves me and I him. Justin would never harm me.'

'Is Captain Devere a privateer?' Lady Fildene frowned, clearly doubtful. 'What is his business? I thought it strange that he should leave you here and go off on some secret mission.'

'It is not secret. He has gone to seek an audience with the Queen…' Maribel's eyes filled with tears. 'Please do not judge him or me, Aunt. I was treated ill by my father and by Captain Hynes. He tried to—to seduce me while I was on his ship. He said he had my father's permission to do as he would with me. If Justin had not attacked the ship, I might be dead, for I would have taken my life rather than live as his thing.'

'My poor, poor child,' her aunt said and held out her arms. 'I am not certain how your uncle will feel about a marriage between you and Captain Devere, for he would frown upon such a trade. Pirates and privateers are the scourge of the seas and cost many an honest merchant a great deal of money. However, you are not to be judged or chastised for you had no choice in all this, my love. Do not fear this man. You shall not be given up to him. My husband will listen to a business proposition if he makes it, but nothing will affect you. I give you my word. You shall not be forced to leave this house against your will.'

'And Justin?' Maribel looked at her uncertainly. She half-wished that she had not told her aunt anything. 'I love him so very much.'

'If that gentleman returns, he will explain himself to your uncle and me,' Lady Fildene said, looking grim. 'If we are satisfied the wedding will go ahead, but he must be prepared to tell us everything.'

Maribel was silent. Her aunt was asking for no more than was due, for she had taken her into her home and treated her kindly, but if she and her husband sought to deny the marriage, Maribel would defy them and run away with the man she loved. She had obeyed her father as a dutiful daughter ought, but never again would she go against the dictates of her heart. She belonged with Justin and she would sail with him to the ends of the earth. Let him only return to her and she would not ask for anything more. Riches and fine clothes meant nothing. Only in her bold pirate's arms could she find happiness.

Chapter Ten

'Her Majesty will see you now, sir. Please come with me.'

Justin inclined his head to the flunky who had summoned him and followed in his footsteps. He had waited every day for the past ten, containing his impatience as best he could, but he knew that he might have been kept waiting so much longer. Some of the gentlemen he had spoken to had already been kept in limbo for far longer. After traversing some steps and a long corridor, the footman paused outside a door, indicating that Justin might enter.

'Her Majesty will be with you shortly.'

Justin thanked him and opened the door. He entered a large room, which had been hung with rich tapestry and was furnished with a beautiful cabinet of carved oak, several footstools and side tables. These were adorned with heavy silver chargers, ewers and candlesticks, an important chair set upon a little dais at the far end. As far as Justin could tell he was alone. He moved slowly towards the dais, then hesitated as he heard a woman's laugh and then a muffled whisper, which sounded like a man's voice. A curtain moved to the right of the chair and a woman came out.

Her red hair was hanging down her back, held only by a little jewelled cap at the back of her head. She looked like the young girl he had met before but her gown was exquisitely sewn with jewels, rows of pearls hanging about her white neck. She stood with one hand behind her back, her gaze bright and inquiring.

Justin went down on one knee. 'Your Majesty,' he said. 'I thank you for graciously allowing me this audience.'

'Have you forgot me, sir?' Elizabeth demanded with a twinkle in her eyes. 'I am still the same Bess you visited and teased, as I recall, when I was but a child and you a friend of Robin's.'

'I was privileged to know you then—and I am honoured to bend the knee to my Queen now.'

'Stand and face me. I have received the gift you sent me. It is a fine jewel and I shall have it mounted in a crown, I think.' Her shrewd eyes narrowed. 'Why have you given me such a precious thing, sir? I believe you must want something of me.'

'I have come to ask for the royal pardon, your Majesty. I was shanghaied and taken aboard Captain Smythe's vessel and eventually driven to mutiny, as I believe you may have been told by others.'

'Captain Smythe has been dealt with and all those

who took part in the mutiny are pardoned by my decree. Mutiny is a serious crime, but the man was a monster and he dared to sail under a royal flag, bringing disgrace to our name. He will do so no more. So, what more have you to tell me, sir?'

'I have sailed as a pirate, Majesty. I attacked Spanish and Portuguese merchantmen—and one English ship.'

'Why did you attack an English ship, sir? I can turn a blind eye if you attack Spanish treasure ships, for that country grows too rich and powerful and in time will seek to rule us. The Portuguese are greedy and will not share their trading agreements, keeping all the riches of the east for themselves. If a privateer wishes to attack ships from these nations I may choose not to know what they do—but I shall not tolerate attacks on English ships by an Englishman.'

'Hynes was in league with an evil Spaniard who tortured and killed men who worked for him in the silver mines. Sabatini intended to sell his daughter to a monster. I rescued her and gave him back his ship, but then he and the Don attacked the island where my ships were anchored, killing and injuring innocent men and women. They stole Maribel against her will, but I rescued her and she has consented to be my wife. This time I did not give him back his ship—and if I had the chance I would see him hang for his crimes.'

'Indeed?' Elizabeth's eyes gleamed. 'You take much for granted, sir. Mayhap I shall make an example of you to teach others what I expect of my young captains.

Perhaps you will be the one to hang. Kneel, Master Devere. I wish to see you penitent for your wicked crimes.'

A nerve flicked in Justin's cheek, but he went down on one knee before her, bowing his head, his eyes fixed on the hem of her gown. 'I know I have behaved recklessly, but I crave your Majesty's pardon.'

She made a sound that he interpreted as a laugh and there was the sound of movement, as someone joined her. He could see a pair of booted feet standing beside her, but did not raise his head.

'Well, what shall I do with him, Robin?'

'It is your choice, but you may one day have need of such men as Devere, Bess.'

Justin did not look up, but he knew that only one man would dare to speak to the Queen in such a manner. Lord Robert Dudley had been one of her most loyal friends during the difficult times when she was at the mercy of her sister Mary's whims.

'Give me your sword, Robin. Raise your head, Master Devere.'

Justin looked up as she brought the sword tip down on one shoulder and then the other. Elizabeth's eyes were bright with mischief. She had become a queen and must be treated with respect and reverence, but as yet there still remained the girl who had loved to laugh and play with her friends. She had been a captive at the mercy of her sister, treated as a bastard and at times in fear of her life, but courage and her own good sense had brought her through. Justin believed that at last England had a worthy queen.

'Arise, Sir Justin Devere. You are hereby made a knight of my realm. If you wish for it, I shall give you papers to sail as a privateer under my order.'

'Your Majesty…' Justin was surprised and overwhelmed—he had not expected such an honour. A pardon was all he had dared to hope for. 'I do not know how to thank you.'

'You were Robin's friend and mine in the past. I am Queen now, but I have enemies as well as friends. There may be a service you can do for me one day.'

'Your Majesty may call on me whenever you wish.'

Justin stood. He offered his hand to Robert Dudley. 'I am glad to see you, sir.'

'And I you, Devere. You must join me for supper. I should like to hear more of your adventures. Especially concerning Spanish treasure ships.'

'Thank you, I shall be pleased to. This evening, if you will, for I leave London almost immediately. The lady I have promised to wed waits anxiously for news.'

'Your uncle wishes you to come down,' Lady Fildene told Maribel that evening. 'Captain Hynes is with him. He has asked if he may speak with you, but he has laid no claims. I have held my peace so far, but do not fear that I shall allow this man to distress you.'

'Must I see him?' Maribel asked. 'I do not like or trust him. He is sly and may try to turn my uncle's mind his way.'

'I shall be with you all the time. Fear not, dearest.

You are under my protection. I promise no harm shall come to you.'

'Thank you.' Maribel smiled at her gratefully. 'I shall come, but you must not leave me alone with him.'

Maribel glanced at herself in the tiny silver mirror that hung from the chatelaine at her waist. She no longer dressed her hair in the Spanish way in ringlets either side of her face, but instead wore it loose down her back, tucked beneath a velvet hood in the manner of an English country lady.

Her heart raced as she accompanied her aunt down the wide stone steps leading to the great hall below. She could see her uncle, a young man who looked very like him and was clearly his son Michael, and Samuel Hynes. A shiver went through her as he glanced up and saw her. His eyes narrowed, gleaming with sudden excitement. Maribel's nerves jangled, but she kept her head high, giving him a haughty stare.

As she and her aunt advanced towards the little group, Samuel Hynes inclined his head to her.

'Good evening, Donna Maribel. I am glad to see you looking so well and none the worse for your adventures. I did not dare to hope that you would be brought safely to your family after that pirate abducted you from my ship.'

Maribel resisted the temptation to look at her uncle. 'Captain Devere is a man of honour. I was his willing captive, sir—for I did not wish to marry your cousin.' She wanted to fling her accusations of attempted rape in his face, but retained her dignity.

'If a pirate can be honourable, I suppose he has acted

in your best interests by bringing you here. I have a letter from your father to deliver to your hand. Don Sabatini insisted that it must come only to you.'

Maribel looked at her aunt, who nodded, then went forwards to receive it. She took the sealed paper from his hand. 'Thank you, sir. If that is all, I shall leave you to your business.'

'I pray you stay a little, lady. Your father's instructions to you are in the letter.'

'My father may no longer command me, sir. I am under the protection of my uncle.' She turned her head, but saw that her uncle and his son were leaving the room. Her aunt had withdrawn to the far side and was staring out of the window. Maribel felt as if she had been deserted, but she resisted the impulse to summon her aunt to her. 'I must tell you that I shall not return to Spain—nor will I submit to unreasonable demands.'

'I believe that Don Sabatini wishes to make amends. If you read his letter, you will discover that he has suffered a seizure and may never truly be himself again. He asks that you will allow me to take you to him so that he may give you his blessing and promises that you will not be forced into marriage.'

'Do you imagine I would trust you after what you did to me on board your ship? You hit me and kicked me as I lay on the floor. You threatened me with all manner of violence—' Maribel broke off as she heard something behind her and saw her aunt leave the room with her son. She had been left alone after all her aunt's promises! Fear coursed through her. 'Do not touch me, sir. I shall scream.'

Hynes moved towards her. 'Your uncle is interested only in the rich contract I bring him. He will send you back to your father and then I shall have what belongs to me.'

'No!' Maribel gave a scream of fright as he pounced on her, grabbing her arm. He pressed his face close to hers, his sneer of triumph making her shiver and tremble. 'No, my uncle would not…he could not…'

'You are quite right, my dear, I would not,' her uncle said, entering by a door situated behind Samuel Hynes. 'When Lady Fildene told me what this evil man had done I could hardly credit it, but when he asked to see you alone I made my little plan to test him.' He advanced on Hynes, his face set coldly. 'I have heard enough from you, sir. You may believe that I am interested in your talk of riches, but I assure you I care nothing for Sabatini's money. He took my sister from me and broke her heart. One letter telling of her unhappiness was all she sent me, but it told me everything. If he imagines I would allow my niece to return to Spain on this false pretence, then he is sadly mistaken. He may be ill, but unless Maribel wishes it she will not leave this house.'

'Damn you!' Samuel Hynes's face turned dark red with anger. 'Her father gave her to me and I mean to have her—whether she wills it or no!'

'You will leave my house instantly or I shall have my men arrest you and send for the militia.'

'You will pay for this—you and that hellcat!' Hynes said and stormed from the room.

'Uncle…' Maribel was pale as her uncle came

towards her and took her trembling hands in his. 'I thought for a moment that you had deserted me.'

'Forgive me. It was the only way, Maribel. I believed your story for I knew my sister was unhappy in her marriage, but I had to be certain just what was happening. I hoped that if Hynes believed you were alone he would say something to betray himself—and he did.'

'I cannot thank you enough for believing in me. Even had I wanted to visit my father I would not have trusted Captain Hynes. Besides, I must wait here until Justin returns.'

Her uncle looked severe. 'And when he does I shall have a few questions to ask that young man, Maribel. He must prove himself worthy of you, for I will not have you wed a pirate. You are a lady and it is not fitting.'

'I am sure that Justin will be able to satisfy all your questions when he comes, Uncle.'

'We shall see, Niece.'

Maribel was thoughtful as she returned to her own chamber. She had been wrong to doubt her uncle and aunt; they were both truly kind and concerned for her. Her uncle had sent Samuel Hynes away, but would he give up his attempts to claim her?

'Oh, Justin…' Maribel sighed. 'Where are you my love? I need you so.'

Something told her that Captain Hynes would not give up just because her uncle had sent him packing.

Samuel Hynes stood looking up at the house high above him. It would be impossible for a small force to scale the cliffs from this position and take the inhabitants by surprise. He had imagined that by wooing the son he might gain the father's trust, but he had lost his gamble. His one advantage was that he had learned Justin Devere was not here. He knew that he might have only one attempt to snatch the girl, because once Devere returned he would guard her too well.

The uncle was a wily old bird and had fooled him into thinking he was interested only in the rich contract he had offered. It might be prudent to give up the contest, let the girl go her way and forget her. He had Sabatini's contract in his pocket, but he wanted much more. Maribel probably did not guess what a wealthy heiress she was or that if she contested her father's guardianship in the courts she could regain all that was hers by right.

Sabatini had let slip far more than he realised in his rage at her capture. Hynes wanted the girl. He intended to humiliate her, to break her spirit and teach her to serve him like a slave. Once he had her fortune in his possession he would probably discard her, but marriage was necessary if he were to gain the riches she could bring him.

Hynes had recently inherited his cousin's title and what was left of his estate, but it was heavily encumbered by debt and of no consequence beside what he might gain if he could force Maribel to become his wife. If Sabatini were to die after they were wed, his fortune would probably come to Maribel and him. It might be possible to arrange a little accident for the proud Spaniard, but it would avail him nothing unless the girl was his wife.

Lord Roberts had needed the fortune she could bring him, but it was Hynes that had suggested sending an early portrait to fool both her and her father. It had made the trick easier when he discovered that Sabatini hated his daughter and hoped to keep control of her fortune even after she was married.

If it had not been for that damned pirate, Maribel would already be his to do with as he wished—and it would give Samuel pleasure to tame the vixen. Once he had her she would soon learn to know her master!

He was determined to have her, and he craved revenge on the man who had stolen her from him twice. He had tried persuasion, but now he must resort to cunning and force. Maribel was safe while she remained inside her uncle's house. Samuel must find a way of enticing her to leave it. He knew that she did not walk out alone as she had sometimes at her home in Spain, but she must long to walk on the beach when the weather was fine. If she thought that she was coming to meet that damned pirate, she might disobey her uncle and slip out alone.

On his ship with his crew to protect him, Devere was impossible to beat, but if he had been in London, as Michael Fildene had obligingly revealed when they were talking before the girl made her appearance, it should be possible to set a trap for him. He was travelling alone and might not be on his guard in his eagerness to claim his bride.

* * *

Justin decided that he would stop at the inn he had stayed at before when making his way to London. He could not hope to reach Maribel before nightfall and it was best to avoid the roads at night; a man travelling alone was easy prey for the bands of beggars and rogues who haunted the roads.

After his audience with the Queen, he had stayed in London only long enough to buy gifts for Maribel, most of which he had had sent to his father's house, along with other things he needed. It was Justin's intention to take Maribel to visit his mother. If his father would receive him, he would visit with his parents until he could find an estate he thought worthy of his wife. If not…perhaps he would take her to court, where he was certain she would be welcomed.

He was still surprised to find himself being addressed as Sir Justin, but did not imagine that a knighthood would weigh with his father. John Devere would not change his mind simply because the Queen chose to find his son's adventures worthy of honour.

At least he could hold his head up high, Justin thought as he dismounted and gave his horse to a groom. In the morning he would speak to Maribel's uncle and ask for her hand.

He was crossing the yard to the inn when he heard something behind him and whirled round. Seeing the three rogues advancing on him, Justin drew his sword. By the look of their faces they were out for more than the gold he carried and he was immediately wary. Once before he had been caught in a trap, his attention on the rogues who were attacking him from the front while another attacked him from behind. It would not happen this time. He gave a low piercing whistle and suddenly men came running towards him from the shadows—several more than he had expected.

'Higgins?'

'You sent word to meet you here, Cap'n. I brought a few of the men with me just in case.'

Justin smiled in the gloom. 'I applaud your caution, my friend. We'll make short work of these rogues between us.' He brandished his sword in anticipation. One of the would-be assassins pointed a pistol at Justin, but before he could press the trigger a knife thudded into his chest and the shot went wide. Seeing they were outnumbered, the two men who had threatened Justin disappeared into the shadows and a third man watching at a distance scowled and melted away.

'What made you think an attack might take place here?' Higgins asked as a couple of shots were fired after the fleeing rogues.

'As soon as you sent me word that Hynes had been seen lingering in the vicinity I suspected that he would try something. He could not know when I left London, unless he had someone watching me, and I had not noticed anything unusual; therefore, it was likely he would try to surprise me when I stopped at the inn. He may have men watching for me at various inns, but if he made enquiries he could have learned that I stopped here before.' Justin's brow furrowed. 'Is my lady safe? He has not tried to harm her?'

'Hynes made some attempt to persuade her to let him take her to his father. Anna told me there was some tale of Sabatini being ill and wanting to make amends. When her uncle left her alone with him, he tried to force her and was caught out. Fildene is no fool, but…' Higgins looked awkward. 'Anna says that he means to question you about your plans before he will permit the wedding. He will not have his niece marry a pirate.'

'Nor would I expect his blessing if that were the case. I believe he will be satisfied. Her Majesty hath seen fit to bestow a knighthood on me and I intend to take my bride to my father's house until I can find an estate fitting for her.'

'I am glad that the Queen pardoned you.' Higgins gave him a hard look. 'What of the rest of us? Are we to receive the royal pardon too?'

'You are all pardoned for the mutiny and Captain Smythe has lost his master's ticket. Her Majesty is willing to grant me letters of marque so that we could sail as privateers if we wished. She told me in confidence that she fears Spain; if that country grows too powerful, its king may cast covetous eyes on England's throne, and, as is well known, the Portuguese merchants will not share the secrets of their trading with the exotic lands of the east.'

'Rich pickings for the taking…' Higgins nodded his understanding for the Portuguese were the envy of other nations who craved a share of their special trading agreements. 'But 'tis not your intention to sail under licence to the Crown, is it?'

'No. I could not ask Maribel to share life on board a privateer. I must make a home for her. She is a lady and deserves to be treated as such.'

Higgins looked thoughtful. 'Me and Anna—we have thought of settling down. We had thought of a trading post on the island, but...' He rubbed the bridge of his nose. 'I have been talking to some folk who think of sailing to the New World.'

'The Spanish grow wealthy on silver and gold stolen from the Incas and other tribes, but you could not compete with them.'

'It is not of gold or silver taken from the earth that these men dream, but of freedom and the wealth of the soil. They say that there are great forests where the game is so plentiful that a man would never starve. They talk of a settlement where they can build new lives for themselves, unhampered by old prejudices and unfair laws—a land where all men are equal and all can work to earn their fortunes.'

'Do you believe such ideals are possible?' Justin asked doubtfully.

'I may be pardoned for the mutiny, but there are men in England with long memories. I could be hanged for stealing a loaf of bread. I might be arrested for speaking out of turn to an aristocrat. I am thinking of buying a cargo and sailing for the New World. I know that there are men who sailed under you who have thought of it too. If men are to settle there, they will need ships to supply them with the goods they cannot provide for themselves.'

'What would you do—set up a trading post?'

'Aye, I've thought of it, but I'll need a regular supply, someone I can rely on to replenish my stocks once they have gone. I don't know what you have in mind for the *Defiance.* There's the *Mistress Susanna,* too—though that was promised to the men.'

'I might pay its price myself, but I am not yet certain of my plans.' Justin was thoughtful as they went into the inn together. 'I had thought to become a merchant adventurer when I was no longer a pirate, but things have changed. Give me a few days to think this over and I will give you my answer.'

'It will take me a week or two to get a cargo together. I've been asking what kind of things will be needed. For a start it will be tools and seed that are most wanted, but the settlers will no doubt take those things with them. I was thinking of other stuff: lamps and crockery, material for women to make new gowns and shirts for their menfolk.'

'You will make a fine shopkeeper,' Justin said and chuckled, clapping him on the back. 'I thank you for coming to my rescue this evening. I shall give your ideas some thought, but for the moment there is still the problem of Samuel Hynes. His first attempt to have me killed has failed, but there will no doubt be others.'

'Why are you looking so upset, Aunt?' Maribel asked as she walked into the parlour and found Lady

Fildene sitting over her needlework, tears trickling down her cheeks. 'Has something happened to distress you?'

'Michael has been telling his father that he would like to join some men who are making plans to sail for the New World. Sir Henry says that we must not hold him if he wishes to go; it is an adventure and he is a young man—but I had hoped he would marry and live here with us. His father had thought he would take over much of the business.'

'I am sorry. You will miss him if he goes,' Maribel said. 'But you have other sons who—' She broke off as the door opened and a maid entered carrying a small tray on which lay a small piece of parchment. She offered it to Maribel, who took it and saw her name inscribed. It had been folded and sealed with wax, but there was no insignia to indicate who had sent it. 'Who gave you this, Jess?'

'A young lad brought it, mistress. He said it was for you and that his master would be waiting for your answer.'

Maribel broke the seal and gave a little cry of pleasure. 'It is from Justin. He says that he will be here later today. He asks that I will meet him on the beach because he wishes to talk to me alone.'

'Show me…' Lady Fildene held out her hand and Maribel gave it to her. 'Is this Captain Devere's hand? Are you sure it came from him?'

'I do not think I have seen Justin's writing before this,' Maribel said and looked at her aunt. 'Do you think it could be a trap?'

'Is this the kind of thing your betrothed would ask you to do? I think it most improper for you to meet any man alone on a beach.'

'I do not know…' Maribel wrinkled her brow in thought. She was remembering the walks they had taken together on a beach, and the way Justin had kissed her. He might long to hold her in his arms and feel that he needed to be sure of her love after whatever had happened to him. 'Justin might wish to be alone with me before he spoke to my uncle. Yet I am not sure. I think I must show this letter to Uncle Henry.'

'Yes, my dear. That would be the best—ask your uncle what you should do.'

'I shall go and find him now.' She hesitated, then, 'You should not cry, dearest Aunt. If Michael understood how you felt, I am sure he would not leave you.'

'But he must not know,' the loving mother said at once. 'You must not tell him, Maribel. If it is his wish, I shall not stand in his way.'

Maribel inclined her head. Her aunt was so generous and she was sorry that her son seemed likely to leave his home. An adventure such as Michael was about to undertake must be fraught with danger—but it would be exciting. To begin a new life in a land where all were equal, valued for their contribution to the community rather than their birth. It was an interesting thought, but she pushed it from her mind as she went in search of her uncle. However, she was told that Sir Henry had gone out on business and would not be back until later that afternoon.

Maribel returned to her own chamber. As the sun began to move round the sky and the time for the meeting with Justin drew nearer she felt restless, unable to settle to her needlework. It was a fine day and Justin might be waiting for her on the beach, wondering where she was and thinking that she no longer loved him. Yet it might be a trap…

Making up her mind, Maribel found a light cape to wear over her gown. She would go down to the beach, but she would not go unprepared. She took out the knife Peg had given her on the island. If the note had come from Samuel Hynes, she would not be as weak and defenceless as she had been once before.

'You had my letter?' Justin asked as he was shown into Sir Henry's counting room. A large table was spread with ledgers and small piles of coin and talents were set out in readiness. 'Forgive me. I was told you were here, but I see you are busy.'

'My steward has made a reckoning of the rents and monies owed for this past month, but we are almost finished now. My servants and labourers will be coming for their pay at any moment but the steward will manage without me. Walk with me, sir. I would talk to you alone. I believe you bring good news with you?'

'Yes, the news is better than I had hoped, sir. I wished to talk to you…to tell you of my plans. Now that her Majesty has seen fit to give me a knighthood I mean to retire from the sea, but I may carry on trading. I have a fine ship and I am looking for a captain to sail it to the New World for me.'

'Indeed, that is interesting,' Sir Henry said. 'You must meet my son Michael—you may have something in common. You have answered my most pressing question, for I did not think I could allow Maribel to marry a pirate—or even a privateer. She is my sister's only child and has become a daughter to us. I want to be sure that she will be happy.'

'It is my chief concern.' Justin inclined his head. 'I have fortune enough to provide a good home for Maribel, to give her the life she is entitled to expect. I have always known that I could not wed her and continue the life I led before.'

'Then we are in agreement.' Sir Henry smiled. 'I know she has been waiting anxiously for your return and I think we should not keep her waiting a moment longer…but there is something else I must tell you. I have received news of Maribel's father. If it is true, he was taken ill of a seizure after a quarrel with someone and has since died—' He broke off as he saw his wife coming towards them. 'Lady Fildene, my dear. Sir Justin hath come to claim Maribel and I have given him my blessing.'

'Then why have I just seen her leaving the house alone?' Lady Fildene looked alarmed. 'This morning she received a letter that was supposed to have come from Captain Devere. I warned her that it might be a trap and she said she would ask you what she ought to do, Henry—did she not come to you?'

'I have been out all morning on business. What did this note say?'

'It asked her to meet Captain Devere on the beach…'

'Samuel Hynes! He tried to have me killed. When the attempt failed he thought he would abduct Maribel instead!' Justin cursed and turned on his heel. 'I must go.'

'I shall come with you.' Sir Henry said. He looked at his wife as Justin set off at a run. 'Rouse the household, madam. We must put a stop to this rascal's mischief once and for all. I should have seen to it before, but I thought her safe in the house.'

'I tried to warn her…' Lady Fildene shook her head at the folly of love and picked up a large brass bell, shaking it hard. As it reverberated through the house, servants came hurrying to answer her call. 'To the beach…to the beach…' she cried. 'My niece is in danger…'

Maribel followed the sloping path to the beach. The sun was bright but there was still a cool breeze from the water. Stopping for a moment to gaze out to sea, she saw the sails of a ship she thought might be the *Defiance*. Had Justin decided to bring his ship here? She had thought it left behind at Dover, but if he had managed to obtain the pardon he hoped might be his, he could have decided to bring his ship here. She was not entirely sure what he intended once he had settled his affairs. Were they to live here in England or perhaps in Italy or France?

Although her visit with her aunt and uncle had been pleasant, Maribel did not think she would care to live as they did for the rest of her life. Their way of life was not so very different from that she had known before she left for England the first time—but sailing with Justin on his ship and her stay on the island had opened her eyes, making her see that there was more to life than sitting in a drawing room in a pretty gown embroidering cushions.

Was she foolish to long for something different? She knew that she might have been more sensible to sit in her room at home and wait for Justin to come to her—but perhaps he had been testing her?

She could not see anyone on the beach, but she caught sight of movement near a rocky point at the far end and thought that perhaps a boat had been beached just out of sight. Her heart quickened. The true reason she had come to meet Justin was that after leaving her aunt and failing to find her uncle, she had wondered if Justin's reason for asking her to meet him was that he had been unable to secure a pardon. Perhaps he was a fugitive in hiding from those who wished to capture and hang him?

Maribel's mouth ran dry with fear, her pulses racing. It was surely the only reason Justin would ask her to meet him in such a clandestine way. She must be prepared to leave with him immediately because his life might be in danger every moment he stayed here!

Reaching the beach, Maribel glanced up at the cliff top once and then began to walk towards the point. Justin must be waiting for her, keeping out of sight until he was certain she was alone.

'Justin…I am here, my love—'

Maribel stopped as several men suddenly burst out from behind rocks that jutted into the sea and had hidden them from her gaze until this moment. She hesitated, her heart catching as she saw their faces and realised that these men were not Justin's. Immediately, she knew that her aunt had been right and she had foolishly walked into a trap.

Turning, she began to run back the way she had come. Her heart was thumping madly because here on this beach she was vulnerable. The ship anchored in the bay must be Samuel Hynes's ship and these men had come to take her captive. How foolish she had been! She ought to have known that Justin would not ask her to meet him alone.

She was breathing hard as she reached the bottom of the path leading back to the top of the cliff. Glancing up, she saw that a man was scrambling down to her as swiftly as he could manage. She knew him at once and her heart gave a little skip. Gathering her courage, she turned as the first of Samuel Hynes's men caught up to her. She whipped out her knife, brandishing it in front of her, sweeping it back and forth as she moved away from the cliff face to the open sand.

'Stay away from me or it will be the worse for you,' she cried. 'I know how to use this and I shall…' Maribel gave a little cry as one of the men lunged at her with his sword. She backed away, because a knife was no match for such a weapon. 'Stay back…'

Four of the men had surrounded her. One tried to

grab her from the back, but she whirled about and slashed his hand, making him yell in pain and retreat. Another man threatened her with his sword, the tip of his blade hovering near her throat.

'Have a care, Davy,' his companion warned. 'He wants her alive and all in one piece. It will be you he flogs if she is harmed.' He glanced over his shoulder, and, following his gaze, Maribel saw that Captain Hynes was near the boat that had brought them ashore.

'Damn the wench!' The first man spat on the sand. 'He swore she would be easy to abduct once he got her here.'

A shout from Justin warned them that he was nearly at the foot of the cliffs. The men swung round to look and all of a sudden a crowd of faces appeared at the top of the cliffs, men and women, all carrying weapons of some kind, had followed and were about to pour down the steep path. Someone pointed an arquebus at the would-be abductors and fired. The shot went wide, for at this distance it could never have hit its mark, but the sound was enough to startle the men.

'Leave her! We shall all be killed…' one of them cried.

The one pointing his sword at Maribel's throat hesitated, then, seeing his friends fleeing, turned and followed as fast as he could in their wake.

Justin reached Maribel before the scoundrel could regain the safety of the jutting rocks. He fired after them and his ball struck home, winging one man in the arm. The man's screams echoed, as he yelled for his friends to help him and was ignored. He fell to his knees, struggled to his feet once more and set off towards the boat, which had already been pushed out into water deep enough to float it. His pleas for help were disregarded as the others began to row frantically for open water.

Sir Henry's household had reached the beach and several shots were fired as the wounded sailor ran into the water, floundering after the boat and eventually falling face down into the sea as another shot struck his back.

Maribel gazed up at Justin as he stood before her, his eyes intent on her face. 'I was so foolish,' she said, catching her breath. 'I should have known that you would never tell me to meet you here. I thought that you might be in danger of your life.'

'And so you risked yours…' He smiled and shook his head. 'If you insist on taking such foolish risks, I must teach you to use a sword or, better still a pistol, my love. Peg's knife served you well—without it they might have had you in the boat before I could reach you—but 'tis no match for a cutlass.' He shuddered. 'It would have served only to delay them, Maribel. Had your aunt not seen you leaving the house I might still have been talking with your uncle and it might have been too late.'

'Justin…' Tears welled in her eyes. 'Forgive me. I have missed you so much. When the letter came I suspected a trap, but I longed to see you and I was afraid if I did not meet you, you might go away and I should never see you again.'

'My sweet, lovely, foolish darling,' Justin said and trailed his fingers down her cheek, wiping away the tears. 'I would never have gone without giving you the chance to come with me. Had I been a fugitive and risked death to come to you I would still have done it— but I am a free man. The Queen has pardoned me and there is nothing to stop us marrying.'

'Justin…' She breathed and moved closer to him. She was longing for him to sweep her into his arms, but at that moment her uncle arrived, sword in hand. 'Uncle…I fear my foolish behaviour has caused you some trouble.'

'Foolish it was, child, for you should have consulted me,' Sir Henry said, but looked pleased with himself. 'I believe we showed those villains that we are not to be messed with, Sir Justin. If Hynes has the sense he was born with, he will sail away and not bother us again.'

Justin inclined his head, but when Maribel looked at him she saw there was a grim set to his mouth.

'Is it true?' she asked. 'Are you now Sir Justin?'

His gaze came back to her and he smiled, putting his arm about her waist. 'Shall you enjoy being Lady Devere?'

'I do not mind what I am called if I am with you,' she declared passionately. 'I will be your lady, your wife or your mistress…just as long as you never leave me again!'

Chapter Eleven

'You must know that I would not,' Justin said. He gazed down at her, his expression serious. 'If I seem distant or reserved it is because I have something on my mind, Maribel. I love you with all my heart. I wrote to your uncle and told him of my coming, but he was out when the letter arrived and I was with him when your aunt told us she had seen you heading towards the beach.' Justin caressed her cheek with his fingertips. 'You uncle has seen fit to allow the wedding. If you will have me, my darling, we shall be wed as soon as it can be arranged. Then I shall take you to meet my mother. After that…'

'You are anxious for my safety,' she said, looking into his eyes. 'Surely I must be safe once we are wed?'

'Yes, of course.' Justin promised. He took her hand and held it firmly. 'Yet still you must take care not to walk alone.'

'You fear that Hynes may try again? Surely he must

know that he has lost? I would kill myself rather than wed him—and it is my fortune he wants.'

'Perhaps.' Justin's brow furrowed. 'We have had news that your father may have died of a seizure.'

'My father may be dead?' Maribel was shocked by the news, but could not grieve for a man she had never truly known. 'God rest his soul. He did not love me, but I would not have wished him dead.'

'Of course you could not.' Justin took her hand. 'He did not deserve a daughter like you—indeed, I have wondered if he believed you were not his child.'

'He believed my mother had betrayed him?' Her eyes opened wide. 'Was that why he hated me?'

'It may have been or he may simply have been driven by greed. But his death has consequences. Even if he has left you nothing of what he owned, your husband's fortune will be at your disposal. I do not think you know the extent of the fortune your husband left you, but I imagine it may be considerable. Until we are wed, Hynes may not be the only man to covet what is yours.'

'Yes, I see. I knew Pablo was wealthy, but I do not care for riches. I was far happier when we lived simply on the island—at least I would have been had it not been for Captain Pike.'

Justin smiled wryly. 'You are too beautiful, my love. Men will always find you attractive, but once we are married no decent man would try to take advantage.'

'Let it be as soon as possible,' Maribel said and saw the gleam in his eyes. 'I want only to be your wife.

Nothing else matters. I do not care about the money. I never did.'

'I promise I shall keep you safe.' Justin bent his head, touching his mouth to hers in a soft kiss that held the promise of much more. 'I cannot wait for the moment you are truly mine.'

'I have been yours since the moment you took me captive.' Maribel smiled at him with love in her eyes. 'My uncle waits. We should go back to the house so that the arrangements for the wedding may be made.'

'You make a beautiful bride, my love,' Lady Fildene said as she gave Maribel a blue lace ribbon for her posy. Maribel was dressed in a gown of pale grey with trimmings of silver, a lace veil over her hair caught with jewelled combs in the Spanish way. 'I wish you every happiness, Maribel. Perhaps you will visit us sometimes?'

Maribel kissed her cheek. 'If I cannot visit I will certainly write to you, dearest Aunt. You have been kindness itself and I wish that I had known you years ago.'

'It has given us great happiness to have you here for this time.' Lady Fildene pressed a gift into her hands. 'This locket will remind you of your mother—it has her likeness inside. It was painted when she was very young and your uncle treasured it, but he says that it should be yours.'

Maribel opened it and saw a young girl who looked much as she did when a year or so younger. 'I shall treasure it always, Aunt—but are you sure my uncle can bear to part with it?'

'I believe he has other keepsakes. He wishes you to have this, Maribel.'

'I must thank him.' She fastened the locket about her neck with a ribbon. 'But he will be waiting downstairs, for it must be time to leave.'

'Yes, we must not keep the gentlemen waiting. Sir Justin will be anxious to see you, Maribel.'

'He loves me. I am so lucky, Aunt. There was a time when I believed my destiny would bring me little happiness, but now I know that I am the most fortunate of women.'

'Yes, my dear, I believe you are.' Lady Fildene smiled at her. 'Sir Justin will take good care of you, I have no doubt.'

'I am certain it is uppermost in his mind.' Maribel picked up her posy of pink roses. 'I am ready.'

Seeing her uncle waiting for her, she went up to him. He smiled and kissed her on the cheek, then took her hand.

'I believe you have found yourself a true man, Niece. He is the proper custodian for your person and your wealth.'

'I know that Justin has no desire to benefit from anything that was mine before I wed him. If my father is truly dead, he will sell my property in Spain and put it to good use elsewhere. I have friends I would like to help—and there are people who recently lost much of what they own. Justin will use some of my money to help them. We have talked of what I wish and he has agreed to do what I ask.'

'It is rare that a man is so uninterested in the marriage portion, but in this case you are right. Sir Justin is heir to a large fortune and has no need of anything you might have owned.'

'I am very fortunate in my husband-to-be.'

'Then I shall write to Spain and confirm what we have been told.' Her uncle smiled at her. 'The groom is waiting. Go to him with an easy heart, Maribel. You will no longer be the target for greedy men who want your fortune.'

'Thank you.' She smiled, kissed him again and went to meet her soon-to-be husband.

'As soon as the wedding is over, you will go aboard the ship at Dover and wait for my instructions,' Justin told Higgins as they stood outside the church for a few moments. 'You need not fear reprisals for yourself or the crew.'

'I have told you that we have a mind to sail for the New World, sir.'

'Aye. I am still thinking of your proposals and will send word once I have spoken with my mother.'

'You have not made up your mind about becoming a privateer? The letters of marque from the Queen would grant us safe passage.'

'I am not certain of my plans yet, but you shall know—as soon as I have spoken to my mother and my wife.' Justin heard the sound of approaching carriages. 'As soon as you can, take Anna and go to the ship. Tell the men that they are free to leave or stay, but I would ask one more service of them.'

Higgins looked at him in silence for a moment, then inclined his head. 'We all of us owe you that, Cap'n. My plans can wait for a while.'

'Thank you,' Justin said and smiled. 'And now if you will excuse me, I have an appointment to keep inside the church.'

Maribel saw Justin standing before the altar waiting for her. He turned his head to look at her and the expression in his eyes made her heart leap. She walked towards him proudly, feelings of joy and anticipation surging through her. She had been his willing captive, but now she would be his wife! They would live together for the rest of their lives!

Maribel glanced about her as they left the church. Bells were pealing and the villagers had gathered to throw rose petals, but she noticed several heavily armed men amongst the crowd.

'Who are those men?' she whispered to Justin.

'Just some men I have engaged to serve us, my love. Nothing for you to worry about.'

Maribel noticed a nerve flicking in his throat and the way his eyes scanned the faces of the villagers and a shiver went down her spine. She knew without being told that he and her uncle had been prepared in case another attempt should be made on her life outside the church. Yet surely Captain Hynes must know that he had lost, for he could not hope to benefit once she was married.

However, she was determined that she would not allow the worrying thought to spoil her wedding day.

She raised her head, smiling at her husband as he led her towards their carriage. Her uncle was giving a reception for them and they would stay under his roof for this one night. In the morning they would travel to the home of Justin's parents.

Maribel was eager to meet his family and yet she sensed that something was not right…that something more than the threat of another attack was playing on Justin's mind.

'I thought that we should never be alone.' Justin said, a rueful look on his face as he gazed down at her. 'Your uncle has too many friends, my love. I wished to be alone with you before this, because we have a long journey before us on the morrow.'

Maribel reached up to kiss him on the lips, her eyes questioning. 'Something troubles you, my love. Something more than Samuel Hynes, I think—will you not tell me what plays on your mind?'

'I said nothing to your uncle, Maribel.' Justin's expression was serious. 'My mother forgave me, as mothers will, without asking my story—but my father feels that I have shamed him. He walked from the room when I told him where I had been and I fear he will not wish to receive us.'

'Justin…' Maribel's heart caught because she knew how much the breach with his father must pain him. 'I am sorry. Surely he will find it in his heart to forgive what you did now that the Queen has given you a royal pardon?'

'My father is a proud man. I think perhaps too proud for his own good. It was he who told me I must leave England rather than shame the family when I was unjustly accused of being a traitor. I am not sure that he will forgive or acknowledge me.'

'I see that it hurts you,' Maribel touched his face with her fingertips. 'What will you do if he refuses to see us?'

'My mother may wish to say farewell to us. After that we shall leave.'

'Where shall we go? I thought you hoped to buy an estate close by your father's?'

'If I did that, my mother would visit us and that might cause an estrangement between them. I could not be responsible for that—so I think we shall leave England.' Justin's gaze was intent as it searched her face. 'Would you mind if we did not live in England?'

'I shall be happy wherever we live. I want only to be with you, Justin.' She held his hand to her cheek and then kissed the palm. 'For your sake I pray that your father can find it in his heart to receive you, but if he cannot we shall leave England and make our home else-where.'

'I thought Italy or France. It would be warmer for you as you have been used to the climate of Spain.'

'Perhaps,' Maribel said, 'but I have been thinking. There is somewhere else we might go.'

'Where? Tell me and—'

Maribel put her fingers to his lips. 'This is our wedding night, Justin. Make love to me. You have not loved me since that last time on the ship and I was but half-alive without you. I long for you to make me whole again. I missed you so when you were away.'

'My beloved…' Justin moaned softly as he buried his lips against her soft white throat. 'You are right. These things can wait. I burn for you. I love and want you so much.'

He bent down and swept her off her feet, carrying her to their bed. Removing the delicate lace nightgown, he gazed down at her body and then bent to kiss her. Maribel gasped as his tongue stroked and caressed the rosy peaks of her breasts, making her arch towards him, inviting him to take her to the heights of pleasure once more.

'I want you so much.'

'I adore you, my darling.'

'Oh, Justin.'

Maribel clung to him as she felt the burn of his flesh, opening to his thrusting manhood and giving a scream of pleasure as he entered her. She had longed for this, for the touch and taste of him, and it was all that she had remembered and more. Their bodies moved together in perfect harmony, reaching a swift and exquisite climax.

She lay gazing up at him, eyes soft and dark with desire. Justin stroked her side, her thigh, her cheek, as they looked into each other's eyes. She sighed and melted with love, her hands seeking the smooth hardness of his back. Her hands caressed him, smoothing over his shoulders and down his back. He bent his head, his tongue seeking out the secret places of her flesh, his touch making her arch and whimper with need until they came together in a slow, sensual loving that ended in a blaze of overwhelming sensation that left both satiated, at peace and soon to sleep.

In the night Maribel woke and turned to Justin. She was sure she had heard him cry out and she leaned over to see what ailed him. As she did so, he woke and looked at her.

'You are here,' he said and reached out to take her in his arms. 'I dreamed that I had lost you…but it was foolish, for you are not as she was, my darling.'

'What do you mean?' Maribel reached out to touch his cheek with her fingertips. 'Not as who was—do you mean the woman you once loved?'

'Yes. Loved, but learned to hate,' he told her. 'She was to have been my wife, but then she died—and before she died she told me that she loved another. He was poor and her family wanted her to marry for wealth and so she took me, but she loved him.'

'Oh, Justin…' Maribel's heart caught with love, understanding how he must have suffered. 'That is why you read that poem so often…' She bent over him to kiss him on the mouth. 'I shall never betray you. No other man could make my heart race as you do. I love you and you alone.'

'I know.' Justin smiled, pulling her closer and rolling her beneath him in the bed. 'Yet the dream was real and hurt me, for I could not bear to lose you, my only love.'

'You will not lose me until death us do part,' she promised and gave herself up to his kiss.

* * *

It was nearly dusk the next day when they reached Justin's home. He came to help her dismount, holding her in his arms and looking down into her lovely face for a moment while the men about them took the horses away to feed and stable them.

'I pray that your father will receive you,' she whispered. 'But if he does not, remember that together we are strong enough to face anything.'

'Yes, I know.'

Justin took her hand and they went into the front hall. A woman gave a cry of pleasure and came hurrying to meet them, her gentle face wreathed in smiles. Maribel looked at her. She guessed that this must be Lady Devere, but Justin's looks did not much favour her. He must get his size and colouring from the father…who was nowhere to be seen.

'Mother…may I present my wife, Maribel?' He held out his hand to her. 'My love—this is my mother, Lady Devere.'

'Ma'am, I am happy to meet you,' Maribel said and curtsied to her. 'I hope we find you well?'

'Indeed you do…and happy to meet you.' Justin's mother studied her face. 'I think my son has chosen his bride well. I believe you will make him happy.'

'She already has,' Justin said. 'My only concern is to be worthy of her—and to build her a home that is fit for her. I am grateful that Maribel has given me her trust and I ask for your blessing on our marriage.'

'It is willingly given.' Lady Devere hesitated. 'Your

father is not here, Justin. He left to visit your uncle's estate only this morning.'

Justin's brow creased. 'He had my letter?' She inclined her head, her eyes reflecting sorrow and disquiet. 'Yet he still went? Then I have my answer.'

'You must give him more time, dearest,' Lady Devere pleaded. 'I beg you not to be bitter or angry. Your father is a proud man. He did not try to forbid me to see you, for he knew that I should disobey him, but he cannot yet bring himself to see you.'

'I would not be the cause of dissent between you. With your permission we shall rest here the one night, for my lady is tired.'

'Your father will be gone for several days.'

'It would be an abuse of his forbearance if we stayed longer, Mother. We shall take our leave of you in the morning.'

'But where will you go?'

'That is up to my lady.' Justin turned to her, his brows arching in enquiry. 'Where would you live, my dearest one? I think Spain might not suit you, for you have sad memories there.'

'Will you truly let me choose?'

'Yes. I shall go anywhere you wish, Maribel.'

'Then…please may we go to the New World? I know that Anna and Higgins wish to set up a trading post in this new land. I hear that it is warmer than England, but much bigger than France or Italy. I believe that a man may take land for himself and make it fruitful if he is strong and he has the will.'

'The New World?' Justin stared at her. 'Have you also heard that it is primitive and wild? There are savages who may take exception to our commandeering land they believe is theirs? It would not be the life you have been used to, Maribel.'

'That is why I have chosen it.'

'I am not sure I understand.'

'I have no wish to sit sewing all day like a fine lady. I want to do the things I learned to do on the island. You could build us a fine house, Justin. Better and bigger than the one we had there—and we could have land that we farm, food that we grow ourselves. In time we may have children and then I may need help with the chores, but I want to be a good wife, to care for my home and family in a way that would be frowned on in gentle society. Think of it—a life where we may work together to build our fortunes. A country that is beginning anew without all the prejudice and unfairness of the Old World. You would help to build it with others of like minds, Justin.'

'To live and work with you would be heaven.' Justin trailed his fingers down her cheek. 'It will be even harder than it was on the island. It will not be a question of whether you wish to work harder than you have before. You may have to do far more in this new life than you did on the island, Maribel. Even though we have money, this new life you speak of will not be easily won.'

'I am not afraid of hard work. I think there are many good people who wish to leave the old countries and go to this new land. My cousin told me that people who feel trapped by laws and prejudice in England and other countries are thinking of becoming settlers. Why should we not be some of the first? We have money enough to buy whatever we need—and your ship can sail between the New and the Old World, bringing us more supplies. We can use some of the money Pablo left me to help others establish themselves, as well as helping the people whose homes were destroyed on the island. We could build a town for others to come and settle. Do you not think it would be a good life?'

Justin hesitated, studying her face and finding no sign of doubt. 'I must confess it has been in my mind to do some of the things you suggest. Higgins asked if I would let him commission my ship to supply the settlement, which he and others mean to start. I know that other ships are being prepared. Indeed, there is no reason why I should not commission others. The more ships we have to bring us the supplies we shall need in the early years, the better. But I would ask you to be certain, my love. It will be a long and arduous journey, much harder than that we took to the island. Things will become easier as the years pass, but at first it will be primitive.'

'I am prepared for long weeks, even months, at sea, and I know it will be difficult at first, but we are young and strong, Justin. I believe that we can make a good life for ourselves. My cousin tells me that the settlements are far from the silver mines that my countrymen exploit.'

'Yes, your uncle is certain there is nothing to stop you selling your estates, and he will see to the business for us. He is a good man and I trust him to treat fairly with you. I believe we shall be free and happy in this brave New World.' Fire leapt in him and he laughed as he gazed down at her. 'You are as courageous as you are beautiful, Maribel. It is little wonder that I lost my heart to you almost from the start.'

'Are you sure you wish to go to such a place?' Lady Devere looked at their faces and sighed as her hopes of seeing her son's children faded. 'Then you go with my blessing, my dearest ones. I have chests of things you may find useful in your new life, Maribel—materials of good cloth, wool and kersey and linens, which will serve you better than silk. Also items of pewter and cast iron that you will need for cooking—and I shall make you a gift of my recipes, which I have written in journals. Had I a daughter I would have passed them on to her, but they shall be for you.' Tears stood in her eyes. 'I shall miss you, Justin—and your lovely wife.'

'We shall send word of how we go on, Mother,' Justin promised and took her hand. 'If my ships trade successfully, I shall purchase others and perhaps one day we may return to England to spend time with you—and you may come to us if you wish. We shall send news of our lives when the ships return to England and you may write to us. Mayhap one day your grandson will visit in our stead.'

'I pray that you find happiness and whatever you both seek in this New World,' Lady Devere said. 'Now come upstairs with me, Maribel. I want you to choose some things to take with you. It is best that you go well prepared for when you land safely—God willing!—it may be months or even a year or more before fresh supplies can be brought. The sea is a fickle mistress and ships do not always arrive when they should.'

'Go with my mother,' Justin said. 'With your permission, Mother. I shall write a letter for my father before we dine together.'

'Yes, you should. Try to forgive him, Justin. I believe he may regret his decision when he learns what has happened here.'

Justin watched as the two ladies went upstairs together. They talked and laughed and he was torn with regret. He was excited by the adventure that lay before him, but he would have liked to make his peace with his father before he left England.

Justin had no doubts that the future would be a success. Years might pass before they accomplished all their dreams. It had taken some years before the pirates had established their houses and inns on the island and who knew what would happen in this new land? Yet the idea had fired Justin with enthusiasm. Maribel's trust in him to make a good life for them was a challenge in itself. He had wondered if he would miss the freedom he had experienced as a pirate, but now he was filled with a sense of adventure.

His mind worked swiftly. They must gather as many men and women of the same mind as they could, for the more settlers the better. He would hire a good carpenter to build a small house for the time being, and then, when he found the right land, he would build something bigger and better. He would also commission several more ships, because one thing the settlers must have was a supply of necessities from the Old World until they could produce all they required. Storms and crop failures could lead to the failure of their bright hopes, but with a fleet of ships to keep them supplied they could survive the first years.

Smiling, Justin sat down to write the letter to his father. He bore no ill will to any man—if he had not been shanghaied and forced to sail as a pirate, he would not have met his Maribel. Yet there was still a small shadow in his heart; he regretted that he had parted from his father with anger between them.

Maribel was standing outside the inn looking towards the sea. In the morning they would embark and then their great adventure would begin. Hearing the sound of heavy footsteps behind her, she turned. Her heart was beating fast; despite her uncle's assurances that she was now safe from any further attempt to kidnap her, she sometimes worried that Samuel Hynes might try to be revenged on them. When she turned and saw the man looking at her, her heart missed a beat for there was such an odd expression in his eyes.

'Did you wish to speak with me, sir?'

'You are the wife of Sir Justin Devere?'

'Yes, I am.' Maribel's gaze dwelled on his face a

moment longer and then she smiled. 'You are Justin's father, aren't you?'

'How did you know? I do not think we are much alike; I think he favours his mother.'

'I don't agree; he resembles you in more than just looks…a set of the mouth that can seem harsh to those who do not know Justin well. You have it too.'

'Do I?' John Devere smiled at her. 'How observant you are, lady.'

'Please, you must call me Maribel. I am so happy to meet you. I know Justin hoped that you would come to take your farewell of us before the ships sail, though he has not said anything of his hopes.'

'You are set on going? I thought that perhaps you were leaving because of my unkindness?' There was a look of unconscious appeal in Sir John's eyes. 'Is it too late to beg my son for forgiveness?'

'I do not think you need to beg for forgiveness,' Maribel said. 'Justin would be happier to part as friends, but he bears no malice in his heart.'

'I have realised that I am much to blame for what happened to him. I sent him away with anger in my heart, but I never ceased to love him.'

'My husband will be happy to hear your words, sir,' Maribel said. She smiled as she saw Justin walking towards him and knew that he had seen his father. 'I do not think he will change his mind about leaving, for all our plans are made, but he will be glad of your blessing, sir.'

'I shall be glad to give it.'

Maribel smiled. She went to meet her husband, kissed him and then left him to make his peace with his father while she talked to some of the other women who were preparing to make the difficult and dangerous journey to a land that they had never seen. Maribel had no doubts or fears concerning the future. She had been frightened of life before she was taken captive by pirates, but now she was bold enough to face anything, as long as she had the man she loved beside her.

'Take a last look at England, my darling,' Justin said, his arm about her waist as the *Defiance* sailed out of port. 'There is still time to change your mind?'

'And disappoint all our friends?' Maribel laughed up at him, her eyes alight with excitement. 'I am not speaking of just the crew. My cousin Michael came with one of my uncle's ships as soon as he heard what we planned and others have joined us. For many of them it is a chance of a much better life, Justin, for they find the bonds of their lives here restrictive. In the New World it will not matter where a man was born; if he is honest and of good heart he will succeed. With God's help and a fair wind we shall find this new land and prosper there.'

'I am sure we shall,' Justin said and bent to kiss her. 'As you know, Higgins and I have commissioned two more ships to sail with us and a cargo that may make the difference between success and failure, for some of our friends come ill prepared. However, it is a brave adventure and I am certain that we shall find a place where we can live happily together; whether it be in the New World itself or an island in the West Indies matters little.' He glanced towards the shore once more and for a moment his expression was thoughtful, almost sombre.

She looked up at him. 'You do not regret what we have done? You do not regret leaving your home? We could have stayed now that your father has forgiven you and mine can no longer threaten us. I shall be happy whatever you decide, Justin. I am excited about our adventure, but I would be content to live anywhere with you. You are not doing this just for me?'

Justin gazed down at her and smiled. 'My home is right here beside me and will ever be while I have you, my love. We shall not speak of these things again. A new life awaits us and we shall make the most of it.'

'Yes, Justin,' she whispered and lifted her face for his kiss. 'The future is ours to make of it what we will—and I know that whatever fate befalls us, we shall be together for as long as we live.'

* * * * *

MILLS & BOON

Historical

On sale 7th May 2010

COMPROMISING MISS MILTON
by Michelle Styles

Buttoned-up governess Daisy Milton buries dreams of
marriage and family life. But Viscount Ravensworth shakes
Daisy's safe, stable existence up. Could the tightly laced
miss ever forgo society's strict code of conduct…and come
undone in the arms of a reformed rake?

FORBIDDEN LADY by *Anne Herries*

Sir Robert came to claim his lady honourably. But Melissa
denied their love and her father had him whipped from the
house. Then, as the Wars of the Roses ravage England,
Melissa falls into Rob's power. He should not trust her –
but can he resist such vulnerable, innocent beauty?

STETSONS, SPRING AND WEDDING RINGS
by Jillian Hart, Judith Stacy, Stacey Kayne

Clara, Brynn and Constance are heading West, looking for new
lives, and three forceful men are determined to keep
these courageous women where they belong – in their towns,
in their hearts and, most of all, in their beds!

millsandboon.co.uk Community

Join Us!

The Community is the perfect place to meet and chat to kindred spirits who love books and reading as much as you do, but it's also the place to:

- **Get the inside scoop from authors about their latest books**
- **Learn how to write a romance book with advice from our editor**
- **Help us to continue publishing the best in women's fiction**
- **Share your thoughts on the books we publish**
- **Befriend other users**

Forums: Interact with each other as well as authors, editors and a whole host of other users worldwide.

Blogs: Every registered community member has their own blog to tell the world what they're up to and what's on their mind.

Book Challenge: We're aiming to read 5,000 books and have joined forces with The Reading Agency in our inaugural Book Challenge.

Profile Page: Showcase yourself and keep a record of your recent community activity.

Social Networking: We've added buttons at the end of every post to share via digg, Facebook, Google, Yahoo, technorati and de.licio.us.

www.millsandboon.co.uk

2 FREE BOOKS
AND A SURPRISE GIFT

We would like to take this opportunity to thank you for reading this Mills & Boon® book by offering you the chance to take TWO more specially selected books from the Historical series absolutely FREE! We're also making this offer to introduce you to the benefits of the Mills & Boon® Book Club™—

- **FREE home delivery**
- **FREE gifts and competitions**
- **FREE monthly Newsletter**
- **Exclusive Mills & Boon Book Club offers**
- **Books available before they're in the shops**

Accepting these FREE books and gift places you under no obligation to buy, you may cancel at any time, even after receiving your free books. Simply complete your details below and return the entire page to the address below. You don't even need a stamp!

YES Please send me 2 free Historical books and a surprise gift. I understand that unless you hear from me, I will receive 4 superb new books every month for just £3.79 each, postage and packing free. I am under no obligation to purchase any books and may cancel my subscription at any time. The free books and gift will be mine to keep in any case.

Ms/Mrs/Miss/Mr ———————— Initials ————————

Surname ————————————————————

Address ————————————————————

———————————————— Postcode ————————

E-mail ————————————————————

Send this whole page to: Mills & Boon Book Club, Free Book Offer, FREEPOST NAT 10298, Richmond, TW9 1BR.